QUEEN'S PAWN TO D4

ROD JOHNSTON

First published in Australia by Aurora House
www.aurorahouse.com.au

This edition published 2025
Copyright © Rod Johnston 2025

Typesetting and e-book design: Amit Dey (amitdey2528@gmail.com)
Cover design: Donika Mishineva (artofdonika.com)

ISBN NUMBER 978-1-923298-58-3 (paperback)

The four main characters of this book, their relatives and colleagues, are
entirely fictitious. Any resemblance to real persons is entirely coincidental
and is unintentional. The one exception: *2025 Reflections – The Journal of
a Concerned Australian* is an autobiographical travel memoir, based on
my actual experiences over a fifty-year period. It is not fictitious. Rather,
it comments on real events as they occurred, without exaggeration or
distortion, as well as my personal opinions drawn from those events.

 A catalogue record for this
book is available from the
National Library of Australia

DEDICATION

*For my grandchildren ... May you all play your
part in making the world a safer and happier place.*

Whoever wins [the Australian Federal Election] on May 3 will face not just a multi-dimensional game of global economic and geo-strategic chess, but possibly an epoch-defining choice for the country.

– ABC website, 19 April 2025[1].

CONTENTS

PART 1

The Opening

In chess, two opposing sides each seek to demolish and dominate the opposition, ultimately capturing their king. The queen is the most powerful piece on the board, with the ability to inflict widespread damage on her enemies, but constantly under attack herself. Sometimes a knight may enter the fray at an early stage, able to jump erratically over others to strike and destroy his enemies with little warning. The opening moves of the game often involve the advance of the pawns, the front-line "foot soldiers, who attack and defend as the need arises, but with only a limited capacity to inflict damage. The white queen's pawn (the one protecting the white queen from a position immediately to her fore) is often trusted with the opening move, advancing two spaces to the square known by its coordinates as D4 ... a move referred to as "queen's pawn to D4".

WHITE QUEEN

The queens are the most powerful pieces on the chess board, able to move any number of squares in any direction to eliminate an enemy. They are second in importance only to the king, and the other chess pieces must obey and protect their queen at all costs.

7:00 pm, 5 February 2030, *Parliament House Studios, Canberra*

Her face uncharacteristically grim, Aurora faltered as she attempted to retain her composure. But the teleprompter was merciless. This broadcast must proceed no matter what, without delay and devoid of emotion, no matter how the news of this incident had affected her. Gathering herself, she focused on the camera.

"Welcome to *Australasian Focus*. Tonight, we question our nation's leader on important issues taking place in the north of our country." She turned to the man who sat across from her.

"Prime Minister, can you reveal the cause of the explosion that ripped through the Torres Strait gas pipeline early this morning? Was anyone injured? Perhaps some of the workers?"

She found herself tuning out as he responded, surreptitiously dabbing his handkerchief to his forehead then stuffing it in the breast pocket of his navy Italian-made suit. He was a smart, fit-looking man with a reputation for being both self-assured and elusive when it came to hard-hitting questions, so she hadn't been expecting the interview to be easy. But she found herself becoming frustrated, angry even, at his ambiguous responses.

During her long career as a national TV journalist, Aurora had reported on many disasters, both natural and resulting from human activity, each progressively cutting a little deeper into her psyche. *What if it involved someone I know?* she often found herself thinking. *Perhaps a close friend, or even a relative? What if it were my own children, or grandchildren, who had been killed?*

Now, as she listened to the Prime Minister's anodyne replies, she brushed such thoughts aside and concentrated on the job at hand.

Aurora's years of experience had given her an uncanny knack of sensing fear in a politician. More importantly, she possessed the forensic skills to probe until she uncovered the deceit that was their stock-in-trade. Evidently, something had this Prime Minister deeply worried. But what was it that had made him so uncharacteristically nervous?

"Well, if you can't explain the cause of the explosion, Prime Minister," she persisted, "perhaps you can at least advise the extent of the damage?"

"It's really too early to say," he replied, his eyes flicking away for a second. "No such reports have been received yet. The advice we've received is that it was just a minor maintenance problem."

After several more attempts to pin him down and get to the bottom of why he was so spooked, she gave up. The Prime Minister refused to elaborate. In fact, he seemed to be in complete denial about any significant incident at all.

"Thank you, Prime Minister, we appreciate your time," she said, catching the look of relief on his face as the camera swung back to focus on her.

What was he hiding? She watched him walk off the set. Or perhaps more to the point ... *what was Australia's Prime Minister scared of?*

An hour later, in the calm of her office, Aurora reviewed the facts – or at least what she understood to be the facts so far. The Torres Strait gas pipeline had been built in 2029 with the aid of Australian private capital, to receive natural gas from Papua New Guinea and transport it across Torres Strait to the far northern tip of Queensland; a farsighted project.

The gas was extracted in the previously lawless Hela Province of PNG (Papua New Guinea) in the far west of the country, then piped through the mountains to the southern coast, where it dived under the short six kilometres of water separating the mainland from Boigu Island.

Despite being so close to mainland PNG, Boigu was legally part of Queensland and, hence, Australian territory. From Boigu, the pipeline submerged and headed due south across Torres Strait, resurfacing close to Bamaga near the tip of Cape York Peninsula. From here, the gas proceeded overland, further south down the peninsula to Weipa, where it powered the huge, recently constructed alumina refinery.

But early this morning, the Thursday Island network correspondent had reported an explosion at the southern terminal of the undersea pipeline. It appeared that a gas-storage tank had erupted, and there was speculation about possible injuries.

And that had been it. The words "national security" had been uttered, but since then, nothing. The Australian Government was being tight-lipped.

Of course, there was plenty of conjecture as to what may have caused it … equipment failure, seabed seismic movement, impurities in the gas … The list was endless, but nothing could be substantiated. What did the Prime Minister know?

Back at her modern penthouse apartment overlooking Lake Burley Griffin, Aurora entered her bedroom, kicked off her high heels and peeled off her stylish lavender linen pants-suit, letting it drop to the floor, replacing it with an unflattering old grey tracksuit. She needed a drink.

Was it too early to call her son? Or too late? She never knew the best time to call, these days. He might be feeding or bathing the kids and feeling harried and stressed. But if she left it till later, she'd be eating into his relaxation time. She decided to risk it. A quick chat with him and the children would lift her mood.

After a few rings he picked up.

"Sorry, Mum, the kids are already in bed. It's too late for them to be talking with Nan."

Nan. That made her feel old. Much older than her naturally attractive fifty-five years. Too old to be the anchor of a national current affairs television program – and certainly too old to be jousting with slippery politicians, night after night. But she was good at it; in fact, she was the best in the country. Over three decades, she'd clawed her way up the journalistic ladder. Now at the pinnacle of her career, she was renowned for her incisive probing and exposure of the dark arts of politics through her award-winning show.

Aurora slumped against the cushions, too exhausted even to reach for the TV remote. Why bother anyway? Just more ads on the free-to-air commercial channels, and more political bias, both right and left, from her own employer. Everyone had an opinion, but nobody had any facts. *Blah, blah, blah!*

Have another glass of wine, she told herself. Oh! The bottle was empty already. Had she really drunk so much in the short time since she'd arrived home? *Is this what my life's come to?* she mused, staring at the blank TV screen.

Her ex had a new wife, her kids were too busy to talk to her, and the grandkids must sleep twenty-four hours a day ... or so it seemed. And work ... ah, yes, work ... the one driver in her life that had relentlessly pushed her forward.

But to what purpose? Ultimately, did anyone really care if the Prime Minister habitually lied, or if the Opposition Leader's popularity score was lower than a limbo bar? Who cared if the country was bankrupt, so long as the sporting finals weren't disrupted by yet another pandemic?

Might as well have another drink. Oh, that's right, the bottle's empty. *Ironic, isn't it, how suddenly the empty bottle seemed like a metaphor for her life*

Aurora groaned, rolled over and crashed to the lounge room floor. She must have fallen asleep on the couch, too exhausted

– and tipsy – to even stagger the five metres into her bedroom. Her head ached. Her mouth was parched. Why had she opened that second bottle of wine? Oh well, another day, another dollar. She had a few hours to get herself together before she had to head back to the studio where she'd present the usual polished version of herself. She was an expert at it. She'd done it plenty of times before.

Gingerly, she forced herself to her feet then weaved her way to the bathroom and stepped into the shower, soaking clothes and underclothes alike. The water was cold, too cold to be enjoyable, and almost made her gasp, but it was just what she needed to clear her head. *Get a grip, Aurora. You have to be on top of your game today.*

Two strong coffees and a few paracetamols later, freshly dressed and groomed, Aurora felt more like herself. Now the haze in her head had evaporated, a little bit at least, she felt confident enough to tackle her emails.

Her laptop screen flickered into life, displaying several dozen incoming emails. She glanced quickly down the list ... nothing, nothing, junk, garbage and nothing. Wait, what was that one? Hmmm. An email from Senator Whitehorse.

Aurora had recently become friendly with Marcus White-horse, one of the twelve senators representing Queensland in the Commonwealth Parliament. Their relationship had started when she'd interviewed him about a line of questioning he'd raised in parliament, mostly to do with development in the north. He was proving to be a new and valuable source of information, while she reciprocated with chatter on the rumours circulating within the Canberra bubble. But who was playing whom? Did she learn more from him, or did he learn more from her? Did it really matter?

"I saw your interview with the Prime Minister," his email began. Judging by the time of transmission, the Senator had been quick to reach out. He must have put fingers to the keyboard as soon as the interview concluded. "I confess that I am worried. There is something not right with this pipeline explosion." So, he too had sensed some deeper-than-usual deceit in the Prime Minister's equivocation. "Perhaps we should exchange information, maybe combine forces and share sources," the email continued.

A strange turn of events. Usually, politicians briefed journalists, leaking information to gain a political advantage. This time, the senator was suggesting the information flow in the opposite direction.

The email went on to explain his plan in detail. Marcus could raise questions in the Senate, but he needed reliable information to base them on. He "… had some resources available within his electoral office, but insufficient to facilitate on-the-ground investigations." Could she please help?

This was like manna from heaven – Aurora's chance to significantly strengthen their relationship and increase the potential for her to receive much more confidential information in return, in the future. This type of information was a journalist's life-blood, more precious than gold, and any means of securing its steady flow must be deemed legitimate.

As she pondered his proposal, her gaze came to rest on the chessboard on the coffee table in front of her, its ebony and ivory pieces staring each other down, ready for the combat of a new game. Aurora and the Senator had recently discovered a common interest in the game and got into the habit of playing remotely, one move per day, communicated by email.

She'd make the first move. But what? Perhaps ... no, too obvious. Or ... no, too bold. Perhaps ...

She turned to the keyboard, typed rapidly and hit SEND.

"We need to meet, somewhere private ... for a quick coffee and a sandwich ... your office this afternoon would suit." Then an impetuous afterthought. "And perhaps I'll ask our Thursday Island correspondent to look into the gas explosion." And at the bottom of the email, Aurora added the opening move of their remote game.

"Queen's Pawn to D4 ... Game on."

QUEEN'S PAWN

*The pawns are the foot-soldiers of the chess board, and the
queen's pawn is the one stationed immediately in front of
the queen.*

To many, the summer heat and humidity of Australia's tropical north are oppressive, but to Digger they were liberat-
ing, offering the opportunity to shed clothing, retaining just
the minimum demanded by decency, and get out and about
in the open. Today in particular he welcomed this assignment,
emailed by Aurora a few hours earlier. It was good to escape
from the claustrophobic confines of his tiny Thursday Island
home office into the fresh air, good to feel the sting of the salt
spray, whipped up by a brisk breeze bearing in from the east, on
his suntanned face.

Last night had been a long one, the first of the three annual
State of Origin Rugby League football matches, broadcast across
the nation, when the men of the north beat the … whatever …
out of those southern wimps. Every year, Queenslanders, no
matter where they currently lived in Australia, united (via the
television screen) in a common cause to demonstrate the supe-
riority of a northern upbringing over southern decadence.

This was the Australian equivalent of civil war, repeated year after year, generally with the same outcome. The Maroons hammered the Blues. The Queensland footballers triumphed over New South Wales yet again. This was a call for celebration with the boys ... a few pots of beer (*schooners*, the southerners would call them) at the very least. After all, as the old marketing campaign had declared, "A hard-earned thirst needs a big cold beer". And yelling at a big-screen television set in the local sports bar in chorus with some good mates had, indeed, been thirsty work.

But that was last night. Today, Digger was heading south in a chartered fishing boat to see just how much he could learn about the situation Aurora had outlined. Standing casually at the wheel, he guided the little vessel further down the coast, keeping the vast blue Gulf of Carpentaria off his starboard beam while he scanned the portside mangroves for saltwater crocodiles.

The vessel edged cautiously south, skirting the tourist resort at Seisia, on past the Indigenous settlement at Umagico, then past another Aboriginal community at Injinoo. Approaching his destination, he scrutinised the shoreline where the pipeline came ashore, and where the huge gas-storage tanks were located. Now coming into view in the distance, a plume of black smoke snaked heavenwards, high over the southern horizon.

Just as the fishing boat edged further towards the smoke, Digger observed a solid speck emerging from the distant haze. Approaching at speed, the helicopter roared into hailing range, the loudspeaker booming a not-so-subtle threat.

"This is a restricted area. Withdraw immediately or your boat will be impounded, and all on board will be charged with trespass on government property."

Perhaps Digger could manage just a few quick photos before he beat a hasty retreat to Thursday Island?

Digger had lived on Thursday Island, or TI as the locals pre-ferred to call it, for a couple of years now. "Digger" wasn't his real name, but he'd always hated "Douglas", the name on his birth certificate. Besides, for several generations the family's first-born male had been nicknamed thus, a tribute to his great-grandfather, a First World War Gallipoli veteran. Before his current role, Digger had drifted in and out of work all over Australia's tropical north, doing a bit of this and a bit of that, including a few things he preferred the Australian Tax Office not to examine too closely.

As a young man, he'd left his childhood home in Brisbane then spent several years in Darwin before moving on to more lucrative employment in the mines of the Pilbara for a couple of years. Similar work in Sub-Sahara Africa had led him to the highlands of Papua New Guinea, the Pacific Islands and, even-tually, to Central Asia.

Although he loved the freedom and excitement of this lifestyle, the uncertainty of mining ventures in such remote areas eventually forced him back to Australia. He'd gravitated north from Cairns, working as a tour-boat crewman out of Port Douglas, then as a maintenance contractor at the Mossman sugar mill, followed by a job as a security guard at the new Weipa alumina refinery.

Eventually, he'd drifted up to TI, jewel of the Torres Strait. Now closer to forty than thirty, Digger had struck it lucky, landing a modest salary and a secure future in paradise as the

resident media correspondent servicing several national networks. Today's assignment, on behalf of Aurora's current affairs
program, was to quietly investigate the gas explosion that
occurred in the early hours of the previous day. He liked working for this network, and he particularly liked its glamorous
anchor. Aurora kept it professional, of course – no flirting, just
friendly – but Digger did enjoy their occasional conversations.

Back in the solitude of his office, a dusty ceiling fan ticking
sluggishly above, Digger flicked through the images captured
on his mobile phone. Yes, there was the helicopter. But what
were those markings on the body? Although the fuselage was
not side-on in the frame, the decal, albeit barely visible, was
apparently a naval pedigree.

The loudspeaker had seemed to warn off trespass on government property. That didn't make sense. Private property, yes.
But the gas terminal was not a government installation. So why
was it being protected by a naval helicopter?

He scrolled further back through the images. There in the
distance was the gas terminal tank farm, and further to the
right was the "snake", that black plume of smoke threatening
to strike all intruders. The smoke wasn't actually rising from the
tanks but appeared to originate a few hundred metres further
down the coast. Now he was curious.

Digger had many friends throughout the north, including a
mate who still worked as a security guard at the Weipa alumina
refinery. In a moment of inspired genius, a quick telephone call
confirmed that, "Yes, there was a break in the gas-flow to the
plant, but, no, it only occurred late that morning".

A good ten hours after the explosion.

Once seen as a shining example of Australian corporate initiative and boldness, the Weipa bauxite mine had never actually been so. Since its opening in 1963, the mine had had huge reserves of "red dirt" stripped from below the topsoil and shipped overseas, to be turned into shining aluminium by foreign manufacturers. Never more than a "rip and scrape" operation, the mine mercilessly pillaged the valuable "dirt" and disposed of it "dirt cheap". During the first quarter of the 21st century, Australia produced almost one-third of the world's bauxite but manufactured only one-fortieth of the world's aluminium.

The COVID pandemic from 2020 to 2022, and the Chinese and American trade boycotts of the same era, had demonstrated the need for Australia to increase its local capacity to produce a whole range of manufactured goods. As this became obvious, all sides of politics embraced the decision to create an additional alumina refinery, here in the far north, on site at Weipa. But it was a feeble, half-hearted effort and the refinery never yielded the promised economic benefit.

The planning of the new refinery was complicated by the dilemma of how to power it. While the conservative government of the day blatantly lied about its achievements in reducing greenhouse gas emissions and, thus, slow global warming, the opposition feared rural electoral backlash and capitulated. Power to the new facility would be provided using carbon dioxide-liberating natural gas, imported from neighbouring Papua New Guinea. Thus, the Torres Strait gas pipeline was born.

In the short term, local industry promoting the increased use of natural gas thrived; however, as the years passed, Australia became recognised as the international pariah it was. Just as a drug-pusher denies responsibility for an addict's drug habit, Australia disclaimed its responsibility for pushing carbon-intensive manufacturing onto the world.

That was five years ago. Over that time, like most of his boozy buddies, Digger hadn't thought much about global warming; in fact, he hadn't thought about much beyond the next footy game. The apathy of the average Australian encouraged the lazy politics of self-interest at the expense of international responsibility.

But now he was a (presumably) responsible current affairs correspondent, Digger was starting to see the folly of such myopic self-interest. He began to understand the frustrations of the small but growing contingent of responsibly minded Australians, who sought to power our industries through reliable renewable energy sources. Years of proven service made solar power, boosted by battery storage, an obvious choice. So, too, was the emerging practice of deep-well geothermal power. Why burn natural-gas carbon when the earth itself is a ball of molten rock, ready to provide unlimited pollution-free power?

Such were the arguments now propagated by environmentalists, but the radicals still demanded more militant action. A small cohort of thugs, pretending to be acting in the interests of the planet, frequently disrupted sensible scientific arguments through their mindless vandalism. Perhaps the current trouble near the gas pipeline terminal was a result of the demanded militancy? Was yesterday's explosion a result of sabotage?

Digger knew he must file a detailed report. But on the spur of the moment, he dashed off a quick text to Aurora, reporting the delay in cessation of the gas-flow, attaching the photos of the helicopter, and describing the smoke plume.

The phone registered the text transmission just as two burly uniformed commonwealth police officers strode unannounced through his front gate and burst into his office. Before he knew what was happening, his phone was seized and his computer impounded, and he was left with a stern warning not to venture south of Seisia until the police gave formal approval for entry into "the danger zone".

The White Queen's Pawn, now in play, had advanced to position D4.

WHITE KNIGHT

The knights, each represented as a horse, range about the chess board eliminating their enemies. While their movements may appear erratic (one place diagonal and one place straight), their ability to pass over friend and foe alike, to eliminate their prey, equips them with an unrivalled element of surprise.

Aurora cradled the cup in both hands, absorbing its warmth through her palms, and took a cautious sip. The coffee was good, the long black kick-starting a spark of interest deep within her and reigniting a smidgeon of the enthusiasm that had once filled every fibre of her being – long since stalled as the last drop of motivation had been sucked out of her.

As she savoured the caffeine's effect, her eyes surveyed the slim, distinguished-looking man sitting opposite. His neat, well-fitting suit and polished shoes betrayed neither ostentation nor stinginess. She'd met him a few times before and they'd become friends – the safest description of their relationship. He was a genuine gentleman, perhaps a decade older than herself. One might mistake him for a mild-mannered, ageing civil servant – there were enough of them in this town – but civil servant he was not.

Marcus Whitehorse was one of the twelve senators representing Queensland in the Commonwealth Parliament, the last to be elected, and the third senator of the Paradigm Party.

A new paradigm ... Australia reimagined.

This slogan had served them well and was amplified by the party's mission statement:

"... a new vision of a cooperative, compassionate and caring world, where self-interest is subservient to mutual interest; a new vision in which countries of the Southern Cross may emerge as the world's peacemakers. It is time to renounce state-promoted violence and to promote respect, cooperation and assistance throughout the region and the wider world."

But there was more to the Paradigm Party's three senators than just a catchy slogan and a well-intentioned vision statement. This group potentially held the balance of power, and the fate of an entire nation could be determined by the voting patterns of this most unassuming man and his two colleagues.

The other two were flamboyant and charismatic, but Marcus was different, deliberate and methodical, with the patience of a marathon runner. Many didn't trust him (too cold and calculating); "Mad Marcus, the man-machine" his enemies called him. He was renowned for his dispassionate dissection of any problem, analysing the possibilities in detail before devising and implementing a strategy with precision and ruthlessness. To friend and foe alike, he was "Whitehorse, the White Knight".

The meeting with Aurora had gone well enough. Now, seated in the sanctuary of his office, Marcus reflected on their discussion. Despite Aurora's emailed suggestion that she "… might ask [her] Thursday Island correspondent to look into the gas explosion …", she now appeared less enthusiastic about this, in response to his proposal for information-sharing. Still, she didn't actually refuse to help, and she'd at last agreed to ask her colleague in the far north to dig a little deeper. Marcus would just have to wait and see what eventuated.

He allowed his thoughts to detour in a direction where they hadn't drifted for a long time. *Yes, she's an attractive woman. A VERY attractive woman. Who knows what might … no, banish the thought. Although she IS extremely attractive. But no, there's more to beauty than mere physical attraction.*

It was now just on three years since his own darling wife had passed away, and he missed her badly. During their fifty-plus years of marriage, they'd been inseparable. Of course, at times they were physically separated, out of necessity – that is part of a politician's burden, after all – but were never spiritually apart. Each could sense the other's emotions, and each would comfort or support the other when necessary. She'd encouraged his political ambitions, just as he'd championed her family and community commitments. They'd been a good team … no, they had been a *great* team. But cancer doesn't discriminate. And now he was alone.

Alone. Such a cruel word.

Alone.

KNIGHT'S PAWN

Like the other pawns, the knight's pawn is a front-line fighter, stationed immediately in front of the knight.

The screen of Cassandra's laptop filled with the parliamentary logo, ahead of the familiar font of an email from Senator Whitehorse. A man of few words, Senator Whitehorse (or Marcus, as he'd instructed her to call him) preferred to communicate with his staff by email, rather than verbally. "It eliminates uncertainty from the intent of the communication," he'd say. Where other politicians preferred the spoken word (no doubt to avoid scrutiny of their email trails), Cassandra's boss was clear. "We have nothing to hide, and plenty to say," Marcus would often comment.

Cassandra squinted a little as she closely studied the brief for her new assignment. A broad grin slowly enveloped her countenance.

"Yes," she murmured. "Yes, this will do very nicely, thank you."

Cassandra had always been a precocious child – or so her domineering mother had often said. While childhood was difficult enough, the teenage period really applied the blow-torch to their relationship. Sparks would fly over the most trivial of tantrums.

"Too much screen time and not enough study," would elicit the response, "I'm still top of my class, so leave me alone".

"You're not wearing that!", was countered by, "I'm sixteen, and I'll dress how I like," while a rift of tectonic magnitude was the predictable result of, "I don't like you spending so much time with … him!"

But "he" came and went, of course, followed by a few more boyfriends; however, Cassandra's relations with her mother eventually repaired.

By this stage, Cassandra's father had long since taken leave of his overbearing wife, started living with his much younger and more accommodating PA (personal assistant), and finally dissolved their marriage. Cassandra, an only child and spoiled by her doting dad, was devastated. So much so that she never forgave him for abandoning her to the mercy of her manipulative mother. She never spoke to him again.

With the onset of young adulthood, teenage traumas subsided and Cassandra began to concentrate on matters of more gravitas than computer games, clothes and boys. She also began to realise she was more like her mother than she'd previously cared to admit. They were both acutely focused on achieving their declared goals.

Her mother allowed nothing to stand in the way of pushing her daughter forward to achieve the career success that, for her, had been truncated by childbirth. Cassandra was determined to seize every opportunity to reach the top.

Empathy was not in their vocabulary. For both mother and daughter, such a sentiment was an impediment to achieving their desired outcomes.

The transition from high school to university was seamless. Cassandra was ambitious, and keen to get on with tertiary education and a career in politics and had no time for frivolities such as a gap year. Such indulgences would have to wait. Work, work, work ... the more you did, the richer the rewards. And she was doing well.

But then, mid-way through her third year, disaster struck. A cataclysm threatened to derail her whole strategy.

A boy, youth, man – whatever you wanted to call him ... a member of the opposite sex – flipped her completely off balance. They attended the same tutorials and were thrown together into a group project by the alphabetical proximity of their surnames. He was adorable, funny, handsome, sexy and ... well, maybe she did let things go too far. That is, until a calamity forced her to confront reality.

She failed an assignment!

That was it. No more boyfriends for Cassandra. She terminated the relationship. Brutally. And he took it badly. What a loser! Couldn't he see that passing exams and a successful career were much more important than ... *that*? Last she'd heard of him, he'd graduated and moved up north, to Darwin to work as a reporter for some second-rate local rag.

But that was long in the past. Four years of hard slog to earn an undergraduate arts degree, majoring in government and economics, and a further two years to secure a master's degree in political science, had ultimately paid dividends. Two years ago, at the mature age of twenty-six, she landed her dream job in Canberra: research officer on the staff of a federal senator.

Cassandra loved her work. It was almost as if she had been ordained for this role by the gods. In Greek mythology, the great Apollo had bestowed the gift of prophecy on Cassandra, the daughter of the ill-fated King Priam of Troy. The art of prophecy was essential, too, for modern-day Cassandra's current employment as a political adviser. Perhaps she should choose to neglect the rest of the ancient story, that the fabled Cassandra had cheated Apollo, and, in revenge, he'd ensured nobody believed her prophecies.

Now, Cassandra's new assignment would provide an opportunity to advance further in the political hierarchy. Senator Whitehorse, Marcus, hadn't been too specific in his email, but apparently the task involved researching and drafting policy on all aspects of the murky quagmire of 21st century international politics, into which Australia had descended during the 2020s. And, joy of joys, Cassandra no longer had to do all the boring donkey work herself. She'd be able to delegate the detailed research to a new assistant.

KNIGHT'S GAMBIT

The knight's gambit requires the early advancement of the knight into the field of battle, moving to position F3. It is a dangerous opening, risking the sacrifice of the knight to obtain an advantage. It requires courage and insight and is not for the risk-averse.

Returning to the harshness of the here and now, Senator Marcus Whitehorse glanced at the chess board centred neatly on the coffee table. This morning, he'd registered Aurora's opening move, and now it was his turn. Respond with a pawn advance? No … too conventional. True to his nature, he'd use a strategy that was sure to destabilise his opponent's resistance. Perhaps Marcus would employ the knight's gambit.

Knight to F3.

Marcus knew something strange was occurring in the Torres Strait. But he also knew a much bigger story was brewing in the United States. Overnight, an old colleague, now based in Washington, told him previously classified information was about to be released by the Pentagon, but substantial additional information remained classified and unavailable. This undisclosed documentation was assumed to contain a bombshell.

How could he find out more? He desperately needed the resources normally available only to a senior veteran journalist, perhaps one backed by a major television network. And hey … he knew just the person. He was currently "in a relationship" – wait, no, that wasn't the right phrase: "in a working friendship" – with such a journalist, through whom he could likely receive and interpret such confidential intelligence. He must, at any cost, he told himself, focus on obtaining the background to this international issue, and let the local story of the gas explosion drift.

As the "quick coffee and a sandwich" of yesterday's meeting receded into Aurora's memory of an otherwise uneventful afternoon, the evening's developments proved to be the complete opposite.

An important story emerging from Washington began to materialise. The "Mystery of the Gas Explosion" piece was bumped by the producer so the so-called "Pentagon Leaks" report could feature as the lead story. It was to be expected. This really was explosive stuff – much more so than a gas leak in the Torres Strait. But before the program went to air, Aurora would need to gain a better understanding of the issues involved.

But, as she discovered, the Pentagon Leaks weren't really leaks at all, but simply the periodic release of briefing documents used by the United States military to keep their elected representatives at least partially informed. Most of the information was already publicly available, but the name (first coined by one of the larger American networks) had stuck. The public throughout the western world loved this stuff. It did not matter that it was mostly a beat up. A lead story dissecting the matter would earn crucial prime-time ratings.

The network's research department had been hard at work all afternoon, producing a stack of background material. To the more analytical minds of academics and their ilk, large simultaneous releases of previously confidential information, such as the papers issued in this case, provide a rare opportunity to plot the trends in international politics, and to hypothesise on the secret strategies devised, but not released, by the military.

The 1945 allied victory, led by the United States, settled a turbulent period of two world wars and heralded the Pax Americana, which had delivered an eighty-five-year period of relative peace and prosperity. Despite sporadic localised wars in Korea, Vietnam, Iraq, Iran, Palestine, Afghanistan, Ukraine, Gaza, Lebanon, Sudan, South Sudan, the Congo and other smaller conflicts, most of the world had been free from external invasion. The 1991 dismemberment of the Soviet Union had left the United States as the sole super-power. This peace inaugurated a world order that championed capitalism over socialism, the victory of money over human resources, and the triumph of globalism over nationalism. But the gains were ephemeral, an illusion that flickered for a while and then disappeared.

Such an environment had also given rise to the resurgence of the mega-economies of China and India, those two giants that, half a millennium earlier, had risen from the ashes and now dominated the world economy. But India struggled, hampered by the entrenched religious bigotry that infected its democratic political institutions and caused it to relapse into internal suppression and discontent.

In the late 2020s, the loosely confederated European bloc had also fractured. Brazil was still a basket-case of corruption; Indonesia still struggled with ever-present forces promoting disintegration; while a multitude of African countries sank into endemic poverty and tribal violence.

China, on the other hand, had surged, buoyed by the stability intrinsic in its socialist one-party-system, adopted in 1949. Chinese business had captured the world market, stared down the American trade tariffs of 2025, and now, China and America vied for world military and economic dominance.

Aurora considered the wide assortment of information that the network's research department had offered at such short notice. However, this exhaustive background, useful as it was for the evening's program, did not explain the atmosphere of urgency around the Pentagon Leaks. According to confidential Washington sources, there were a series of top-secret Pentagon strategies, but the sources could not, or would not, reveal the detail of the strategies, only that they were significant in the context of the drama currently unfolding in the South China Sea.

How much could Aurora reveal during the broadcast? More to the point, how much *should* she reveal? Not much, she was advised by the producer. Disappointed, Aurora glanced at her notes as the evening's filming began. Her concentration drifted a little as she spoke about the more mundane aspects of the situation: the historical development, the current tension, the wavering public opinion in various hotspots, the strident assertions from Beijing, and the stern warnings emanating from Washington. Then, perhaps just a little intrigue to close the program.

Undisclosed Washington sources have described the United States' strategy as a chess game, in which various scenarios are played out with all the skill of a chess master.

A chess game, Aurora mused. She and Marcus now had a common interest that transcended their shared pastime, venturing into the machinations of international politics.

OPENING

Each game of chess is generally described in terms of an opening, a middle game and the end game.

For the second time in as many days, the senator requested a meeting, but this time in a less conspicuous location. With the changes in circumstance, he now deemed it prudent to aim for as much privacy as possible. Aurora and he had driven separately some distance out of metropolitan Canberra, up the Barton Highway in the direction of Yass to the hamlet of Hall, where they met in a small coffee shop.

"Thank you for the text message and photographs from your correspondent regarding the Torres Strait," he said as they waited for their order. "They will prove very useful at the appropriate time, I'm sure."

Aurora nodded and smiled briefly as the server set their coffees in front of them. She was about to respond when he continued.

"I have a request to make, a favour to ask. But let me deviate. First, let us talk about your program last night, the so-called Pentagon Leaks. During the past six months, my research officer has been digging into old copies of Hansard and other documents. Don't worry," he added when he noticed her concern. "They're all publicly available, mostly from the early 2020s, from about ten years ago. We need to find out what these Pentagon Leaks mean for Australia."

He paused to take a sip then continued.

"I was impressed with the resourcefulness of your Torres Strait correspondent, and his ability to ferret out information, use his initiative – and to take risks. I mentioned I have a request. And this is it. Would you please prevail upon your correspondent to come down to Canberra and accept a temporary secondment to my office? I would like him to work with my research officer, to brief her on the strategic issues facing northern Australia and help her put the Pentagon Leaks into a local context."

Aurora looked taken aback.

"I can ask him," she said, draining her cup. "Meanwhile, how about we go for a drink? I could do with one after that!"

Cassandra was a typical millennial, born with two umbilical cords. The first, through which she had received her mother's life-giving sustenance during the first nine months of her existence, was severed immediately after childbirth. The second remained intact, sustaining her through childhood, teens and early womanhood. She was inseparable from her smartphone, tethered to it (metaphorically) by an invisible vital cord. It was essential, the means to her survival, the fount of all knowledge and source of eternal wisdom. Without her phone, she'd surely perish.

Cassandra's thumbs danced over the keys, which glowed in the subdued lighting of the waiting room. Aurora had kept her waiting for well over ten minutes, so why not use her phone to Google this enigmatic woman with the exotic name? *After all, she reasoned, time is money, and money is power. With no time to waste, why not use it wisely?*

"Aurora, Roman goddess of the dawn", Cassandra read, "was also known as Eos, Zorya or Ushas, depending on whether the ancient culture was Greek, Slavic or Hindu." The name, *Aurora*, incited imaginings of the exotic, with its many modern manifestations – queen, princess and heroine of adolescent animation, right through to adult film fantasy.

Just then the queen herself appeared, gliding in to fill the tiny space of the waiting room, her honeyed voice welcoming yet commanding at the same time.

"Cassandra, it's lovely to meet you, at last. Marcus speaks very warmly of your dedication and insight, and I'm sure we'll become close friends. Please … come into my office."

The younger woman had to consciously prevent herself from bending a knee in homage. She found her tongue, at length.

"Thank you," she rasped out, as she dutifully followed the legendary journalist into the inner sanctum.

Fastidious. That was Marcus Whitehorse in one word, and Cassandra knew that he would insist she obtain a signed receipt as she handed over this confidential file, too sensitive to trust to email. The business quickly executed, both could now relax.

"Tell me, Cassandra, what attracted you to the senator's service?" Aurora asked, seemingly genuinely interested. And so Cassandra quickly related the tale of her recruitment – not a particularly long or interesting story, but to the point.

Sensing Aurora had perhaps imbibed a few too many midday merlots, Cassandra was emboldened to make an enquiry of her own.

"Aurora … excuse me, but I hope you don't mind me calling you by your first name? I'd love to better understand how you gather your intelligence for all those stories you break."

Aurora hesitated. "I'd love to share that sort of information with a bright young girl like you, Cassandra. We'll be working closely for quite a while. Incidentally, Aurora isn't my first name. It's actually my middle name … the family name given to the eldest girl for several generations. When I started on breakfast television, the PR (public relations) people decided that Aurora, with its association with the breaking dawn, would sound much more appropriate than my first name – Jane. Plain Jane, you might say."

"So, are you named after the Roman dawn goddess or after the queen of fantasy TV?" Cassandra joked.

"Nothing as exotic as either of those," Aurora laughed. Sensing a willing listener, she launched into a full explanation of her heritage. "I am actually named after a ship, the British steam yacht, SY (steam yacht) *Aurora*, which disappeared in the South Pacific more than a century ago. Let me tell you the story. My grandmother was born in 1917, but she never knew her father. Her mother was a widow whose parents had died and whose younger brother was serving in the Australian forces in Gallipoli and Palestine. My grandmother's father was a sailor, a Russian crew member of the SY *Aurora* during its voyages to Antarctica to provision Douglas Mawson's expedition and the British-Australian bases. As you probably know – or maybe young people no longer learn their history? – Mawson is famous for his 160-km lone trek to safety, after his two companions, Belgrave Ninnis and Xavier Mertz, perished. Ninnis plunged to his death down a crevasse, and the starving Mertz succumbed to poisoning from eating the livers of their huskies.

"My great-grandfather was on the SY *Aurora* again in 1915, when she was trapped in sea ice, drifting about 3,000 km for nearly a year. When the ship finally docked back at Newcastle, my great-grandparents met and ... well, you know, they were never actually married. He left again on the SY *Aurora* when it sailed for Chile. He promised to return, but he never did. This was wartime and the ship was, presumably, sunk by mines laid by the German raider, the *Wolf*. My great-grandmother was devastated. She never married, and she raised her only daughter as a single parent. That was pretty hard in those days. Ever since then, the daughters in our family have been given *Aurora* as their middle name."

"That is incredibly sad! Did they ever hear of the ship again?" Cassandra asked.

"They recovered just one lifebuoy, with the name of the ship. And then, ten years later, a man walking on Tuggerah Beach, south of Newcastle, discovered a wine bottle that had been engraved in 1912 with a sketch of the SY *Aurora*, and the names of eight of the explorers. Apparently, the bottle was on the ship when she went down in 1917."

Cassandra barely hesitated before projecting a little of her academic prowess into the conversation.

"There must have been so many ships named *Aurora*. After I finished my PhD – it was on the Russian Revolution, you know – I travelled to Russia. It was after the Ukraine war had abated, so travel was OK then. Despite their humiliation, the Russians were still very militaristic, and they made a big thing of one of their old warships, a cruiser also named *Aurora*. From what I remember, it was one of the only three Russian naval ships to survive the Battle of Tsushima Strait in 1905, when the Russians were decisively defeated by the Japanese navy during the Russo-Japanese War."

She paused for a moment, then continued, "But the *Aurora* went on to see action in both the First and Second World Wars, and even her guns were commandeered for use on land, during the desperate defence of Leningrad. But the most significant part of the *Aurora*'s' history was that it fired the first shot in the 1917 Russian Revolution – a blank, fired towards the St Petersburg Winter Palace. And now the Russians have restored the old ship, and it's a symbol of Russian naval heritage."

"Yes, I know that story well," Aurora replied. "By some strange coincidence, my great-grandfather's brother served on that warship throughout the whole of its life. While my great-grandfather served and died on an *Aurora* of peace, his brother served and lived on an *Aurora* of war. It seems so wrong. Perhaps that's why I am so anti-war. But hey – such a depressing subject! Let's talk about something more uplifting. Boyfriends, for example … how many do you currently have? Come on, Cassandra, spill! Let's lighten the mood a bit. Let's have a drink."

EN PASSANT

A pawn that moves two squares forward can be taken on the following move by an opposing pawn that's directly next to it. When opposing pawns pass, only one can survive ... pawn en passant.

Cassandra was angry. Who the hell was this dude ... this ... this *bloke*, who had referred to her as "perky"?

Perky ...? What on earth did he mean? Cassandra had definitely heard Digger use that adjective. She hadn't meant to listen in on the phone call to his Darwin mate, but she'd distinctly heard him describe her as "perky". She Googled it. ... *Bubbly ... lots of energy ... always smiling ... cheerful disposition.* She smiled, relieved. *Perhaps he was right. Perhaps I am. kind of,* she mused. *Perky, perhaps, but naïve ... never.*

Cassandra knew this could be her big break, the chance to establish her credentials as a potent political player, one who could seize an opportunity, take a risk and make her mark. She may be just a pawn in the big game, but pawns progress, and pawns can have devastating impact. Her boss, Senator Marcus Whitehorse, seemed to place a lot of trust in this bloke, Digger, and was determined to thrust him into her domain. So, she had to use him as best she could, to get the result that would catapult her up the political food chain.

Cassandra was determined to find out more about Digger's background, what made him tick. Marcus had asked her to do a routine security check on him, so she felt justified in digging deep. Research was one thing at which she excelled.

Ignoring the official channels available to a senator's assistant for this sort of check, Cassandra decided to try the internet. A routine query to an ancestry site yielded Digger's heritage, going back generations, while a scan of the Australian war service records told of several generations of military duty.

One record attracted her attention. Apparently, Digger was descended from a soldier imprisoned by the Russians in 1922. 1922? Of course. British, Americans, French and Australians had been fighting in support of the White Russians in the aftermath of the Bolshevik Revolution.

As the Red armies swept to victory, many foreign fighters serving with the White-Russian forces were either killed or captured. And it appeared Digger's forebear was one of these, captured in Central Asia, imprisoned in Bukhara and, at last, exchanged in a prisoner swap.

For some strange reason, this story seemed familiar. Tossing and turning all night, Cassandra couldn't dispel the sense of familiarity of the narrative from her consciousness. In the morning, sleep-deprived, she remembered and headed straight for the filing cabinet containing the reams of hard-copy research material she'd accumulated for her thesis on the Russian Revolution.

There it was. A letter, written over a century ago, archived with the other papers she'd meticulously scoured for facts. The last letter from a White-Russian czarist official, written to his only surviving son, while imprisoned in Bukhara in 1922, before his execution at the hands of the Red Communists. With the letter was another document, the *Journal of a Russian Patriot*, published much later in the 1960s, and detailing the naval activities of the czarist official's second son.

Cassandra skimmed the lengthy journal. Although it wasn't the document she was searching for, it did contain a lot of useful background details, describing the political and military situation of the time, from the late 1800s through the Russo-Japanese War, the First World War, the Communist Revolution, the Russian Civil War and the Second World War.

The White-Russian czarist official had formerly been the governor of the Central Asian provinces, today's Uzbekistan and Kyrgyzstan. He'd moved there with his family in the mid-1800s and had been at the focus of the gradual Russian domination of the region. He had two boys and two girls. The girls were both widowed during the revolution and were living in poverty in Tashkent, the capital of Uzbekistan.

The letter had been written to the second son, a Red Russian naval officer, the first son appearing to have been lost at sea in the South Pacific. It touched on the "Great Game" intrigues, during which Britain and Russia vied for control of Afghanistan, Tibet and adjacent territories, and the disastrous Russian naval defeat during the Russo-Japanese War of the early 1900s.

Bukhara Ark Fortress, 1922

My dearest son,

I write amidst the melancholy of this most dread prison, the "bug-pit" dungeon, beneath the ruined Bukhara Ark Fortress. It was from this same hole 80 years ago, in 1842, that they dragged British Colonel Stoddard. I can picture it even now. The curved blade would have flashed in the morning sunlight, as it hovered momentarily mid-air, before descending to the back of the poor colonel's neck, thus ending his life. So too, Captain Conolly met a similar fate. I live in constant fear. Will my fate be that of Stoddard and Conolly, or will my captors assign me to a long one-way journey to Siberia?

1922 has not been a good year for me, but the Reds, your Russian communist masters, keep me alive, in the hope that I, a senior White-Russian civil servant, ever loyal to the Czar (God rest his soul), may yet prove useful to their cause. Although I do not know what fate awaits me, there is little sign that my end will come soon. Time is both my friend and my enemy. I value the time that I have, but there is little to relieve the endless hours of boredom that I now endure. So, I write. I write memoirs, I write history and I write philosophy. And most important, I write to you, my dear son, knowing that I may never see you again.

We all thought that the war would be over in a few months, that the crazy Kaiser had bitten off more than even the hungriest wolf can devour. But we had not counted on the incompetence of the French, British and (sadly) our own Russian generals and politicians. The ineptitude on all sides was staggering. For example, I was stunned to read that, although British firms had been constructing ships for the Ottoman navy under contract for many years, in August 1914 that insatiable war hawk, Winston Churchill of the British Admiralty, unceremoniously seized (without compensation) two newly built Turkish battleships, Sultan Osman and Reşadiye. This decision, inevitably seen by the

*Turks as "British treachery", was instrumental in sway-
ing Turkish public opinion in favour of aligning with
Germany, and led directly to the Dardanelles naval fiasco
and the abortive Gallipoli Peninsula campaign. Perhaps I
am underestimating Churchill and his cronies. Forcing the
Turks into the opposing camp gave the British and French
the perfect opportunity to prosecute war against the Turks,
rather than work with them to defeat the Germans and
Austrians. The British Army, supported by the Arab Revolt
(popularised by their hero, Colonel Lawrence), rolled back
Turkish control of the Levant. This gave the British and
French the ideal opening to dismember the Turkish empire
and seize the valuable Middle East oilfields.*

*The notorious and secret 1916 Sykes–Picot Agreement,
between the British and French, effectively partitioned
the Levant among these powers, and saw the establishment of puppet Arab states in Arabia, Palestine, Syria
and around the Persian Gulf. It was all about the oil
– black gold – the lubricant of modern industry. I can
vouch from experience that this type of ruthless partition
and subjugation of native peoples always leads to dis-
sent. Who knows how history will unfold in this volatile
region, and what brutality will erupt, during the next
century ... or longer?*

Cassandra paused to ponder this observation. Ceaseless
wars during the 20th and 21st centuries in Palestine, Israel, Lebanon, Syria, Iraq, Iran and other Levantine countries bore testimony to the accuracy of this prophecy. As a university student
of the 2020s, she was aware of the Palestine genocide and the
ravaging of Iran, Iraq, Lebanon and Syria.

This was heavy going. The letter had been useful for her Russian Revolution thesis, a first-hand account of an official who suffered the ultimate price for loyalty, but how was it relevant to that country bumpkin from Australia's deep north, whom Marcus had seen fit to foist on her as an assistant?

Another coffee helped her to focus – and then she struck gold as she read further.

I share my cell with a forlorn British soldier, or perhaps I should correctly acknowledge him as he insists … an Australian soldier. I do not understand these people. He was born in that far-off wilderness on the wrong side of the globe, apparently the great-grandchild of convicted felons, whom the British had deported to that "Siberia of the South". There is no doubt of his courage and his loyalty to his mates. He will support his friends, even unto his own death. While he fiercely retains an anti-authority insolence, he nevertheless "signed up to help his mother country", and he follows their orders without question. Despite being ruthlessly blooded by the appalling carnage of the Turkish killing fields, and despite the British military incompetence that sentenced thousands of his compatriots to early graves, he is again following them into another military disaster. This foreign Central Asian civil war offers no credible threat to his antipodean homeland, yet he is here. He is again blindly following his bungling imperialist masters, and yet again he is betrayed. Perhaps these Australians are incapable of thinking for themselves. As I said, I admire their courage and loyalty, but I do not understand these people.

I asked his name, but he simply drawled, "Mate, just call me Digger". My puzzled brow extracted the further explanation that "digger" was slang for "Australian soldier", although I have since learned that the term originally referred to the migrants, from many countries, who scratched in the Australian dirt for gold, some 70 years previous. Despite being called "Digger", he seemed to suffer particularly severely from the claustrophobia of our shared underground hell-hole. But talking seemed to relax him, so he talked, hesitantly at first … but then he talked and talked and talked. Digger was just 19 the first time he killed someone – the day Australia went to war. In the cold, dark pre-dawn of 25 April 1915, he was one of the first to struggle from the icy Aegean onto the Gallipoli shore, the killing field later to be known as Anzac Cove. Digger told of his many mates who met their Maker on the first morning – too many for a young man, for a mere teenager. All were tragic, but one in particular shook him to the core.

A 23-year-old sergeant had taken Digger under his wing. Before enlisting, the sergeant had been a teacher and was, therefore, used to leadership. He also had a good knowledge of military matters, as his father was a Boer War veteran who had risen to the rank of major. The sergeant had volunteered early in 1915. Enlisting as a private, he rose quickly through corporal to the rank of sergeant. They were among the first wave of Australian troops that struggled ashore before dawn and up the steep cliffs flanking the beach. Dodging machine-gun fire, they scaled the first ridge, and after 20 minutes were about 800 metres inland. The troops still sheltering on the beach had been warned not to fire before daylight, because unseen Australians were already scaling the cliffs ahead of them. Then ... disaster. The sergeant was struck by a bullet – in the back. He knew he had been shot by a fellow Australian and was heard to say, "It is hard luck being hit by one of our own men". A stretcher-bearer dressed his wound in an abortive attempt to thwart death. An energetic, charismatic young man, revered by his men, loved by his parents and adored by his siblings, had passed from this world, without children, without grandchildren and without fulfilling his potential for human contribution. All that stretched before him, just moments earlier, had now perished.

Digger witnessed many more deaths that day, and each day of the following eight months. Both Turks and the invaders, many of them just boys, killed and were killed. He would never know the death toll of that Gallipoli invasion. I have subsequently heard estimates of 87,000 Turks, 21,000 Britons, 10,000 Frenchmen, 8,700 Australians, 2,800 New Zealanders and 1,400 Indians. The wounded numbered twice the number who died. And for what? After a fruitless eight months of carnage, the invaders, who had come ashore along the coast at Anzac Cove, Cape Helles and Suvla Bay, retreated, leaving Gallipoli to the brave Turks who, at enormous cost, had successfully defended their homeland.

But it was not over for the Australians. Blooded by Gallipoli, many were deployed to the murderous western front, cannon fodder for the disastrous trench warfare of northern France and Belgium. But Digger was fortunate. He had been raised on a sheep farm (a station, he called it) and was quite a good horseman. After withdrawing from Gallipoli, Digger seized an opportunity to transfer to one of the cavalry brigades that constituted the Australian Mounted Division – or as he called it, the "Australian Light Horse".

The Light Horse had seen action (without their horses) in Gallipoli and had been withdrawn, along with the rest of the invaders. After regrouping in Cairo, under the direct command of their own General Chauvel, they joined British General Allenby's push east out of Egypt, across the Sinai wastelands and into the southern Levant. Destination Damascus. As 1916 turned to 1917, Digger was in his element … a horse, a rifle, the open air and the opportunity to kill Turks. He was particularly fond of telling of his participation in the action at Beersheba, adjacent to the southern Judean foothills.

The Light Horse emerged from the Negev Desert, waterless and thirsty, approaching the strongly defended wells at Beersheba. They were desperate for a quick battle. If they delayed, the defending Turks would destroy the wells, and the march to Damascus would stall. At 16:30 that afternoon, 800 Australian horsemen of the 4ᵗʰ Brigade of Chauvel's Light Horse charged three kilometres across open ground into heavy machine gun fire … and into history. The Australian Light Horse seized the town and the wells of Beersheba in the last great cavalry charge of a major war. It was the stuff of legend, and Digger never tired of recounting the detail and the elation of the victory.

*Mature people should pragmatically consider armed con-
flicts, weighing the human costs (on both sides) against
the potential benefits (if any) that might accrue from the
prosecution of the battle. But it appears that Digger and
his countrymen act from instinct alone. It is as if they were
born myopic, unable to see past the immediate situation,
into the broad sweep of history and the damage caused by
the violence that they pursue. Digger has adopted a per-
verted pride in his suffering, and he is addicted to war. I
pray, for the sake of his countrymen, that future generations
can curb this war lust and take a more mature approach to
the resolution of foreign conflicts, particularly those that do
not directly threaten them.*

*Unknown to Digger and his mates, there was political
intrigue afoot. As Chauvel's Light Horse bore down on
Beersheba, British Colonel T.E. Lawrence was scheming
with Arab Sheikh Faisal (bin Al-Hussein, bin Ali Al-
Hashem) for the dismemberment of the Turkish empire and
creation of a far-reaching Arab state. But unknown to Lawrence and Faisal, British diplomat, Sykes, and his French
counterpart, Picot, had already arranged an alternative
acquisition of territories that benefited their own countries.
Reacting to domestic political pressures, the British have
declared their intention to create a Jewish state amidst the
hostile Palestinian lands. How naïve are these people? Can
they not see that this will cause Jewish-Palestinian conflict
for decades into the future – perhaps centuries?*

*Betrayed by the British and French, Faisal had to abandon
his dream of a Pan-Arab state and settle for a subservient*

kingship of the newly created Iraq. Meanwhile, his tribal enemies, the Al Saud, are being favoured by the British power brokers as the rulers of the Arabian Peninsula. Further north, the Turkish hero of Gallipoli, Mustafa Kemal, has successfully displaced the disgraced Young Turk leadership triumvirate of Enver, Jemal and Talaat. As I write, it is clear that Kemal will also dispense with the ineffective Sultan Mehmed VI. There will be great turmoil in the dismembered Turkish empire, genocide against the Armenians in the east, displacement of Greeks from Asiatic Anatolia, and an exodus of Turks from the hostile European lands west of the Bosporus. Old scores will be settled and there will be great bloodshed.

Poor Digger. He is bewildered by these machinations of international power politics. But I have had recent news of an even more perverse nature. The Basmachi rebels are a Turkic people, who are resisting the Russian Reds, further to the east in the Fergana Valley. In their desperate struggle, the Basmachi are supported by the British. But the Basmachi are currently led by none other than Enver Pasha, the discredited former Turkish leader. Whereas Digger and his countrymen once fought in support of the Russians against Enver and the Turks, they now are fighting against the Russians and supporting Enver and his Turkic bandits. When I explained this to Digger, he just wept. He finally realised that the years of killing had been for nought.

Yesterday the prison guards dragged Digger away, presumably on his way to meet his Maker. I do not know what happened to him. To the end he maintained his sense of humour, joking with me right up to the moment when they dragged him out of our shared pit.

"We have been through hell together, mate," he called back. "So I guess we will meet in a better place next time!"

I think that we both sensed that his life had been a terrible waste ... killing and more killing, just to end up being killed ... and what did he achieve? If he died, he would have died alone and unmourned, in an alien land far from home, without wife or children, and failing to make any meaningful contribution to advance humankind – unless you count cracking a few jokes. I hope his death was quick ... or perhaps (just perhaps) he may have survived. But either way, I never saw Digger again.

It so unsettled me that I could not sleep. The icy stone floor of the dungeon sucked the warmth from my aching body, and my mind was wracked with a kaleidoscope of horrifying images ... blood and gore, swords, guns, bombs, and the whole arsenal designed to deliver death and destruction. But finally, I must have slept, although that afforded no relief. I dreamed, but the dream turned to a nightmare ...

I am at peace in a green field in my beloved Central Asia, when I sense danger approaching on all sides. From the north, a huge bear bounds across the steppe, from the south a ravenous lion descends from the mountains; in the western sky I see an eagle circling and, in the east a fiery dragon is stirring. I am running, desperately running, but I find nowhere to hide. The first to catch me is the bear. I fall to the ground as his huge claws rip at my flesh. The pain is unbearable and I cry out for help. Soon the lion is menacing the bear, and my hopes of survival soar. But the bear beats off the lion, which is forced back through the mountains whence it came. The bear continues to devour my flesh, and I fear that I will surely die. But then, from the sky swoops the eagle. Its powerful beak and claws torment the bear, which finally withdraws. I am saved ... but no! Now the eagle tears at my limbs, and the pain is worse than that inflicted by the bear. And when I fear all is lost, I see the dragon slowly but surely emerging from its eastern lair, breathing fire and consuming all in its path, as it approaches. The eagle and the dragon face each other; each has a vice-like grip on my arms. I am being ripped apart. And then ... then ... No, I can remember no more.

I must have woken then. Another day, another nightmare. I pray that this letter may find its way to you, perhaps when your ship, our great naval cruiser Aurora, is back in ~~Saint Petersburg~~ Leningrad. It appears to have nine lives ... survivor of friendly fire in the North Sea on its maiden voyage; survivor of the Tsushima Strait disaster near Japan; and instigator of the revolution, firing at the Winter Palace. But take care, my son. Despite the coincidence that your brother's ship, a steam yacht, was also called Aurora, God saw fit to sacrifice him to German mines, beneath the South Pacific somewhere off the Australian coast. I do not want to lose two sons.

I pray that you will somehow receive this letter, for I do not know whether I will have the opportunity to write again before my fate is sealed. Remember, I love you.

Your most affectionate father ...

Cassandra stared in disbelief at what she had just read. That closing paragraph: *... your brother's ship, a steam yacht, was also called "Aurora", God saw fit to sacrifice him to German mines, beneath the South Pacific somewhere off the Australian coast.*

This was identical to the story Aurora had told Cassandra the day before – that the women of her family all had the middle name Aurora, in memory of the ill-fated ship of her missing Russian great-grandfather.

Could this coincidence be true? Did it mean that the White-Russian official who had shared a cell over one hundred years ago in Central Asia with Digger's great-grandfather was actually Aurora's great-great-grandfather? Did that mean that Aurora's great-grandmother (who had had a relationship with a Russian sailor) and Digger's great-grandfather (a soldier in the bug-pit) were sister and brother? No way!

But here was the proof.

She smiled as she replaced the letter in the file, but this time labelled with a prominent yellow sticky note marked KEEP.

Knowledge is power.

Who knew when this knowledge might prove useful?

CHESS ALONG THE SILK ROAD

… chess was so widely played along the Silk Roads that there are a number of theories as to how it evolved. One theory is that an early game similar to chess called Chaturanga originated in the northern Indian Subcontinent during the Gupta period (~ 319–543 CE) and spread along the Silk Roads west to Persia … similar strategy board games such as Xiangqi in China, Janggi in the Korean Peninsula and Shogi in Japan have been exchanged and played along the Silk Roads where they are still played today …

The earliest reference to the game comes from a Persian manuscript of around 600 CE, which describes an ambassador from the Indian Subcontinent visiting King Khosrow I and presenting him with the game as a gift. From there it spread along the Silk Road to other regions including the Arabian Peninsula and Byzantium. In 900 CE, Abbasid chess masters al-Suli and al-Lajlaj composed works on the techniques and strategy of the game, and by 1000 CE chess was popular across Europe, and in Russia where it was introduced from the Eurasian Steppe …" [23]

Marcus motioned for Digger to enter his office and take a seat beside Cassandra. This was the final step in confirming Digger's appointment to the senator's staff as Cassandra's assistant. For all intents and purposes, it was the job interview.

Marcus had developed a unique style for interviewing potential staffers, designed to draw out their ideas on the most obscure of topics – a test of their resourcefulness and flexibility.

Cassandra herself had been put to the test when she'd been interviewed (not so long ago), and Marcus had asked for her thoughts on the probable role of the British Government in forcing Türkiye into World War 1 on the opposing side, so that they, colluding with their French conspirators, could assume control of the Levant oilfields from a defeated nation.

You must be joking! Cassandra had thought at the time. Marcus already knew that Cassandra's thesis subject was the 1917 Russian Revolution, and he knew she had researched, as background material, the international politics of that era. She'd disclosed that in her written job application. Early 19th century Turkish politics was a related subject, even though it didn't impact directly on the Russian Revolution. Thus, Marcus's request gave him an opportunity to see how she could extrapolate a little peripheral general knowledge to explore, and evaluate, alternate hypotheses relevant to a specific historical event. Now it was Digger's turn to squirm under this same spotlight.

"So, Douglas, please tell me a bit about yourself, your travels, what motivates you, that sort of thing," Marcus began.

"Please, Senator, call me Digger. Everyone else does. It's a sort of family name ... you see, each generation from my great-grandfather down has been called Digger, even though it shows 'Douglas' on my birth certificate and passport."

"Okay, Digger. And you can call me Marcus, at least while we're in the office. I can see from your CV you've written articles for a travel magazine about recent developments in, say, western China and beyond after the COVID crisis of the early 2020s. Perhaps you could start by telling me about your visits to China's Xinjiang Autonomous Region, Kyrgyzstan and Uzbekistan. For example, why you were there, what you observed, what you experienced and what you learned. Take about, let's see, twenty minutes – and maybe throw in a bit of history to provide context. Educate me, entertain me ... nothing too difficult!"

And so, Digger began the most important speech of his career.

"Sure, that sounds like a challenge. I know from your published memoirs that you, Senator – sorry, I mean, Marcus – have also travelled in Xinjiang, over a decade ago, during the period of deteriorating security, but while the Chinese government was still allowing foreign visitors, albeit closely monitored.

"I visited western China in 2028, about twelve years after you did. That means the worst of the Uyghur insurgency in the region occurred between our two visits. In your own memoirs, Marcus, you described yourself as old enough to understand the demise of the ailing British Empire, supplanted by the American global hegemony which pervaded the late 20th century, and the Pax Americana. You also observed the end of the Cold War, the dissolution of the USSR, and the ultimate failure of an expansionist Russia in its bellicose invasions in Manchuria, Afghanistan and Ukraine. That same period also featured the pointless American militaristic adventurism of failed wars in Viet Nam, the Balkans, Iraq and Afghanistan, together with countless other covert intrusions into the governments of small countries around the world. But, for me …" and here he broke off and glanced towards the office window.

"For me, the most appalling fiasco of international politics was the 2023–2025 failure to arrest the merciless killing of over sixty thousand Palestinians by the Israeli Defence Force as revenge for the murder of 1,200 Israelis."

On this subject, emotion overwhelmed Digger's normally controlled demeanour. He paused, cleared his throat and then continued.

"Your travel memoirs preceded my own witness and recording of the economic warfare waged during the past decade – the rise of China through the late 20th and early 21st centuries, and its ultimate defeat of the capitalist mercantilist economic protectionism of Trumpian America.

"Although it was starkly obvious to many wiser heads in 2024, an ill-informed insular American majority failed to embrace the reality of a huge difference between what a politician promises, to get elected – or re-elected in this case – and what he can actually achieve, even if he *were* genuinely trying to achieve some tangible benefit for the broader American public.

"But more importantly for Australia, our own government failed to recognise these changes in global relationships. Like the American population, the Australian electorate couldn't comprehend that populism cannot replace sound policy. The subsequent election of Australian governments by a public ignorant of real-world situations ensured that Australia would, like a faithful puppy, continue to mindlessly tether itself to its American master. This meant that during this same period, Australia virtually guaranteed it'd be drawn into the vortex of the next world war, through reliance on its various American alliances and military cooperation arrangements."

He stopped and glanced first at Marcus, who sat listening intently, then at Cassandra, who appeared to be nodding off.

"I believe that our own views probably align in condemning the second Trump presidency as the period that rammed home – to any observant witness – the American failure as a world leader ... economically, militarily and, most importantly, morally."

Marcus gave the slightest of nods but did not comment other than to indicate Digger should continue.

"I have made these observations as a prelude to replying in detail to your invitation to comment on my own travels in China, particularly in Xinjiang in the west of the country, and in neighbouring Kyrgyzstan and Uzbekistan. In other words, I have sought to provide some context for my own observations.

"Although my visas stated I was a tourist, which I genuinely was, I'd been encouraged by a colleague – I believe you know Aurora – to use this opportunity to research and report on the progress of the China-Kyrgyzstan-Uzbekistan rail link construction project. Many Sinophobic Australians take fright at every Chinese initiative aimed at improving their trade and transport links, and I saw it as important to write a soundly based opinion piece on this enterprise and what, if anything, it'd mean for Australia.

"Of course, I had to be very careful to ensure I didn't stray across the murky boundary into illegal intelligence-gathering. The Chinese government still imposes severe penalties on suspected spies. I was diligent in ensuring all my enquiries were restricted to publicly available material, that I didn't photograph any rail infrastructure or military establishments, and that my notes were typical of a tourist's diary. Fortunately, one's memory can fill in a lot of blanks around an accurate framework provided by airline bookings, train tickets and photos of mountains and rivers.

"As I'm sure you are aware, the China–Kyrgyzstan–Uzbekistan rail link is an integral part of China's Belt and Road Initiative, the BRI. The proposed six-year construction program for the Kyrgyzstan link was announced in a small village near Jalal-Abad at the end of December 2024. It's part of China's attempt to provide secure transport links between China and Europe, the Middle East, India and, eventually, to Africa ... routes that don't rely on sea passage through the disputed South China Sea and the precarious Strait of Malacca, between Sumatra in Indonesia and Malaysia and Singapore, or land routes across the vast expanse of a potentially hostile Russian steppe. As you know, without the BRI land transport corridors, China's international trade would be extremely vulnerable to American disruption in the event of a full-blown trade war ... or worse.

"Let me briefly describe the history of trade along the ancient Silk Roads over two millennia. That ancient network of trade routes originally connected the Chinese Han Dynasty of two millennia past to their ancient contemporaries, the Roman Empire, and subsequently to its successors."

Digger paused again, seeking endorsement for what he feared may have simply been considered "waffle". Cassandra, as he'd half expected, looked bored, but Marcus waved for him to go on with another slight nod of approval.

"Commencing about 4,000 years ago, China had been developing self-sufficient, inward-looking civilisations through the successive Xia, Shang and Zhou dynasties, which eventually succumbed to fragmentation during the Warring States period.

The short-lived Qin dynasty finally emerged ahead of its competitors, uniting the country with its capital based in Xi'an.

"During the subsequent 400-year Han Dynasty, a unified China flourished, as did the overland trade along the Silk Roads, linking the Chinese east with the European west. This trade survived for a thousand years over numerous dynasty changes at both ends of the Silk Roads, as well as en route. Notably, trade continued under the Mongol disruptions of the thirteenth century, and it was only during difficulties associated with Turkish expansion in the fifteenth century that both Chinese and Europeans began to consider sea routes as an alternative to the existing land routes. And this's where it starts to get interesting ..."

There was an expectant hush in the room as Digger took a big gulp of chilled water. Downing his glass, he went on with his tale again.

"Where was I? Ah, yes ... The Chinese and European approaches were very different, and the results reflected this. On the one hand, the European initiatives were driven by a small group of self-motivated adventurers in the service of a small number of relatively small competing countries. First the Portuguese, then the Dutch and British came. The French, Russians, Americans and Germans all joined the feeding frenzy, each willing to ruthlessly demand more unequal trade concessions from China.

"On the other, the Chinese initiatives were centralised and bureaucratic. Under the Ming dynasty, the sea voyages of Admiral Zheng He were terminated, with the bureaucracy systematically stifling the international inquisitiveness of Chinese maritime traders.

"Just when Europe was expanding from the 15th century onwards, China was *contracting*. The effect was gradual, but inevitably fatal. The Qing Dynasty appropriation of power in 1644 failed to arrest this decline, and by the time the Europeans appeared in force, China was ripe for exploitation.

"China declined while the West expanded. China suffered two centuries of exploitation and humiliation, and this, I believe, is what drives modern China's quest for security and prosperity.

"One of the most telling examples of this exploitation resulted from the increased commodity trade with the Chinese in the 17th and 18th centuries. This stimulated a craving by the British public for Chinese tea. It became a habit matched only by the Chinese addiction for opium. The British solution was simple … initiate the two Opium Wars to force the Chinese to accept Indian-grown opium as payment for Chinese-grown tea. Drug trafficking has a long history."

Marcus smiled slightly at Digger's attempt at levity. He had quoted Marcus's own words from his published journal. Marcus gestured for Digger to continue. Cassandra shifted uncomfortably in her seat, her eyes beginning to glaze over. This Digger character certainly knew his stuff, but he was droning on for much longer and in more detail than she had during her own "interview".

"My trip commenced in Shanghai, which is – to use your own terminology – a miracle of modernity and a symbol of the hard work of the Chinese people. True genius can only be measured from the outcomes that result, and, in my opinion at least, the true genius of modern China was Deng Xiaoping, who led his country between 1978 and 1989.

"Through his embrace of a market economy, albeit within the context of an authoritarian government, China emerged from poverty and has steadfastly progressed towards prosperity.

Following the competent leadership of Jiang Zemin and Hu Jintao, Xi Jinping took control and accelerated the process. The spectacle of Shanghai's glittering Pudong district by night when viewed across the Huangpu River is a worthy testament to the collective leadership of Deng, Xi and other visionaries."

Digger now sensed that Marcus was intrigued with the narrative. He knew the Senator took a close interest in train travel through foreign countries, having embarked on many such trips in remote parts of the world. Marcus took a sip of his coffee, Cassandra shifted again in her seat, and Digger continued confidently with his monologue.

"Train travel through China is no longer the uncomfortable trial it was in earlier times. Modern trains speed along elevated tracks with an efficiency that would be the envy of any modern airline. Although yet to reach full commercial potential, magnetic levitation, or maglev, for short, high-speed train technology has extended from speeds of over 400 km/hour, which was initially achieved on Shanghai's Pudong Airport line, to speeds in excess of 600 km/hour.

"However, my trip to Ürümqi in the remote north-west Xinjiang Autonomous Region was via a more sedate thirty-nine hours spent on conventional high-speed electric trains travelling from Shanghai, through Nanjing and Xi'an to Lanzhou, and then on via Turpan to Ürümqi. But I also took time to stop and soak in the culture and history of several cities en route.

"Nanjing had served as the capital of several Chinese dynasties and kingdoms over the millennia and was capital of the republican Kuomintang government of Chiang Kai-Shek until 1949. It'd also been the base of the rebel Taiping Heavenly Kingdom in the mid-19th century, and capital of the Japanese

Wang Jingwei puppet government. It suffered many atrocities leading up to, and during, the Second World War.

"Xi'an, Chang'an of old, had at various times been the capital of the Zhou, Qin, Han and Tang dynasties, supplanted only by Beijing during the Mongol Yuan dynasty in the late 13th century. Caravans would set out westwards from Xi'an with their precious cargoes of silk and other commodities.

"Today, however, tourist interest centres a little further east on the mausoleum complex of the Terracotta Warriors. These were unearthed in 1974 – 6,000 clay warriors and their 40,000 bronze weapons, faithfully guarding the resting place of the first Qin emperor, Qin Shi Huang, for over two millennia, testifying to his imperial magnificence. Or so it seemed."

Digger broke off, before resuming in a more contemplative tone.

"But what is magnificence? Despite Qin Shi Huang's proclivity for violence and his reputation for ruthlessly crushing his enemies, his dynasty lasted only fifteen years, from 221 to 206 BCE, before being supplanted by the Han Dynasty. Ruthlessness and vanity do not guarantee longevity, it'd seem.

"On arrival in Ürümqi, I wasted no time checking into the moderately priced Bingtuan Hotel overlooking Hongshan Park, where I was visited by the security police, who were quick to establish contact with me – a rare western tourist.

"My movements around Ürümqi were in no way restricted, but as reported in your own writing a decade earlier, I too noted military convoys moving down the highways and through the city streets, as well as the army post just outside the hotel's main entrance and frequent army patrols through the residential parts.

"While ongoing military activities seem to suggest now, as then, a general crackdown on the populace at large, the military concentration around tourist infrastructure indicates a response to targeted terrorism, something that's seldom been reported in our Australian media.

"The north-eastern Dzungaria region, which as I'm sure you know is inhabited by Tibetan-Buddhist Dzungar nomads, and the south-western Tarim Basin – inhabited by Turkic-speaking Muslim Uyghur sedentary farmers – existed separately before being united by the Qing Dynasty in 1884 to form the province of Xinjiang.

"This effectively reinstated the Chinese political control that'd previously existed under the Tang dynasty between the 7th and 10th centuries of the modern era. The Tarim Basin, of course, is rich in oil and gas, and China seeks to supply approximately a fifth of the country's consumption from this region.

"Ürümqi is impressive. It's a large, modern city of over five million people, mostly Han Chinese, originally from the east. Xinjiang itself now has a population close to 30 million, roughly half Han Chinese and half Uyghur and other ethnic groups.

"For years, the Chinese government's been concerned with Islamic fundamentalist separatism propagating throughout the Uyghur communities, and the police, army and security services have been omnipresent for a long time. The Uyghurs are linguistically and culturally Turkic and Muslim, but the Han Chinese speak Mandarin and mainly adhere to Buddhism, Confucianism or Taoism.

"It's a complicated situation, really. Although religious practice is tolerated, the government of the People's Republic of China does not formally endorse or support any religions.

"Meanwhile, the Uyghur separatist movement claims the region was invaded by China in 1949 and has subsequently been under Chinese occupation. The 2005 Tulip Revolution in neighbouring Kyrgyzstan ushered in a period of political instability throughout the region, with China's Xinjiang region suffering increasing Uyghur militancy and acts of terrorism.

"This threat was exacerbated by the 2016 bombing of the Chinese embassy in Bishkek, Kyrgyzstan's capital, and the return of the fundamentalist Taliban regime in Afghanistan in 2021. Human rights organisations reported the severity of the Chinese government reaction to what it claims to be Uyghur terrorism, but more recently the increasing wealth and development in the region means the previous separatist threat, and the reactive repression, is slowly receding.

"Anyway, back to my story ... My plan had been to switch to the train that traverses around the north side of the Tarim Basin in the shadow of the Tian Shan mountains, skirting the Taklamakan Desert, and terminating – at least for the time being – in Kashgar. But I must confess I became a victim of my own honesty, or perhaps naivety is a better choice of word, when I foolishly listed my profession as journalist on my visa application. Journalists, of course, are the last people the Chinese security service wants to see in western Xinjiang!

"So, because I could go no further in Xinjiang, I continued by bus overland into Kazakhstan, before turning south through Charyn Gorge to Karakol in eastern Kyrgyzstan. Once there, I took the opportunity to venture into the mountains beyond Jety Oguz, to the south towards China, and then Shaban, to the north towards Kazakhstan. I continued west around the northern side of the Issyk-Kul Lake – which is stunningly beautiful, by the way – to Bishkek."

Digger knew from his perusal of Marcus's published journal that he'd spent some time in this remote region, and would be familiar with, and hopefully interested in, the observations of a fellow traveller.

"After a two-day break, during which I just rested and relaxed, I continued south for an arduous nine-hour drive through the western end of the Tian Shan mountains to link up again with the proposed China–Kyrgyzstan–Uzbekistan railway at Jalal-Abad, before crossing into Uzbekistan and then on to Tashkent via the Fergana Valley. From Tashkent I resumed the role of a normal tourist, high-speed train to Samarqand, before continuing to Bukhara and Khiva.

"So, my main observations garnered during this trip, and by considering wider history are as follows.

"First, any developed country that tries to hide behind isolationism and its economic equivalents, such as tariff walls, is doomed to stagnation and decline. The withdrawal of Ming China from 15th century trade has now been replicated in the 21st century by the United States and will, over time, result in the same stagnation.

"That said, there are better ways to encourage and foster those industries that are key to national survival. These include eliminating those supply-side costs and taxes from which international competitors are already exempt. A sensible adjunct is to boost free tertiary training in STEM-related professions.

"Second, a China that seeks fair trade with Australia, and is prepared to militarily protect those trading arrangements, is not Australia's enemy.

"And finally, Australia must be prepared to engage with a host of different trading partners, including India, Japan, Korea, Indonesia, Viet Nam and the other countries of South-East Asia. It isn't a zero-sum game."

Digger finished his monologue; Cassandra rolled her eyes, while Marcus nodded his appreciation. He was impressed and, later, over another coffee, said so. Digger had nailed it. It was clear to Marcus this "can-do", "knockabout" Aussie larrikin was capable of astute observation, as well as the formulation of insightful conclusions.

After his busy morning meeting with Digger, returning missed phone calls and answering countless emails, Marcus took a few minutes to rest. Alone now in his office, he cradled his coffee cup in both hands and sipped slowly. An early-morning coffee had been a ritual he'd practised for many years with his wife. Now, often, he indulged in the beverage alone.

Ah … coffee.

As the effects of the caffeine diffused through his body, his thoughts returned to a happier era … a time of adventure, when he and his wife had set out to conquer the world. During their long marriage, they'd travelled widely, seeking to learn more of the cultures on each of the continents. He still enjoyed flipping through old photos or browsing his travel diaries. Before she'd passed away, his wife had encouraged him to set out these experiences in a more formal memoir, the one to which Digger had referred.

Marcus mused that even when young, he'd been concerned by what he perceived to be the major political threat of his lifetime: the excesses of authoritarian regimes around the world, the fragility of liberal democracy and the dysfunctional role of the media. *While vote-rigging, intimidation and torture were the most obvious abuses inflicted by governments,* he reasoned, *surely ordinary people must also accept responsibility for compliant obe-dience as their freedom of independent thought was progressively eroded?*

Media laziness and bias should be at the forefront of our con-cerns. So, too, must the public guard against intellectual laziness. We mustn't allow ourselves to be brainwashed by a biased media, he reminded himself.

The morning's meeting with Digger, listening to his nar-rative, had been refreshing as well as productive. As these thoughts crowded into his consciousness, Marcus returned to the problem that currently confronted the Australia he loved.

People get the government that they deserve, and it is they, the people, who must guard against the threats to liberal democracy.

PAWN PROMOTION

A pawn that reaches the end of the board can become any piece you want (just not the king or another pawn) – pawn promotion.

And so it was that Digger joined Senator Marcus Whitehorse's Canberra staff, albeit temporarily. Nevertheless, it would be a pleasant break from the torrid north. It was all a bit cloak-and-dagger, he felt. The letter of appointment described the job as "… a temporary appointment as Assistant to the Research Officer, providing grassroots feedback on government development initiatives in Australia's far north". But what Marcus had told him privately, not reflected in the letter, was different.

"There's something fishy about Australia's current action within the Quad alliance," Marcus had said. "The leaked Pentagon documents hint at some hidden strategy, but the government is tight-lipped about it. I believe it has something to do with the military bases in Australia's north, and perhaps beyond. You have on-the-ground experience and contacts in that region, so your real brief, Digger, is to provide me with enough information to ask the right questions in the Senate."

"What is the purpose of your visit to Timor Leste?"

"Tourist ..." came Digger's nonchalant reply as the bored immigration officer searched for an unused page in his tattered passport. The inefficiency of the old-fashioned immigration system was somehow comforting. The description of "tourist" attracted less scrutiny than the cover story he'd use during his stay: *I am an expert working for an Australian not-for-profit NGO.* And it certainly attracted less scrutiny than the real story: *I am here to prepare a report for an Australian senator on the extent of recent Chinese political and military influence in Timor Leste.*

Despite initial goodwill engendered by Australia's early support for Timorese independence from Indonesia, Australia had repeatedly managed to sour the relationship.

In 2004, the Australian Secret Intelligence Service (ASIS) had bugged a room next to the Timor Leste Prime Minister's office during negotiations concerning the Timor Gap oil and gas fields, to benefit Australia. When the deception was exposed in 2012, the Australian Government denied the bugging and subsequently prosecuted the whistle-blower.

Throughout the 2020s, Australia continued to disadvantage Timor Leste regarding gas processing, denying the opportunity to treat the gas on-shore in south-facing Betano Bay.

Aid was curtailed, resulting in an inevitable Timorese appeal to the ever-willing Chinese. *But what price did China demand,* Digger pondered. *What was the trade-off? Was the new Betano Bay gas plant the only installation that had been built by the Chinese, just a short 670 kilometres across the Timor Sea from Darwin?*

Digger shouldered his daypack as he exited the international terminal. He was used to travelling light; no messing around with bulky baggage, which would inevitably go missing on even the shortest of international flights.

He'd been here before, between the bouts of civil unrest that had plagued the early years of this infant nation. While recent improvements were everywhere, much was familiar. The Cristo Rei, a gigantic statue of Jesus, arms outstretched, still gazed over the long sweep of the serene Dili Harbour, backed by the now-peaceful city. There were a few more medium-rise buildings, a sprinkling of bars and restaurants, and a handful of new hotels, but much remained from yesteryear.

Digger wasted little time checking in at his hotel but set about establishing his cover, an NGO employee on official business and an enthusiastic part-time tourist in his spare time. Quick visits to the Immaculate Conception Cathedral, the Government Palace (which now served as the Prime Minister's Office), the Pura Girinatha Hindu temple, and the Cristo Rei statue, provided an itinerary worthy of any tourist. A traditional Portuguese meal and a quick drink in the bar, presaged an early night in bed. Tomorrow would be a busy day.

The next morning, Digger set about establishing the bona fides of his assumed identity: an expert in carbon sequestration and tree-planting projects, an activist dedicated to arresting climate change and an enthusiastic employee of a charitable not-for-profit NGO.

Multinational oil and gas producers paid handsomely in aid grants to the governments of developing countries for the carbon credits they earned through their sponsorship of carbon sequestration in tree plantations. While such schemes paid big dividends to small developing countries, they simultaneously alienated large tracts of scarce arable land. A specialist consultant in such matters had unquestioned access to many parts of the country, and Digger had sufficient knowledge and confidence to pass as a credible authority to all but a real expert. He engaged a local guide and set off to inspect several such projects.

The first was west of Dili, along the coast to Liquica and then up the river past the village of Metagou. Here, on the mountain slopes overlooking the serene Savu Sea and the Indonesian Alor Archipelago beyond, local farmers now tended multiple hectares of seedling and mature eucalypts, each earning precious foreign currency for the Dili-based government.

For the fortunate few thus employed, the income was good, but for the many unemployed, the loss of subsistence agricultural land had made life tough. Digger soaked in the peaceful atmosphere, photographed the plantations, and listened enthusiastically to the employed, and sympathetically to the unemployed. But this visit to Liquica was simply part of his cover as an agricultural specialist. The real mission, observing military activity, would start tomorrow.

As they re-entered the outskirts of Dili, Digger, glancing at the passenger side mirror, noticed a little Chinese Changan car with a broken headlight. He'd first glimpsed it in Liquica and here it was again, still behind them – some distance back, but replicating every turn they made. It remained until they reached Digger's hotel, when it vanished. Coincidence? Perhaps.

Or perhaps not.

Rising early the next morning, Digger took a brisk walk beside the crystal sea lapping the foreshore of Dili Harbour. The peace of this idyllic setting permeated his soul, and his bare limbs absorbed the warmth of the sun as he strolled beside the calm waters. This was why he loved the tropics. He sucked in the clean, balmy air with its slight hint of salt spray.

Pleasant as it was, he must return to reality to begin his real mission. Today's journey would be much longer than yesterday's – and much more important for the fulfilment of his clandestine project. Again, under the guise of inspecting tree plantations, Digger and his guide would ascend the tortuous hairpin bends of the road that wound over the hills south of Dili.

Setting off after breakfast, they stopped for a quick coffee in the tiny township of Aileu, then headed south towards Maubisse, their objective no longer the eucalypt-covered hills but the highly secretive Chinese-funded off-shore gas treatment plant at Betano Bay.

Betano Bay had a long association with Australia. Here, the 2/4th Commando Squadron had landed in the dark days of 1942 to reinforce the Australian Sparrow Force guerilla fighters in their struggle against the occupying Japanese imperial forces. From here, also, they were evacuated several months later.

And in Betano Bay the ill-fated first HMAS *Voyager* grounded, and was scuttled, during those landings. Somewhere beneath those sands, washed by the Arafura Sea, lay the corroding bones of a valiant Australian warship.

All seemed to be proceeding to plan but then, as they rounded a sharp bend, there, across the road, was a makeshift barricade, manned by a pair of armed security guards.

"I am sorry sir, but I cannot let you pass. This road is closed." It was spoken in perfect and polite English, albeit with a Timorese accent.

And there, a little further down the road, partially obscured by the overhanging branches of trees, was the little Chinese Changan car with its broken headlight.

THE PIN

*A pin occurs when a defending chess piece is under attack
but cannot move without exposing a more valuable piece.*

On his return to Canberra, Digger reported directly to Marcus, neatly avoiding any contact with Cassandra. The venom that'd poisoned their initial relationship had now festered into a full-blown infection. He despised her, and she him.

Marcus, with the wisdom of years, recognised the tell-tale signs, and had sought to reconcile the two. But reconciliation had proved too difficult, and all he could do was separately instruct each to swallow their pride and focus on the common goal that could only be achieved through mutual respect and cooperation. Slowly, the atmosphere softened … a bit.

Marcus was disappointed that Digger's quest to observe the Betano Bay gas installation had been thwarted, but he remained upbeat. Perhaps Digger would be more successful on his next assignment.

In the meantime, Digger decided to call on Aurora, his friend and mentor. On arrival at the studio, he was conducted directly to her office. But on entry he was shocked.

Before him sat a broken woman, sobbing uncontrollably. Her office was a mess, papers strewn everywhere, some on the desk while others littered the floor. An empty red wine bottle had rolled under the desk, pushed there as the door had opened against it. Another lay, almost empty, balanced precariously on the edge of the desk, while an empty glass lay on the floor beside the weeping woman.

After considerable effort and exercising all the patience he could muster – showing a compassion he hadn't previously demonstrated – he coaxed from her what had triggered her breakdown.

On the floor lay a ripped envelope, and on the desk, a formal letter typed on the network's official letterhead. It was brief and to the point. ... *direct you to cease all communications with Senator Marcus Whitehorse henceforth. Failure to do so will result in disciplinary action."*

Aurora was pinned. She loved her job, but she also feared the network and the faceless powerbrokers who manipulated its policy.

Digger did his best to console and comfort her, while she slowly calmed and began to explain the context of her dilemma. It seemed that Digger's visit to Timor Leste hadn't gone unnoticed, and the powers-that-be had moved quickly to shut down any controversy.

"Which powers, exactly?" Digger asked. "Can you give me any names?"

Aurora shook her head.

"Who knows? Just 'the powers'."

Obviously, they were aware of his connection to both Aurora and Marcus, and this had triggered the gag.

Digger tried to convince her to immediately apply for a day of compassionate leave. After all, she was a long-standing employee who'd suffered a deep personal shock. But Aurora was having none of it. They, whoever "they" were, wouldn't keep her from her chosen profession.

Finally, Digger prevailed, and Aurora agreed to apply for one day of leave. But first, he must take her home. Digger supported her as she negotiated the office door, the corridor, the fire door and the emergency exit stairs. He bundled her into the back of a hastily summoned Uber and whisked her off to the safety and security of her apartment.

Digger knew Aurora had grown close to Cassandra in recent weeks, so, swallowing his pride and ignoring the warning in the letter, he telephoned the girl. To her credit, she came immediately. Both agreed that, for Aurora's sake, they'd keep this incident confidential, confiding only in Marcus. The senator would know what to do.

REINFORCING THE QUEEN ATTACK

Early attacks by the white queen, such as the queen's gambit, are sometimes effectively repulsed by the strategic use of the black knights, the thugs of the chessboard. When the queen is under attack, all of her allies must rally around for her protection. Without the queen, the game is lost.

When she struggled out of bed the next morning, Aurora had a gut feeling it was going to be another bad day at the office. She woke late, with a feeling of dread in the pit of her stomach and her head thumping like the bass drum of a heavy metal band. Unable to face solid food, she opted for a liquid brunch.

Her aching guts and the nausea rising in her throat made it tempting to not go in to work. She'd call in sick, she decided. But that wasn't a great idea in the circumstances. She knew "hangover" wasn't on the list of acceptable post-COVID reasons for absence. She stumbled into the bathroom, fuzzy-headed and confused.

Slowly, a semblance of normality took hold as the cold shower jolted her back to partial reality. Aurora towelled dry, retrieved yesterday's clothes from the wash basket, ordered a ride-share and at last made it into the studio. But as she'd predicted, the day seemed destined to end in disaster.

What felt like an endless age in make-up resulted in such a thick application of a pale-coloured foundation to mask the blotchiness of her skin that she ended up looking like a Japanese geisha. She knew she looked awful.

Gazing at her reflection in the mirror, she felt sickened at how far she'd fallen. The "goddess of the dawn" – the Aurora – had morphed into the Medusa, the Greek gorgon of darkness, with snakes substituting for hair and a visage so hideous that mere mortals would turn to stone at the sight of her.

Not a good look for the camera – and her producer obviously thought so too. A heated argument ensued.

"Take the day off, Aurora. No. Take the week off. Actually … take the month off. I don't care!" he bellowed, as he metaphorically slew the gorgon. "In fact, I don't want to see you again until you've pulled yourself together. Don't come back until you hear from us. Chloe, get in here! I need you to cover for Aurora. Quick smart!"

Shocked, her eyes filling with tears, Aurora realised she was being suspended … indefinitely. Her career, her whole life, had been torn apart in the space of a few seconds.

Marcus was appalled when he was alerted to the fate of his friend. He knew instinctively there must be more to Aurora's suspension than her alcoholism, and this was soon confirmed by his assistant.

Cassandra may have been an impetuous young political climber, but she was also a good researcher with an ever-expanding web of informants. According to her, Aurora's intemperance was just a convenient excuse, the perfect ploy for a cleverly orchestrated government-ordered operation to remove from public view a journalist – the only journalist, in fact – bold enough to challenge their fictitious pronouncements.

Time for Marcus to intervene.

As it happened, Marcus was scheduled to ask a question without notice in the Senate. Coincidentally, this threat to freedom of the press directly impeded his own aim to alert the Australian public to the impending sinister developments in foreign affairs. He must carefully tailor a question such that Aurora's suspension could be quietly reversed, without specifically drawing attention to her case.

He stood up.

"Can the Minister confirm the Australian Government's commitment to freedom of the press? In particular, will the Minister confirm that the Australian Government, its members and their staff, have never sought to influence the staffing decisions or editorial policies of media? Is the Minister confident that the reporting of foreign affairs is balanced and unbiased?"

Next day, Aurora's suspension was lifted.

QUEEN'S PERIL

Survival of the queen ensures that future attacks can be most effective.

It wasn't over yet, though. Another day brought self doubt, drowned by another night of alcoholic overindulgence. Her suspension lifted, Aurora went back to work and survived another evening ordeal in front of the cameras.

Stressed and miserable, she decided to clear her head by walking home from the studio, stopping off at the local bottle shop on the way. But it'd been raining heavily in Canberra – just as it seemed to rain constantly in her head – and Aurora had neglected to take an umbrella. Now, back at her apartment, she was soaked.

Too weary to summon the energy to change into dry clothes, she simply kicked off her shoes, poured herself some wine and collapsed on the couch, her mind in a turmoil. She could not erase the guilt and shame that crowded her thoughts, chasing away any chance of relaxation. She was a fraud, she convinced herself. Despite the appearance of being a caring and compassionate opinion-maker, deep down she knew she'd been a disappointment as a wife, irresponsible as a parent and a failure as a grandparent.

Self-opinionated and too focused on her career, she'd allowed her ambition to overshadow the important things in life, the reason for her existence – the care and nurture of her children and her grandchildren, the generations to whom we must bequeath a better world.

After a few more drinks, she succumbed to her exhaustion, and slumber quickly turned to sleep. But sleep turned to dreaming, and her dream became a nightmare. Waking in fright, she couldn't return to sleep, so she spent the rest of the night tossing and turning in a cold sweat.

She must have dozed off again, because the next thing she knew, the sound of the alarm was reverberating through her aching head with the intensity of a jackhammer. She was late for work – again. She struggled from the couch, threw down some coffee and stripped off her still damp clothes. She hurriedly donned some crumpled dry ones, raced out of her apartment door and headed for the exit. And then it happened ... a piercing pain, shooting through the whole of her upper body. As she stumbled, consciousness departed, although not before she had one last fleeting thought.

Was this her end?

When Aurora awoke, she was neatly tucked up in a hospital bed, with tubes protruding from places better not mentioned. There by her bedside sat her son, daughter-in-law and two grandchildren. Concern was writ on their faces and they looked as though they'd been crying.

"We thought we were going to lose you," her son confessed. "At first we thought you'd suffered a massive heart attack, but thankfully it's not that bad. They're saying you passed out because of a serious bout of pleurisy. Probably exacerbated by ongoing stress – but they told us the main factor is the … um … I mean … um … well, they called it alcoholism. But they say that after a few days' rest, you'll be OK."

Aurora felt her eyes well with tears as he continued awkwardly. "We love you, Mum. We love what you do and what you stand for. But most of all, we love you because you love us."

"I love you too, Nan," blurted out her five-year-old granddaughter, as she laid her cheek softly on Aurora's free hand.

"And me too, Nan," piped up her little brother with a cheeky grin, so warm that it could melt a glacier faster than you can say global warming.

As the family continued to talk, Aurora felt her world righting itself again. Now, she could see a way ahead – and it looked brighter than it had in a long while. Waving goodbye as they left her to rest, she knew for certain everything was going to be all right. Her life's work hadn't been in vain, after all. Her family knew and understood her suffering. More importantly … they loved her.

The queen's peril had passed.

BISHOP'S OPENING

"Bishop's opening" describes a game in which white advances their king's bishop to C4 in the second round. Black may respond in several ways but must be wary not to fall into a deadly trap laid by the white player.

Burdened by concern for his friend's mental welfare, Digger was reluctant to embark on his second mission. But Marcus had been firm.

"Your assignment is of national importance. Don't you worry about Aurora. There are ways and means to thwart the bullies. I'll look after her, and by the time you return, she'll be her old self again."

The flight into Port Moresby's Jackson International Airport was uneventful. Digger had visited here several times during the past decade, mostly en route to other, more remote parts of the country to work with volunteer groups and local community-based organisations, building clinics, schools and other village infrastructure. The work had been difficult, and at times dangerous, but the satisfaction of seeing the health and education of the locals improve was worth the effort.

Transferring to a local flight to Mendi, capital of the Southern Highlands Province, was fairly easy: out the door of the modern international airport, a sprint along the footpath, and in through another door to the domestic airport. Here was another world, with the press of local people milling around expecting their flight would be called next, despite predictions to the contrary on the cluttered departures board.

Ostensibly, Digger was here to visit the Senator's old friend, the bishop, whose diocese extended both east from Mendi into the remote mountains and west into the lawless, mineral-rich Hela Province. Marcus and the bishop had become friends over a decade earlier, when he'd accepted an assignment to assess and report on damage to the diocese's schools, hospitals, housing and churches, caused by the powerful earthquake that devastated Hela and Southern Highlands Province.

But the continuing earthquake tremors weren't the only problems confronting them at the time. Hela was a hotbed of tribal warfare, pitching clan against clan in an escalating cycle of violence. In years past, the bow-and-arrow technology had limited the scale of injury and death, but more recently the increasing availability of guns had introduced a more deadly factor into each clash.

Nor was the violence limited to tribal warfare. Politicians encouraged their own supporters to execute acts of intimidation and thuggery aimed at the supporters of opposition parties.

Exacerbating this unrest was a seething undercurrent of resentment by locals, evicted from their traditional land by rapacious mining companies, yet denied any meaningful share of the enormous wealth being extracted. This was the region of abductions, when unwary expatriates were seized and spirited away, to be released only on payment of huge ransoms.

Under such conditions, the United Nations relief agency had withdrawn its staff, and aid had dried to a trickle. Yet, despite all the dangers and difficulties, the bishop's staff of expatriate and Indigenous clergy and sisters continued to labour in these perilous conditions, dedicated to their vocations as pastors, teachers and health professionals. Marcus had been inspired by their commitment, and he was confident Digger would be similarly impressed.

The bishop never took any action contrary to the interests of his adopted home, but he also well understood the reason and urgency of Marcus's request for assistance. He respected and agreed with Marcus's view that the interests of both Australia and PNG relied heavily on a clear understanding of both the overt and covert activities occurring in this remote and lawless part of the country. So, rather than delegate the role to one of his many employees, the bishop decided to accompany Digger on this journey west into the uncertainty of Hela Province.

He'd driven this road many times, through the astounding beauty of the tree-covered mountain ranges of the western highlands. But this beauty masked the hidden risk of armed robbery by gangs of local bandits, a danger endemic in this lawless region.

Setting out just as the sun appeared over the tree-lined crest of the eastern mountains, the bishop and his passenger, Digger, drove south from Mendi through the magnificent scenery along the few stretches of sealed road, before turning north-west.

From here, the unsealed and progressively deteriorating road climbs steadily through the tiny settlements of Nipa and Margarima, each with a history of local violence stretching back many years.

Here, at Margarima, during Marcus's visit over a decade earlier, he and the bishop had witnessed first-hand the makings of a violent tribal encounter. As they'd slowed to enter the town, a crowd of about fifty local youths, stripped to the waist, painted and adorned with feathers, had surged up the road from the opposite direction. Replete with a variety of weapons from bows and arrows to lethal firearms, they were bent on doing battle with their tribal enemies. Fortunately, they'd merely milled around the now-stationary vehicle before resuming their quest, leaving the car and its occupants unmolested.

For decades, this had been one of the most dangerous journeys in PNG. Even a bishop wasn't immune to robbery and assault. But this time, the journey was without incident. As the road climbed, the vegetation thinned, changing progressively from lush temperate forest to sparse alpine grasses. After passing over the 3,000-metre Tari Gap, Digger and the bishop again descended to the Hela provincial capital, Tari.

The town hadn't changed much in ten years. A few new buildings, some built to replace those destroyed in the earthquake, and others springing up to service the burgeoning population; but mostly the unpaved roads, burnt-out shells of houses, untended shops and ruined warehouses told a sad story of decline and decay – a decade of corruption, violence and neglect.

With nothing to see and less to do here, they set off south along the dusty development road as it snaked up out of the valley in a series of precarious bends, to run along the ridge, down again to the valley floor, and up again with monotonous repetition. At last, they entered Komo, a large village set high on the plateau.

From this village, in 2023, a gang of youths had set out on a rampage of rape and violent assault near Mount Bosavi. The gang eventually seized an Australian academic and his three female assistants working in the region, and held them for ransom.

Although the four were rescued, the brutality inflicted by the gang appalled even the most callous critics of the inability of local police to curb highland violence. That incident, though now long past, still served as a potent reminder of the fragility of peace in this lawless region.

But Digger was here on a mission, commissioned by the Senator to check for any unusual activity in this mineral-rich region. High up on the ridge to the east of Komo stretched a four-kilometre airstrip, the longest one in PNG, built solely to service the mining industry. It still hosted a string of transport planes ferrying miners and machinery in and out.

To the west, perched on the ridge on the opposite side of the deep valley, balanced the Hides 4 Gas Conditioning Plant. With its double-razor-wire security fencing, a string of brooding watchtowers and constant patrols by armed guards, one could almost believe it to be a huge, high-security prison. The gigantic flare tower beamed out a hellish warning of fire-and-brimstone retribution awaiting all those who participated in evil or sorcery.

The original intended purpose of the facility was much more benign – to separate and treat the natural gas, condensate and water before the gas was piped 700 km south to the LNG (liquefied natural gas) Plant near Port Moresby – the same gas that now crossed Torres Strait and found its way down the Cape York Peninsula to the Weipa Alumina Refinery.

But Australia wasn't the sole customer for PNG's most lucrative export. Another, more recently constructed pipeline now snaked its way north to the coastal town of Wewak. The gas piped here was destined for export to the steel mills of China.

The Australian Government's failure during the 2020s to provide the PNG government with meaningful royalties had resulted in a Chinese offer that significantly undercut the rapacious Australian contract.

Similarly, the offshore gas supplies close to Timor Leste had also been lost when that government successfully secured Chinese funding to construct a local processing plant, which now exported to energy-hungry China. The resulting significant reduction in secure gas supplies for the Australian alumina refinery so threatened its economic viability that, half a decade later, it was struggling.

Alumina processing wasn't the only mineral-based industry to suffer, as China sought to secure reliable mineral and energy sources other than those provided by a belligerent Australia.

During the 2020s, Chinese steel mills made huge investments in north and west Africa, to develop and export the precious red-brown iron-ore mineral to their own factories. Australia and its traditional competitor, Brazil, were now obliged to reduce the export price for iron ore to such an extent it was hardly worth extracting.

While progressive Australian governments had dreamed of local green steel manufacture, conservative politics fanned the fears of "governments picking winners", and the result was stagnation and an Australia that now languished with the losers.

Travelling these roads was both uncomfortable and dangerous. The mining company staff seldom ventured beyond the safety of their compounds, and the locals remained surly and suspicious of strangers.

After a long and tiring journey, Digger and the bishop welcomed the opportunity for a restful night in the security and relative comfort of the staff quarters within the Komo church compound. The next morning, refreshed after a good night's sleep, and with little untoward activity to report, Digger decided it'd be wise to return, via Tari, to the relative safety of the bishop's base in distant Mendi.

As their vehicle rounded one of the switchback bends, a large truck appeared out of nowhere, heading straight for them. The bishop swerved towards the edge of the road, close to a sheer drop. Fortunately, their four-wheel drive vehicle lodged in the drainage ditch on the brink of the cliff. The truck braked and paused. Reversing lights appeared, but still the truck paused. Then, as suddenly as it'd appeared, it was gone.

Shaken, Digger and the bishop emerged from their stricken SUV. They stood staring at it for some time. Luckily, in PNG local villagers are always close by and, despite the obvious tensions pervading the regions, men of the church are well respected for their selfless, life-long devotion to their people.

In no time at all, a dozen strong men had extricated the car from the ditch and set it back on the road to Tari and, thence, out of Hela Province and back to Mendi.

The next day, having bade farewell to the bishop, Digger settled back as the plane climbed up over the rugged ranges on the return flight to Port Moresby. They'd been lucky to escape a potentially serious truck accident. Why had the driver appeared to consider reversing, only to change his mind and continue without even enquiring as to the extent of damage? The question kept him occupied until the plane landed safely at its destination.

KNIGHT FORKS

A knight is able to attack two or more pieces at the same time (a fork) and cannot be blocked by other pieces that may be in the way.

Marcus understood he'd sent Digger into a potentially dangerous situation in PNG. The preliminary report of a "road accident" involving an Australian ex-pat and a bishop in Hela Province had disturbed him. But now he'd heard from Digger in person that all was well, with no damage done, Marcus could breathe more easily. The warmth of his study helped calm him, and soon his thoughts had left the young PNG adventurer for the nostalgia of his own adventures of yesteryear.

Just as European colonial powers were retreating from Asia in the decades following World War 2, so too were they exiting Africa, leaving in their wake a poor, under-developed, tribally heterogenous and violent continent, and a score of newly formed countries. Marcus and his wife, both young, idealistic and naïve, had been drawn into this situation. They had spent two years working and touring in Europe and now sensed the "dark continent" was beckoning them, urging them to use their skills for the development of this place before returning home to Australia.

Zambia is in the heart of central-southern Africa, land-locked by Zimbabwe, Botswana, Namibia, Angola, Congo, Tanzania, Malawi and Mozambique. In the mid- to late-1970s, violence, poverty and corruption surrounded this isolated small country.

In 1975, Angola and Mozambique were abandoned by Portugal, their colonial overlord, resulting in violent civil wars as left and right factions, puppets of the superpowers, battled for control.

Namibia, or South-West Africa as it was then known, was controlled by the apartheid regime of South Africa, which used it as a base to invade Angola.

Zimbabwe, then known as Southern Rhodesia, had proclaimed a UDI (Unilateral Declaration of Independence) from Britain, with a white-minority government prosecuting a bloody but unsuccessful war against its neighbours.

The Democratic Republic of Congo was infamously renowned for the corruption and brutality that plague it to this day, while Tanzania, Malawi and Botswana were then desperately poor. Zambia, however, was relatively stable and life for ex-pat professionals was reasonably comfortable.

For Marcus and his wife, the year in Zambia was one great adventure, with lifelong friendships formed that would lead to a network of acquaintances around the world. They visited most corners of the country: the isolated and rarely visited Northern Province, including the soaring Kalambo Falls and the new, Chinese-built TAZARA Railway, Kafue Game Reserve, the resource-rich Copperbelt Province, and Kariba Dam, shared at that time between Zambia and its enemy, Rhodesia (now Zimbabwe).

But the highlight was the magnificent Victoria Falls, "Mosi-oa-Tunya", "The Smoke That Thunders", reputed to be the world's largest waterfall, based on the combination of its 108 metres height and 1,708 metres width. To stand only metres from the rushing water, however, just upstream of where it plunges into the depths of the gorge that snakes away downstream, is an experience that makes such dimensional statistics irrelevant. To feel the power and hear the thunder is humbling, and so it was for Marcus and his wife.

After three years of adventure in Europe and Africa, they returned home to the peace and isolation of Australia to settle down and start a family. After they left, the war between the Rhodesian minority government and the various guerrilla organisations escalated.

In 1978, cadres of ZIPRA (the Zimbabwe People's Revolutionary Army) shot down an Air Rhodesia passenger plane near Kariba Dam. Only eight passengers survived, thirty-eight having been killed in the crash and ten survivors, including men, women, and children who'd initially survived, were machine-gunned to death.

Rhodesian retribution was swift and coordinated, with the launch of Operation Gatling on 19 October 1978. The Rhodesian Army and Airforce attacked guerilla bases inside Zambia, killing well over 1,500 people. As part of this operation, the airborne Green Leader Raid bombed a base at Westlands Farm.

Many years later, Marcus stumbled across an internet recording from 1978 of the Green Leader's voice, supercharged with testosterone and oozing adrenalin, as he released the bombs that killed hundreds of his fellow humans at Westlands Farm. Marcus had found it truly chilling to listen to the Green Leader gloating over the destruction and death he'd just delivered. Surely, no provocation could justify the brutality of such revenge.

While Marcus knew the casualty numbers were small compared to those of many other wars, the proximity of this atrocity to his and his wife's former home at Lusaka struck a chord.

How traumatised must be the relatives of the over 60,000 people murdered during the Palestinian genocide and Lebanon invasions? Marcus thought, as he sat in the peaceful surrounds of his office. *What about the hundreds of thousands of deaths resulting from the Russian invasion of Ukraine? And these were just examples of well known conflicts. Many other fierce conflicts raged throughout the world, particularly in Africa, but they attracted little media attention.* That the media should keep the public in the dark over such devastation was a situation that appalled him.

He reflected on the wisdom of attacking the current problem on several fronts – Cassandra would provide thorough in-depth research, Digger could verify the situation on the ground in neighbouring countries, Aurora would concentrate media scrutiny where necessary. He, meanwhile, would work with his fellow politicians to effect change.

He roused himself from his rumination. Time to get to work.

CHECKMATE WISDOM

"Checkmate wisdom" is the application of chess philoso-
phy to everyday life situations, including the importance
of the journey, rather than simply the destination. It pays
due attention to teamwork, strategy and learning from
mistakes. Like a chess king, the leaders of society must be
protected by the teamwork of their most-trusted lieuten-
ants. Each chess game offers valuable insights into the
problems, solutions and decisions that confront us all.

Both "checkmate wisdom" and the "wisdom of Solomon" had been conspicuously absent from Australian foreign policy leading up to the events of 2023.

At that time, the governments of Solomon Islands and the People's Republic of China entered into a security arrangement, triggering a tsunami of strategic concerns that submerged the Australian foreign affairs community and helped to wash away the conservative government of the day.

Now, almost a decade later, Digger peered out of the window as the jet banked to starboard, buffeted by some minor air turbulence, then levelled and began its slow descent into Honiara International Airport. Known locally as Henderson

Field, this airstrip had been the scene of some of the most brutal fighting between the desperate Japanese and American forces during World War 2, as both sought strategic advantage in the Solomon Islands.

Honiara had changed little since his last visit. The untidy port stretched along the northern shore of Guadalcanal, littered by a clutter of inter-island ferries and merchant vessels. Mimicking this seaborne chaos, the waterfront was strewn with non-recycled plastic drink bottles and other refuse.

As expected, road traffic had increased, and it still crawled along the choked road from the airport into the town centre. The huge stadium, built by the Chinese to indulge the Solomons' national vanities of the 2023 Pacific Games, now stood forlorn, its once-green gardens now sprouting weeds from the surrounding brown desert. Potholes had returned to the access roads, and rust now transformed the previously bright paint of the metal fence to a blotchy orange hue. The physical discord there reflected the underlying, but obvious, friction between the Indigenous Guadalcanal residents and the sizeable settler population from the neighbouring island of Malaita.

Digger booked into a rundown three-star hotel hidden away in the backblocks of the capital. He didn't want to draw attention to his visit, so he'd shunned the up-market hotels closer to the waterfront. At this time of night, the street stalls were closed, so he opted for a Chinese meal in a sleepy backstreet café before returning to his ageing hotel room for a lukewarm shower in the mouldy bathroom and retiring for an uncomfortable night on a lumpy bed, no doubt accompanied by an assortment of bed bugs. One night in this dysfunctional capital was more than enough for Digger, and after a sleepless night he was restless to resume his westward journey.

The cramped, twin-engine propeller-driven aircraft he boarded was in sharp contrast to the huge passenger jets that dominated international travel. Brief landings at Seghe and Munda on the island of New Georgia revealed the decade of deterioration that'd followed the airport upgrades funded by the initial Chinese aid package of the 2020s.

Memories are short, Digger reflected as he gazed through the small window on his right. Few now recalled the intensity of the Chinese efforts to influence and penetrate the Solomon Islands' Western Province.

The aircraft approached its destination, the runway that ran the length of the small island, a short ten-minute ferry journey from the Western Province capital, Gizo. As the plane descended, Digger caught a glimpse of Kolombangara Island, the "sleeping lady", so called for its unique profile, through the starboard window. More recently though, it'd become known by a more sinister name ... the "sleeping dragon".

For years, the Chinese had sought a foothold in the critically important Western Province, and Kolombangara was ideal. Rising out of the glistening sea to 1,770 metres – three-quarters of the height of Australia's highest mountain, Mount Kosciuszko – the island dominates its neighbours. Its deep-water port, airstrip and proximity to the rebellious Papua New Guinea province on Bougainville Island enhanced its strategic significance. And now, despite previous rebuffs, Kolombangara hosted a Chinese so-called "timber plantation".

Still travelling light, Digger shouldered his daypack and walked the short distance to the dilapidated jetty to board the hotel ferry. The Gizo Hotel, now showing its age, was renowned for its casual atmosphere, local seafood cuisine and the magnificent view from the upstairs bar and dining room across the water towards Kolombangara. He only had time for a quick meal at the bar, unusually crowded with raucous Americans. He'd have liked to linger, but he was here on a mission.

Digger had previously volunteered with an Australian NGO, building village water-reticulation and sanitation schemes on the neighbouring islands of Ranongga, Vella Lavella and Simbo. Those projects had long been completed, and the program abandoned due to lack of funding from the Australian Government. His cover story: he was visiting these islands to review the long-term effectiveness of those forsaken projects. But, of course, the real reason was to assess, for the Senator, the potency of the Chinese naval facility – the "timber plantation", on Kolombangara.

Powered by its huge outboard engine, the five-metre fibreglass boat Digger hired literally flew from crest to crest, the driver sitting in the stern, his hand lazily twisting the throttle and occasionally adjusting course as deep waves rolled across the thirty kilometres of open ocean between Gizo and Simbo Islands.

Schools of tiny flying fish skimmed across the crystal-clear water, guiding the vessel towards the volcanic peaks of Simbo. Here, the seismic stability is precarious. Sitting on the edge of the Woodlark tectonic plate, villages on Simbo Island were devastated by the 2007 earthquake and obliterated by the tsunami. But memories are short, and thermal springs and smoking fissures were now the only reminder of the earlier destruction.

Digger's visit to Simbo was brief; a chance to touch base with an old friend, a carpenter he had worked with many years previously, the opportunity to view the thermal springs and,

depressingly, to observe first-hand the poverty that still permeated this poor community.

Departing to the north, Digger crossed the narrow but
treacherous strait separating Simbo from Ranongga. Making
landfall in the village of Lale, he proceeded up the coast to
Obobulu and Buri.

Here, Digger stepped ashore briefly and visited some more
old friends, local people he'd worked with to construct and
maintain water and sanitation projects for the area.

But that, too, had been long ago. The underfunded,
neglected water supplies had long since failed to deliver the
precious aqua into the villages, while the over-flowing pit
latrines had been abandoned in favour of defecation in the
bush. It was depressing to see that this region, once so well
serviced by an Australian not-for-profit organisation, now
languished in poverty.

Even the poorest of places can inspire through their natural
beauty, though. In the late afternoon on Buri headland, as the
golden orb of the sun descends slowly into the glowing western
sea, all worldly cares, like the fiery star itself, are extinguished in
the majesty of this moment.

Digger headed north next, up the west-facing "weather"
coast of Vella Lavella Island, visiting several villages along the
way before swinging east into "the Slot", a passage of protected
water that runs the length of the Solomon Islands. At last, the
true objective of his mission, Kolombangara, loomed into view.

Camera clicking, Digger directed his skipper to follow the
long eastern coastline of Kolombangara, past Jack Harbour,
Bibiu and the deep-water port of Ringgi. Here, the activity was
frenetic. Chinese-flagged ships lay at anchor, and he saw large
concrete structures set deep into the still waters. *This* was the

information the Senator was seeking ... *click, click, click* – and here they come. The security boats.

Hastily exiting under the cover of rapidly approaching darkness, Digger's boat headed back towards the safety of Gizo Island and the small township. As blackness enveloped the little vessel, they were forced to reduce speed and carefully plot a course across the open water past Kasolo Island.

As the boat approached Gizo, Digger remembered it was also known, both locally and internationally, as Kennedy Island, in honour of the late John F. Kennedy. Here, on 1 August 1943, the American torpedo boat *PT 109*, commanded by Kennedy, had been rammed and sunk by the Japanese destroyer *Amagiri*. Kennedy and most of his crew survived, but it'd been a close call.

Digger settled back as the lights of the town came into view. But abruptly, *bang!* An object, travelling silently and at speed, slammed into the side of the boat.

DEVELOPMENT

"Development" is a fundamental concept of chess opening theory. The number of chess pieces in active play can be assessed comparatively, by counting the number of active pieces developed by each side. To some extent, development is reactive. What one player does is affected by what the opponent does. Therefore, development proceeds differently in different openings.

Digger and his pilot were in luck. It was only a short night swim to Kennedy Island and an uncomfortable couple of hours on the beach until dawn. From there, the lone island caretaker could radio for another boat to pick them up and return them to civilisation. The price of a new boat and motor, together with a sizeable monetary inducement, ensured the pilot's silence. Amazingly, he only recalled hitting a partly submerged log before his craft slid into the briny deep.

Back in Canberra, Digger reported in detail to Senator Marcus Whitehorse, and later, he briefed Cassandra. Although she showed little interest in his Solomon Islands adventures, she was keen to brief him on what she referred to as an "emerging situation" in Darwin.

Hidden away in a recent press clipping was a single paragraph, innocently drafted and crafted by an investigative journalist from the *Darwin Navigator*, one of the few independent newspapers in the country. The *Navigator* had a reputation for ruthlessly revealing scandals and corruption throughout the country's north. No secret was off-limits, and the paper had frequently been censured in the Federal Parliament.

The article concerned a disturbance that occurred outside the American consulate in downtown Darwin: local university students demonstrating against the presence of American marines stationed at various bases in and around Darwin.

After a couple of days of ineffectual shouting, the demonstration assumed more sinister tones. People entering the consulate were pelted with food, and in the dead of night, the building's external walls were graffitied. The police made a few token arrests, dragging off some of the ringleaders, which only served to intensify the vehemence of the demonstration.

Then an unusual twist of events occurred. Instead of letting the police handle the increasingly ugly situation, the American Consul decided to address the crowd; not the most sensible of actions. The already animated throng escalated their protests, and argument led to abuse. The Consul stood his ground, but eventually reason turned to reaction.

The paragraph that caught Cassandra's eye read:

> *... The demonstrators continued to throw food and hurl insults at the consulate officials. Finally, the Consul lost his temper and, contrary to all the conventions of diplomacy, shouted back at the demonstrators, "You should thank us for being here. Chess is still a better game than xiangqi ..."*

Unfortunately, a twenty-six-year-old arts master had no idea what *xiangqi* was, but a quick Google search showed it was a Chinese strategy game, similar to modern chess. What did the Consul mean? A meaningless insult, or a more subtle declaration, signalling a sinister message to senior Australian officials?

Cassandra realised from the by-line that she and the journalist who'd filed the story had been friends at university – no … more than friends. That had been a long time ago but still, his insights might be useful.

Cassandra decided to send Digger to Darwin to interview her journalist friend and report back. At least that would get him out of her hair for a while, so she could get on with the real work. With her usual lack of tact and subtlety, she gave Digger his marching orders, demanding he report back to her, only her, and no-one else. Her move didn't go down well.

"Look, luv, I'm not a pawn in your political power play!" he retorted.

And with that, he stormed out of the room.

PAWN SACRIFICE

Pawn sacrifice, as the name implies, is the deliberate sacrifice of one or more of a player's pawns. The purpose is to open an attack on the opponent's king, by deriving a space advantage by removing the opposing king's pawn cover, or by otherwise leaving the king undefended.

The hot breeze off Darwin Harbour gusted in over Larrakeyah, up Doctors Gully and along the Esplanade. Most people would wilt from the oppressive humidity. But not Digger, glad to be back in his hometown, the place where he'd lived most of his early adult years.

During the past twenty years Darwin had changed almost beyond recognition. Digger strolled along the Esplanade, reflecting on the memorials to the World War 2 servicemen and women who'd rushed to the region at the time – the only time Australia had been under attack.

It had shocked the government of the day, so much so they'd suppressed the information. Such secrecy hadn't changed much in ninety years. The Australian Government was still paranoid the voting public would turn on the politicians if they really understood how negligent their leaders had been.

He pondered the past. Several Australian towns had been attacked during the dark days of World War 2. But the two air raids on Darwin, on 19 February 1942, had been the most devastating. Two hundred and forty-two Japanese aircraft had pounded the city, the port and the ships anchored there.

The government wouldn't reveal the extent of the damage or the number of casualties, but estimates ranged from a minimum of 250 to a possible maximum of twice that number. These two raids were the first of over one hundred smaller air raids on Australian towns and military assets, yet still the government of the day remained tight-lipped.

Digger walked past the Legislative Assembly Building and Supreme Court, pausing to reflect on the decisions and judgements on Indigenous issues that had been debated and considered here, then descended the steps of the escarpment to the Fort Hill Parkland below. He sauntered past the entrances to the secretive World War 2 fuel storage tunnels, past the university building, various hotels and the convention centre. Here he lingered a while, breathing in the atmosphere of the tranquil inner harbour and exhaling the Canberra muck that had so polluted his consciousness. At last, he made the long walk out along the timeless Stokes Hill Wharf.

This was his favourite part of town. Fish still congregated far below in the clear water lapping the piers, almost daring the fishermen to hook them. Towards the end of the wharf, locals and tourists patronised the six-star restaurants and the utilitarian fish-and-chip stands. Some dined in, enjoying world-class cuisine, while others simply enjoyed their take-away meals, as they bathed in the retreating rays of the setting sun.

That silly little girl in Canberra had sent him here on a fool's errand. He'd seen her type before and knew her game.

Extract as much information as she could about the comings and goings of the north, get rid of him for a few weeks, and then claim credit for all he'd revealed.

But he was having none of it. He'd make the best of this trip to Darwin, treat it as a holiday, a chance to renew old acquaintances, get in a little fishing and, who knows, perhaps "she" might care to pick up where they'd left off. The "she" in question was not some jumped-up Canberra political schemer, but a real woman, one of substance and spirit whom he'd last seen in Darwin fifteen years before. Had it been that long?

There, silhouetted by the fading sun, she sat on a bench, gazing over the serenity of Darwin Harbour. He approached, sat down opposite, and reached out his hand to touch hers.

"Digger, it's really good to see you again after all this time." But as she spoke, she glanced past his shoulder to the man and two children approaching, arms laden with fish and chips. "Let me introduce you to my husband and children."

It had been a bitter blow. But then, what else could he expect after so many years? As the evening progressed he played along, making polite conversation and expressing his gratitude for meeting again to reminisce about shared times past. Long past. And yes, he was delighted to meet her two charming children, and hear how well they were doing at school. And her husband – I'm sorry, what was his name again? – must be incredibly busy with his practice. So many patients to see at this time of year.

"And me? Oh, I am just here on business for a couple of days. Yes, I'd love to catch up again sometime … although, of course, I rarely get back to Darwin these days. But it was lovely to see you again."

Inside, he was gutted. After such a disastrous evening, he consoled himself, a trip to the pub was well deserved.

And so began a three-day bender.

The phone jolted Digger awake; the Senator didn't sound annoyed, although he should have been. Digger had effectively wasted three days of an important assignment.

Marcus again explained the gravity of the situation. Digger was there to find out as much as he could about the American Consul's reference to "chess" and "xiangqi". Surely, it wasn't some meaningless slip by a furious diplomat facing down an angry crowd? There had to be more to it than that. Perhaps a subtle barb, intended to prick the awareness of senior Australian policy-makers.

Digger apologised for his tardiness, promising to get back on the job and report back tomorrow. Yes … he understood. Time was critical.

Cassandra had provided Digger with the contact details of her ex-boyfriend … ex-fellow-student, that is. He was more than helpful, offering to arrange a clandestine meeting with an anonymous contact from inside the consulate. Secrecy was paramount, so the meeting took place in the dead of night on a small yacht moored off the Fannie Bay foreshore. Discreetly departing via the Trailer Boat Club ramp, the short speed-boat trip took just a few minutes. Digger sprang to the deck of the yacht with the agility of an alley cat, waving off the speed boat, which departed rapidly into the gloom, with instructions to return in one hour.

Making his way cautiously to the hatch, Digger went below deck. To his surprise, huddled in the corner of the cabin was a diminutive bespectacled youth – no, he must be older than that – a diminutive bespectacled young man. After a few moments of introduction, they got to work. Time being of the essence, Digger didn't bother to read the documents in any detail. Rather, he concentrated on photographing and transmitting what appeared to be the key pages.

Click and send ... and the fifteen photos of the summary, each marked "top secret", were safely dispatched to the Senator. The images had barely left his burner phone, instantaneously travelling through cyberspace to Marcus's email server, when the cabin door splintered with a thunderous, deafening clap and a thick cloud of dark smoke.

Instinctively, Digger pitched the burner phone through the open porthole into the dark depths of Darwin Harbour. As the smoke cleared, two burly, balaclava-clad thugs stormed in, one of them yelling in a distinct Texan drawl, "Y'all put your hands where we can see 'em! Assume the position! NOW!".

American agents. That could be either good or bad. Digger's mental question was soon resolved. It was to be the latter.

He never saw the consulate contact again. Who knows what became of that poor devil? If he was lucky, he'd spend a couple of decades in the Guantanamo Bay hell-hole, conveniently secreted away from the piercing glare and scrutiny of the domestic American media, and within the heartland of a hostile Cuba. But there could be worse outcomes for those deemed traitors by the Americans.

And what of Digger, an Australian citizen, in his home country, acting in his own country's interests, on the written instructions of an Australian senator? Surely these agents knew they couldn't abduct or kill him. After all, *they* were foreign guests in his country. But realistically, when did such diplomatic niceties and local laws restrict the activities of American agents?

Digger could sense they must be under strict instructions to ensure he couldn't interfere with current events. Securely manacled and hooded, effectively immobilised and blinded, he was hauled from the yacht to the deck of a waiting cruiser. He heard the throb of the diesel as it kicked into life. For three hours that seemed like an eternity, the cruiser bounced from wave to wave. When it hove to, Digger was bundled into a dinghy and transferred at high speed to some unknown shore then unceremoniously dumped among the mangroves.

"Let's see how many more lives this cat really has. He was supposed to be dead in the water last time, up there in the Solomons, but, shucks, here he is again," drawled one of his captors.

"Shut up, Tex," snapped the other in a clipped Bostonian accent. "Yo tok too much."

A searing pain ripped through Digger's shoulders and the base of his skull, and he knew he'd been struck from behind with some heavy object, perhaps an oar. His knees buckled as he momentarily lost consciousness. But he was lucky. Although the blow had been directed fully towards his skull and would have been fatal had it connected, the darkness meant it fell mostly on his shoulders, only glancing off the cranium.

He fell face-down into a shallow pool, and the cold water quickly jolted him back to semi-awareness. Instinct told him to roll out of the water, but logic dictated otherwise. He sucked in a mixture of air and slimy ooze and allowed his body to go limp, while they removed the handcuffs and ripped the hood from his head. There'd be no evidence of his abduction.

The outboard motor roared as the dinghy disappeared into the gloom. Digger lay prone for a long time, unable to think or make a move. Eventually, he rolled away from the water, spluttering and coughing up a mouthful of briny sludge. Acute pain wracked his upper body, and a ringing noise distorted his hearing, almost obscuring the receding high-pitched whine of the outboard as the dinghy returned to the cruiser. He lay there for a long time.

At length, he struggled to his knees and turned to face the open sea, just as the cruiser, dinghy in tow, disappeared around the point. So, this was to be his fate: marooned on some croc-odile-infested shore, beside an old, damaged and unseaworthy tinny, with an Esky full of booze, half-a-dozen empties and some broken fishing gear. His captors had planned well. If his body was ever found, it'd be assumed a drunken fishing trip had gone wrong, resulting in a fatal crocodile attack.

Digger knew the risks. He must get himself away from this mud flat and onto the high ground of the shore. A glimmer of hope rose from the depths of his memory. He'd been here before, many times, on fishing trips during his youth. He rec-ognised the distinctive shape of the point and the disposition of the offshore islands. Even the very mangrove-peppered tidal mud flats were familiar.

He also recalled a rough track ran through the mangroves to a small fisherman's hut, a mere 800 metres further along the shore. And more good fortune, the low tide had reduced the width of the channel separating him from the shore to a mere fifty metres.

Taking care not to disturb any wildlife, particularly reptilian, he waded through the perilous passage to the probable position of the path. It was still there! And so was the hut, just as he remembered. It'd been a close call, but he reached safety.

Pawn sacrifice? Not this time!

THE GLIGORIĆ SYSTEM

The Gligorić System involves the advancement of the white knight to G4, the signature move of champion player, Svetozar Gligorić.

Marcus and his wife had loved chess. That was how they had met in high school, two nerds – or was that two geeks or weeds? – who enjoyed the lunchtime moves of the chess club more than the cut and thrust of the school sports oval.

While he'd built up a reputation as a defensive player, she'd proven much more adventurous. He tended to favour games in which he could safely deploy strategies such as the King's Indian Defence, always opening by moving his beloved white knight to position F6, but she introduced him to more aggressive developments. She'd encourage him to further advance his prized stallion, for example, white knight to G4. Although such skill was well beyond his mastery, Marcus warmed to the idea of his valiant white knight charging into the fray where others feared to venture.

Marcus reflected on their agreed strategy. It was indeed adventurous, a high-risk gamble, but one the four of them must take.

Digger was now safely back in Canberra, providing a detailed statement of his Darwin misadventure via an affidavit dictated to a reputable senior counsel, whom Marcus knew he could trust.

Cassandra was ensconced in a safehouse, surrounded by mountains of paper, computer files and digital records of countless other references. Hidden deep within this treasure-trove of data was a handful of gems, those documents that shed light and lent credibility to the top-secret images Digger had dispatched from the yacht. It was too early for her to assemble a comprehensive picture of the current international developments, but she was getting close.

For the moment, Marcus must buy time. He chose to address the Senate, alluding to the unfolding international intrigue, but without being too specific. This was the Senate's final sitting day before the scheduled break, and a nuanced question to the Minister for Foreign Affairs and Trade would serve to flush out further information. While he couldn't yet disclose the final details of their findings, he could set the scene through a provocative speech the government wouldn't be able to bury.

Aurora, now significantly recovered from her recent "illness", would deliver the killer blow to the broadest possible audience. She'd use her national broadcast to demonstrate the ineptitude and deceit of decades of successive Australian governments, of both the left and the right persuasion.

Their agreed hope was not only that they'd maximise the embarrassment of the political parties, but also effect the kind of meaningful and lasting policy-change that would stabilise

Australian security and promote the nation's role as an international peacemaker. A dove, rather than a hawk.

The clock was ticking as the Senator rose to speak. As was customary during such a speech by a crossbench senator, the red chamber was poorly attended. But that didn't matter. The objective was to place those questions his staff had identified as being crucial on the parliamentary record, Hansard. So he began, formally addressing the Senate President.

"Madam President. I thank the honourable senators for the opportunity to address this chamber on a matter of some considerable urgency, namely the deteriorating international situation to our north, now threatening Australia's security. But first, a little history ...

"Up until the early 2020s, Australia thrived in the prosperity of a relatively peaceful world. China and the United States drank from the common cup of international trade. But during the '20s, relations between the two superpowers took a sharp turn for the worse.

"The bellicose behaviour of the first Trump presidency had been replaced by the cautious approach of the Biden administration. But unfortunately, the well of international cooperation was poisoned during the second Trump presidency. Whoever drank from that source would surely suffer. Year after year, relations worsened. America sought to 'contain' China, to restrict its access to world markets and limit its movement along the sea lanes.

"Successive Australian governments, both right and left, Liberal and Labor, in their role as 'deputy sheriff', were

complicit, blind to where this increasing belligerence was leading … to a potential superpower conflict or, to put it in more
stark terms, to World War 3.

"What would it take to convince these two superpowers
to pull back from the brink? We'll come to that question
in a while. But there are many more twists and turns to
unfold first."

He paused as a slight shuffling of feet from the bench
opposite drew his attention back to his sparse audience.

"As the Australian hawks cemented their subservience to
the American eagle, they unnecessarily provoked the sleeping
Chinese dragon. When China exerted its rightful sovereignty
over its Hong Kong enclave, clamping down on those who
sought to undermine Chinese authority, Australia criticised it.
When China sought to eliminate Uighur separatism from its
Xinjian Autonomous Region, Australia championed the separatists. When China revived the 'One-China Policy', for five
decades the stated aspiration espoused by Taiwan itself, Australia cried 'foul'.

"Australia joined the Quad, together with the US, Japan
and India, with the stated aim of 'containing' China, and the
Chinese, quite rightly, saw Australia as a threat. AUKUS
(Australia, the United Kingdom, and the United States) signalled our antagonism, and the nuclear submarine purchase
confirmed our hostility. No wonder the Chinese now consider
Australia to be their mortal enemy, an existential threat to their
very survival.

"The Chinese reaction was predictable, although most
Australians did not recognise it as such at the time. In 2020,
China imposed a series of tariffs on imports from Australia.
Coal, barley, beef, lamb, wine, cotton, lobsters and timber were

all affected[4], and it took a change of government and several years to have them reversed[5].

"As a demonstration of their ability to project power into Australia's environs, Chinese warships circumnavigated Australia in early 2025[6], followed by closer contact during the 2025 federal election.

"While the sensationalist media beat up the story as Chinese 'provocation', the Australian prime minister of the time, quite correctly and rationally, admitted that such incursions were a proportionate response to Australia sending its own warships to the South China Sea and through the Taiwan Strait[7].

"The presence of Chinese vessels wasn't the only alarming revelation made in the heat of the 2025 election campaign. On the same day, there were reports in the Australian media of a request by the Russian government to deploy their bombers in the Indonesian province of Papua[8], and an agreement by the Timor Leste government to join Chinese-led military exercises in the region ... although it did insist it would only do so if the activity was 'not directed at any perceived hostile entity'[9].

"Even the disasters of the second presidency of Donald Trump failed to elicit any commonsense distancing of Australia from the American military machine. Australian politicians, responding to myopic public sentiment, remained wedded to the bully.

"Chinese resentment of upstart Australia lecturing them on human rights festered, slowly turning to a hatred that provoked their next moves in the international chess game. China now resolved in earnest to isolate Australia strategically, to neutralise us as detrimental to their own prosperity, and to punish Australia for its hypocrisy and temerity."

Marcus paused again to sip from a water glass then turned to the Senate President, who was observing him solemnly over the rim of her bifocals.

"You may recall, Madam President, that in the 1990s Australia championed the secession of Timor Leste from Indonesia in an effort to secure a more favourable sea-bed boundary and provide us with access to greater quantities of the Timor Sea natural gas.

"Notwithstanding the Australian duplicity, Timor Leste survived, albeit as the poorest country in Southeast Asia. But in the late '20s, and in response to Australian hostility, China poured billions of dollars of aid money into that tiny country, ostensibly seeking nothing more than to construct a port and gas plant sited at Betano Bay. This sleepy part of the south-eastern Timor coastline had been the site of the Australian commando landings during World War 2, and the wreck of the Australian destroyer, HMAS *Voyager*, still lay corroding under the sand. Now a huge Chinese naval base has emerged, just a short 650 kilometres from Darwin.

"Not content with securing the Indian Ocean approach to Australia, through Betano Bay, China then proceeded to seduce Papua New Guinea with massive packages of tied aid. Starting with the construction of the Mount Hagen international airport, China consolidated its influence with the construction of a new port at Wewak on the north coast, serviced by a pipeline and road up into the mineral- and gas-rich western highlands.

"By opening this northern corridor, the Chinese effectively siphoned off many of the minerals that could have otherwise flowed south towards Australia.

"But not content with crippling the Australia–PNG trade, the Chinese then took the opportunity to enhance their so-called 'fishing facility' on Daru Island in Torres Strait, immediately adjacent to Australian territory. Here, they also constructed a submarine guidance and communication facility."

Marcus cleared his throat, then continued:

"As the '20s proceeded, aspirations for Bougainville independence from Papua New Guinea gained traction. An ignorant Australian public, ill-informed by a mischievous media, put pressure on the gullible politicians to support secession. Thus, as independent Bougainville was about to be born, PNG hostility towards Australia was magnified.

"An opportunist China sought to replicate its Betano strategy, this time by constructing a large naval base on Buka, at the north end of Bougainville.

"But it gets worse, I'm afraid. I've recently received information of significant naval activity in the deep-water port in Kolombangara, in the Solomon Islands' Western Province.

"Thus, the net is complete … Betano in the west, Daru in the north, Buka in the north-east and Kolombangara in the east. Where once China could've been our good friend and trading partner, it's now our sworn enemy. Like a jilted lover, their parting gift was a necklace, strung tightly around our northern neck, one that could easily choke us off from the rest of the world.

"But that's all history and context. Let me turn now to the current situation in the Taiwan Strait. As you know, Australia's deeply involved in the Quad manoeuvring, to force a war between Taiwan and mainland China. The Taiwan-based Chinese don't want a war. They know they'll be the ultimate losers. Although a small minority, a tiny minority of Taiwan-based Chinese still aspire to militarily conquer the mainland, no-one takes them seriously. A larger number exist who just want to be left alone.

"However, like the mainland Chinese, a sizeable proportion also see unification as both inevitable and, ultimately, beneficial. So, if the Taiwan-based Chinese themselves are of a mixed view, why are we, thousands of kilometres away in a different hemisphere, bent on provoking an international conflict?

"I call on the Minister for Foreign Affairs to explain to the Australian people: What is our involvement in the current developments to the north?"

And the reply?

"The Minister will take the question on notice and reply in due course."

And so develops the Gligorić System ... *White Knight to G4.*

FINAL STAGES

*During the final stages of the game, players move their
pieces decisively to achieve their ultimate goal.*

Spread out on the desk were several documents, some up
to ten years old, others more recent. Some were copies of
Hansard, detailing speeches to parliament made by politicians
from all parties; some were academic papers; and some were
contemporary newspaper articles and transcripts of television
broadcasts.

But they all had one thing in common. They all dealt with
the inexorable deterioration in the Chinese–Australia relationship from 2020 onwards, as successive Australian governments
withdrew from the reality of Australia's geographical and multi-
cultural make-up.

Cassandra looked up from the dual screens as Digger set
down another coffee on the far edge of the desk. He hadn't
completely forgiven her for sending him off, poorly briefed and
ill-prepared, on such a hazardous quest. He'd almost died, saved
only from the jaws of death – from the teeth of the deadly saltwater crocodile – only by his own local experience and fortitude.

But he had to admire Cassandra's commitment to her task. She laboured incessantly, poring over the screens and documents for hours, oblivious whether it was day or night. Once he'd dared to suggest they take a couple of hours off to grab a take-away curry and sit in the park, but that resulted in a curt, "I'm too busy for that!"

As Digger retreated to his own corner of the office, Cassandra spared him a momentary glance and a muffled, "Thank you".

She knew she'd treated him badly, failed to brief him with even the most basic background and rundown of the resultant risks. She'd almost got him killed. And she was generally rude to him. She was ashamed. But he was tough, real tough. To have survived his ordeal, he had to be quick-witted, clear-headed and, above all, brave. She hastily brushed aside such sentiments.

"I'd better get back to work!" she chided herself.

Cassandra's first task was to assemble the background material and consolidate it into a succinct narrative. She began to piece together the evidence of the intricate web of lies and deception that had plagued Australian foreign policy for decades. Nothing was what it seemed. Of the many instances of false intelligence – in other words, lies – Cassandra chose just two to demonstrate the high-level duplicity. She purposely chose both from the distant past, to drive home the point that this deception had been going on for decades.

On 2 August 1964, in the Gulf of Tonkin – possibly within North Vietnamese waters – the USS (United States Ship)

Maddox was engaged in a brief naval skirmish with Vietnamese torpedo boats. The Americans claimed they were attacked again in the same area two days later. Based on this second incident, America escalated its involvement in the Vietnamese civil war.

The outcome was a decade of war, over a million deaths – *over a million!* – and the ignominious defeat of the Americans and their allies, including Australia. And what of this second Gulf of Tonkin incident, US justification for entering the war? It was proven in 2005 to be completely spurious. In other words, it never happened.

A second instance of mass deception led directly to the 2003 military invasion of Iraq – the infamous "weapons of mass destruction" ruse. American intelligence agencies claimed the Saddam Hussein regime was manufacturing and stockpiling huge quantities of chemical and nuclear weapons, which provided the justification for America and a host of acolytes, including Australia, to invade Iraq. So where were these weapons of mass destruction?

Nowhere. They simply didn't exist.

Next, she must assemble more contemporary data.

For months, tension had been building in the Taiwan Strait as the United States concentrated its naval might into the disputed region. The resolve of the government of the Taiwanese Republic of China appeared to be weakening, and America was set on decisive action to maximise its influence in the region.

As with all things Chinese, history is long and confusing, but never forgotten.

To an outsider, however, the terminology was confusing. The Republic of China was declared in 1912 from the remnants of the disintegrating Chinese empire of the Qing Dynasty. Initially led by Dr Sun Yet Sen, the Kuomintang, or Nationalist,

Party and the newly created Republic of China seized power. On Sun's death, both the party and the power devolved to his deputy, Chiang Kai-Shek.

The Japanese occupation during the period 1936 to 1945 disrupted the ascendency of the Kuomintang government and led to civil war, during which the Nationalists, led by Chiang Kai-Shek, battled the Communists, led by Mao Zedong.

Eventually, in 1949, the Nationalists were expelled from the mainland to the offshore Chinese island of Taiwan, leaving the Communists in control of the mainland. Both claimed to be the legitimate government of China – the whole of China, including both the mainland and Taiwan. For the next six decades, the Kuomintang and its allies and successors maintained a One-China policy, vowing to return to the mainland and reunite China under their rule.

But as surely as power follows economics, the tables slowly turned. The government of the People's Republic of China, the mainland-based Communists, also claimed to be the legitimate government of a united China. Their claim was the same as that of the Republic of China, the Taiwan-based Nationalists, who'd also been making the same claim for sixty years.

Who among us really understood these claims and counter-claims of sovereignty of a people split by politics, but united by culture? Cassandra mused.

And amid this confusion, the US was preparing to execute World War 3, potentially a nuclear holocaust in which there'd be no winners.

As she turned to recent events closer to home, Cassandra began to comprehend the seriousness of the incidents that had occurred during the past nine months.

The Torres Strait explosion was not about greenies and gas, but something much more sinister.

The "Pentagon Leaks", that were coming to life in the documents on her desk, confirmed the longevity of US strategies.

The Consul's reference to chess was indeed a warning of a threat to Australia, but was that threat from the Chinese or from the Americans themselves?

Nestled among the other documents strewn about the table was one of pure gold, a shabby fifteen-page print, stapled in the top left corner, with each page containing a blurred photograph of a summary extracted from a much larger document, titled *Queen's Pawn to D4.*

This was Digger's message from the yacht, immediately preceding his abduction. It explained the significance, the awful significance, of an American strategy known as such.

Initially, she'd thought it was about silencing the White Queen, the goddess of the Australian airwaves, Aurora, by eliminating her acolyte, the Queen's Pawn, Digger. But that was not the case at all.

The title of the file was significant. So too was the date embedded in the footer of each page. It revealed that the original document was created in 2020, when the ruling British monarch was Queen Elizabeth II (the White Queen) and her Pacific pawn was Australia (the Queen's Pawn), whose government would mindlessly follow any and all instructions from a superior super-power.

And where, or what, was D4? Perhaps it was any advanced position, such as the Taiwan Strait, that Australia would occupy militarily when so instructed by its "betters". The cynicism was appalling, exceeded only by the ongoing Australian foolishness and gullibility.

For the next two days, Cassandra worked feverishly to finalise her report, then immediately emailed the completed document to the Senator as they'd previously agreed.

They were now entering the final stages of the game.

CHECKMATE

Checkmate is the conclusion of a successful chess game, when one player eliminates their opponent. For the loser, there is no possible escape; for the winner, the sweet taste of victory.

Marcus slowly opened the laptop, reflected for a while, then typed in the closing paragraphs of his testimony. For some time, he'd been recording his innermost thoughts as they motivated his political manoeuvring.

Many recognised that, on international affairs, he was a "dove" struggling to survive among the Canberra "hawks". But few understood the life experience that had shaped this apparent pacifism, the reluctance to commit to arms when diplomacy was still within reach.

No matter what the outcomes of the following few months, this testimony would provide that explanation. It would, hopefully, outlive his mortal "three score years and ten", plus another score if you were lucky.

Marcus mentally analysed and re-analysed the scenarios that would unfold in the next twenty-four hours. Aurora was busying herself rehearsing the opening lines of her telecast. In a few moments, she'd descend two floors to the studio to confront the Prime Minister via a video-conferencing link.

Cassandra and Digger, meanwhile, sat brooding, staring at each other from opposite corners of the tiny room, each lost in their own reflections on the calamitous events of the past fortnight. What they'd uncovered was appalling, and each knew the future of Australia hung in the balance.

A smile flickered across Digger's broad face as he recalled the good times in Darwin: the footy, the fun and the friends; the babes and the booze. But the smile disappeared quickly as he pondered the city's dark history. Darwin had a tumultuous past, a chequered childhood of criminal connections and a violent adolescence as it bore the brunt of failed foreign policies and diplomacy. It had almost been destroyed by bombs in 1942, the most intense bombing of any part of Australia, ever. And to compound these disasters, Cyclone Tracey had devastated most of the city's buildings in 1974.

Of course, the real lesson of Darwin's history had been that, with maturity and commitment, a city and a people can bounce back. Digger now recognised his own personal development mirrored that of Darwin. *There is more to life than sport and revelry. At some time, we must grow up, to assume our responsibilities as mature adult world citizens, and to commit to the welfare of others.*

Across the room, Cassandra was also immersed in self-doubt. She'd allowed her selfish objectives to cloud her judgement, to endanger the life of a colleague and to prevent her from acting quickly in the broader interests. Her determination to climb the thorny vine of success had prevented her from seeing the bigger picture, and stifled the exercise of her responsibility to quickly inform the Senator of the unfolding disastrous situation. In the future (if there was to be a future) she resolved to put the good of others ahead of her personal agenda.

Aurora paused and put down her notes. She knew enough now, and it was all bad. She had a job to do, an important job, one which would affect the course of a nation. She must publicly confront a prime minister on national television and demand an explanation of the appalling situation into which the nation had been unknowingly plunged.

This was no longer about feeding her personal ambition or enhancing her public profile. This was for her grandchildren, those darling innocents who relied on the older generation to soberly perform their life's work in a selfless, professional manner, devoid of personal aggrandisement.

Marcus smiled as he scanned the room, contemplating his three compatriots who'd been drawn to this common cause. Each was different, an individual, with their own strengths and weaknesses.

He thought again of his dear, departed wife. She'd been constantly at the forefront of his mind these past few weeks. *What would she advise? What would she do?* Her commitment to her fellow humans had always been his inspiration. He'd been able to achieve some important things in his long career, but it had only been possible with her love and support. And now he was alone. No ... perish the thought. He was not alone. He had the memory of her love and inspiration to guide him, to work with these three companions to make the world a better place. He must ...

"It's time," Aurora broke into his thoughts. "I must go down to the studio and get ready. You can all stay in this office and watch the broadcast on the wall screen."

And she disappeared through the door.

7:00 pm, 9 July 2030, Parliament House Studios, Canberra
Aurora stared into the teleprompter.

"Good evening, and welcome to this special episode of *Australasian Focus*. We will shortly cross to the Prime Minister … but first some devastating background.

It has now been revealed, by reliable sources, that the explosion that occurred six months ago close to the gas terminal near Torres Strait was, in fact, at a secret submarine communications facility on an adjacent property. Not just the location but the very existence of this communication base has been vehemently denied by the Australian Government for years.

"It has further been revealed that the base was destroyed by a missile, fired from a Chinese submarine, which sailed from Betano Bay in Timor Leste, a week earlier.

"We have it on good authority that the attack was retaliation for a similar attack in the Taiwan Strait, launched from an Australian warship under American orders.

"We understand that the purpose of the attack near Torres Strait was a warning, intended to show the Americans China is prepared to take drastic action to protect their claim to Greater China … to Taiwan, in other words.

"The recent so-called Pentagon Leaks revealed that since the beginning of the 21st century, America has referred to Australia as 'the Queen's Pawn' – a reference to the fact that Australia, under our previous monarch, failed to become a republic when we had the opportunity.

"Apparently, the Chinese and the Americans both view Australia as a mere pawn in the much bigger game of international politics. An expendable pawn, at that. The Chinese, wisely, are reluctant to attack any part of the United States for fear of massive nuclear retaliation. But they, quite correctly, have assumed that attacking Australia can provide a potent demonstration of their resolve without the risk of starting World War 3.

"The American strategy of Queen's Pawn to D4, formulated just before the AUKUS agreement, was a calculated American risk of advancing an Australian submarine or surface warship – in preference to an American one – into the Taiwan Strait disputed zone.

"Clearly, the Australian defence planners, politicians and public all failed to understand the enormous relational damage that would result from the repeated taunts and provocations inflicted on China by Australia, and the hypocrisy of blindly obeying American instructions to escalate any and all conflicts they deemed to be in their interest.

"For decades, the Chinese repeatedly warned Australia not to meddle in their affairs. And now we face the –"

Aurora stopped mid-sentence as the teleprompter went blank. From off-camera, the producer rapidly approached with a handwritten note. Was this the anticipated court order to cease transmission, equivalent to the dreaded D-notice of days past? No.

There is a breaking story of overwhelming importance. The teleprompter will be back up in a moment ... the note informed her.

"I have just been informed of breaking news as this transmission goes to air. We are immediately crossing live to the Prime Minister."

Her face uncharacteristically grim, Aurora faltered as she attempted to regain her composure. But the teleprompter was merciless. This broadcast must proceed, no matter what, without delay and devoid of emotion, no matter how the news of this incident had affected her. Gathering herself, she focused on the large monitor on the opposite wall.

"Prime Minister, can you advise the cause of the explosion that has just ripped through Port Darwin?"

Checkmate.

PART 2

The Middle Game

CASSANDRA – THE KNIGHT'S PAWN

Knight's Pawn – 2030

The bombshell of the Port Darwin explosion had shaken all four members of the team. They decided that each should take a couple of days to separately collect their thoughts, consider their commitment to exposing the truth of both explosions, and refresh their resolve to facilitate a change in Australian foreign policy.

Cassandra retired to the solitude of her tiny Canberra apartment, the scene of so many late nights poring over the mountains of data she'd acquired during recent months.

Cassandra loved reading Greek mythology, which may have seemed rather strange for someone of her age, but it had been her passion since her early teens. She was captivated by the tragedy surrounding the fate of her namesake, the ill-fated princess of Troy.

While the actual characters portrayed in Homer's *Iliad*, and in subsequent retelling of the story, may or may not have been real people, Troy certainly had been a real city-state. Founded around 3,600 BCE, adjacent to the Dardanelles on the west-facing coast of Asia Minor (now Türkiye), Troy had risen progressively to be a great trading city. Commanding a strategic position, ancient Hittite Troy was the envy of the Mycenaean

Greeks[10], who coveted the wealth amassed by the great city through its control of trade[11].

The Cassandra of mythology was the most beautiful of the three daughters of King Priam of Troy and his wife, Queen Hecuba – so beautiful that she was desired by the god, Apollo.

Initially, Cassandra wasn't interested in Apollo's advances, but she eventually agreed to his proposal when he promised her the gift of prophecy. Sensing the power that would accrue from such a windfall, Cassandra accepted Apollo's offering, but then reneged on the arrangement, refusing his amorous advances. While the angry god did not withdraw his gift, he obtained his revenge by ensuring that nobody would ever believe her prophecies. And so it was.

Although ancient Cassandra accurately predicted the siege and eventual destruction of Troy by the Greeks, she was unable to convince her father or brothers of the impending danger.

And the rest is history – or at least, myth. Troy was destroyed, the legendary Cassandra was raped by Ajax the Lesser, and ultimately carried off by the victorious Greek leader, Agamemnon, with whom she was later murdered[12] .

Like the daughter of the Trojan King Priam, the modern Cassandra suffered greatly from the frustration of being able to accurately forecast the outcomes of many personal and public situations, based on her research into previous similar scenarios, but was unable to convince anyone of the validity of her predictions. While rational analysis of such a situation might invite reflection on the interplay of fate and free will, less-rational obsession with the phenomenon may, unfortunately, lead to depression.

As this situation persisted over many years, Cassandra became more depressed, at one stage approaching the cusp of mental illness. During one of these bouts of self-doubt and futility, Cassandra decided to use the Greek *psi* symbol, the trident, Ψ, as her own insignia. She was aware that *psi* is often associated with precognition, clairvoyance, extrasensory perception and other psychic attributes, so it seemed appropriate[13] [14].

Solace from the Past

"What am I doing? Why am I doing it? Am I just wasting my time?"

One might assume the elderly ponder these questions, but the young seem to be burdened by the immediacy of such doubts. Probably, the elderly have no alternative but to accept their life choices. It's too late and too much effort for them to correct past mistakes. But for the young, nothing's cast in stone, and it's never too late to change direction, although to do so is to admit the past, perhaps, has been a waste of time.

In 2030, so it was for Cassandra. She was now in her late twenties, and her dreams of a successful political career appeared to have been shattered by the recent turn of events.

She was without focus or purpose. She'd reached the stage of life where she could either take the easy path and opt out of her current situation, or take the more difficult option and stick with the current path of political intrigue and struggle. In times of severe melancholy, she'd reflect on the words of William Shakespeare's *Hamlet*.

To be, or not to be. That is the question: Whether 'tis nobler in the mind to suffer the slings and arrows of outrageous fortune, or to take arms against a sea of troubles, and by opposing, end them.

Cassandra's childhood had been difficult, as an only child, bullied by her mother and pampered by her father. At age six, she was devastated when her father, whom she adored, decided he could no longer tolerate his domineering wife, and found solace in the arms of his personal assistant. The divorce cut Cassandra to the quick. No more loving, caring, gentle father; and worse, no more protection from the ambition of her over-bearing mother.

Throughout her early childhood, Cassandra had suffered the humiliation of never being quite good enough, never achiev-ing excellence and never performing to perfection. Her reaction had been palpable precociousness. As she entered her teenage years, Cassandra started to develop more effective defences, the precocity of childhood morphing into the aggression of adoles-cence. While many teenagers display rebelliousness, Cassandra was downright hostile.

Although she now excelled in all her school subjects, per-formed brilliantly on the sporting field and starred in extracur-ricular activities, she was arrogant and obnoxious to her mother, teachers and anyone in authority. Her scholastic achievements were exemplary, but her personal relationships were a disaster.

Preoccupation with social media was endemic among Aus-tralian teenagers during the first two decades of the second mil-lennium, and Cassandra wasn't immune. Arguments with her mother would start with criticism.

"Too much screen time and not enough study!" would trig-ger a typical response.

"I'm still top of my class, so leave me alone!"

But what drove her mother to her wit's end was Cassandra's developing an unhealthy interest in boys. While her mother was no saint and her father had succumbed to adultery, Cassandra took flirting to an extreme. The issue came to a head just after Cassandra's sixteenth birthday, when she planned to attend a rave party with a couple of her least-restrained friends, girls with unsavoury reputations. Emails among the girls came to the attention of one of the other mothers, who complained to Cassandra's mother that she was "out of control".

Her mother was livid. Apart from accusing the other woman of indulging in a case of the pot calling the kettle black, and stating her own daughter was no saint, her mother turned on Cassandra, initiating a shouting match with comments like,

"You're not going out."

"Yes, I am, and you can't stop me."

"You're not wearing that!"

"I'm sixteen, and I'll dress how I like."

Doors were slammed. Crockery was thrown. In the end, Cassandra stormed out of the house and disappeared for over twenty-four hours. Her mother was in despair until a sullen Cassandra crept back to her room.

The situation was saved by an unexpected turn of events. In early 2020, COVID19 came to Australia, and the country went into lockdown. Within a short period, movement, including fraternising with other teenagers, became severely restricted. Cassandra had no choice. No more socialising, no more rave parties, no more life as she knew it.

With no idea of how long the lockdowns would last, Cassandra vowed to beat the system. If she couldn't go out, then she'd withdraw from normal teenage activities. She'd show them all by becoming the most successful student ever to emerge from the New South Wales education system. She remained surly and rude, but she performed even better scholastically.

Cassandra reluctantly became aware she was her mother's daughter. They both shared the same intense determination to achieve their respective goals. Both refused to tolerate opposition to their respective visions of a future of their own making. Both were ruthless in their methods in imposing this vision on others; and both exuded an arrogance that repelled their more sensitive contemporaries. Empathy did not reside in their lexicon. They considered compassion a weakness, a barrier to success.

As COVID19 subsided and subsequent spikes in community illness proved little more than inconveniences, Cassandra finished high school. By now, she'd developed an obsession with high academic achievement and easily matriculated with a tertiary entry score that guaranteed her a place in any university she chose.

To beat the system, she realised, you have to get inside it. The way to get inside it – the political system, that is, the one where the real decisions are made – is to excel in a degree in political science. She could then join the staff of some politician and get her foot in the door.

It didn't matter much to her who the politician was, or what they stood for, provided they could wield some significant power. Perhaps a crossbench senator would be her preference. Once she'd set her sights on this goal, achieving it became the sole focus of her early adulthood. Work hard, excel academically, avoid social distractions, and, above all, don't succumb to romantic interests.

The first three of these resolutions were easily achieved, but not so the final one of romantic abstention. Cassandra's near-downfall came during the second semester of the third year of her undergraduate course. They met in the temporary intimacy of a tutorial room while waiting for the tutor, who, as usual, entered late. The juxtaposition of their surnames on the class register had ensured they'd both participate in the same project group, be forced to share each other's knowledge, experience and insights in the pursuit of a subject pass mark – or, in Cassandra's case, better than a mere pass.

As expected, she'd done brilliantly in her assignments and examinations. He'd not done so well. But he had other qualities. Adorable, funny, handsome and sexy were adjectives that she, in uncharacteristic momentary lapses of resolve, had allowed her confused, hormone-affected brain to apply to her new friend. And just as all lapses of judgement result in penalties, too much time flirting and not enough studying resulted in a subject fail.

How could she, Cassandra the brilliant, have allowed this to happen? She wouldn't permit a recurrence. No more boyfriends, no more romance, no more fun. She couldn't believe it! From that point on, she vowed to sacrifice all to achieve her goals: first, university brilliance, and then political employment.

And what of that loser boyfriend? He was terminated by a stinging text message. *Don't bother contacting me again.* He took it badly. But a university campus isn't so big that they could escape occasional contact. Gradually, avoidance yielded to a polite nod, then to a forced *Hello* and, eventually to a shared coffee.

But that was all; Cassandra would grant nothing more. Their final contact was at the graduation ceremony, seated side-by-side as dictated by the alphabetical immediacy of their surnames. She was about to commence her master's degree, while he was preparing to take up employment in Darwin, working as a lowly reporter for some parochial local news outlet.

Cassandra graduated with first-class honours and immediately enrolled for a master's degree in political science by
research and then a PhD concentrating on the same topic.
Her subject was the evolution of 21st-century Russian aggression, with particular attention to the historic claims (on
both sides) that had led to the recent disastrous war between
Ukraine and Russia.

She was in no doubt of the evil intent and cynicism of the
Russian President Putin, but was also sceptical of the inflexibil-
ity of the Ukrainian position during the lead-up to the conflict.
It was apparent that significant sentiment in favour of secession
existed in the Russian-speaking east of the country.

The first phase of the war began in 2014, when Russian-
speaking secessionist paramilitaries, supported covertly by
Russia, seized several towns in eastern Ukraine. The Ukrainian
armed forces were unsuccessful in fully evicting the separatists.

Then, amid worldwide condemnation, Russian forces
marched into Crimea and consolidated their hold on the
region. Cassandra knew there was no justification for the subsequent 2022 violent Russian incursion in an effort to annex
the Donetsk and Luhansk regions, similar to the events of 2014
in the Crimea[15].

While Cassandra's research didn't lead her to doubt Russian culpability for the extensive loss of life on both sides of the
conflict, she did question the commonly held opinion that a
mutually acceptable solution couldn't have been reached prior
to the Russian annexation of Crimea in 2014.

Similarly, she imagined more effort to negotiate a solution
could have been exercised during the period of increasing tension and violence in the eastern part of Ukraine, between 2014
and 2022. Even without the advantage of hindsight, it should

have been obvious to all that the sacrifice of thousands of lives wouldn't change what became the outcome.

Cassandra extrapolated to other disputes her conviction of the need to explore every possibility of negotiated settlements before resorting to an irreversible outbreak of brutality and warfare. Predictably, she deduced that resorting to violent aggression is never acceptable. Less obvious, particularly to her thesis supervisor, was her conclusion that recourse to bloody, robust defence, before exhausting all reasonable alternatives, is also undesirable.

During her research, Cassandra had obtained many previously private diaries and letters, written after the 1917 Russian Revolution. These documents provided a wealth of background data on the aspirations, fears and tragedies that befell a range of ordinary eastern European people during 100 years of revolution, warfare, political intrigue and violence.

Among the numerous papers were a translated diary with the title *Journal of a Russian Patriot*, and a translated letter, dated June 1922, written from the Bukhara Ark Fortress in modern Uzbekistan. Both documents were written within the designated time-frame of her research, and both shed some light on the lives of ordinary Russians as they navigated the treacherous currents of world politics and war during the 20th century.

But now, in 2030, these two historic records had also assumed some considerable significance for Cassandra's good friend and colleague, Aurora. It had become apparent the letter was written by Aurora's great-great-grandfather, a senior White-Russian bureaucrat, in 1922, shortly before his execution, while *Journal of a Russian Patriot* had been written in 1960 by his youngest son, Aurora's great-grandfather's brother, a naval officer who'd survived the Russo-Japanese War, the First

World War and the Second World War. In the spirit of their deepening bond of friendship, Cassandra passed copies of both documents to Aurora.

The Art of Divination

Throughout her academic endeavours, Cassandra had developed and honed her researching skills to razor sharpness. But she'd also developed the unique skill of being able to predict future events, using a combination of publicly available statistics and other data, tempered by an understanding of historical geopolitics.

Ever conscious of the phrase "lies, damn lies and statistics", popularised by Mark Twain when he, incorrectly, quoted British Prime Minister, Benjamin Disraeli[16], Cassandra avoided unrestrained extrapolation of raw data devoid of interpretation. She'd diligently interrogate the assumptions and validate the source of all data before using it to predict future developments.

Throughout the 2020s, the use of so-called "artificial intelligence" (AI) in a range of activities became widespread. Like all her contemporaries, Cassandra had fully embraced the technology, but with some reservations. While there existed many definitions and commentaries on AI, one suitable summary, in her opinion, was:

AI refers to the capability of digital computers or robots to perform tasks typically requiring human intelligence. These tasks include reasoning, learning, language understanding and problem-solving … While AI has achieved human-level performance in specific tasks

... it still lacks the flexibility and general knowledge of humans across broader domains.[17]

Cassandra recognised that while computers are rational and logical, humans are not necessarily so. Some human decisions are best based on logic, but others may be better based on feelings of love, anger, compassion and empathy. These were humanity's motivators, the things that spurred people into action, encouraging them to step outside their comfort zone and engage in otherwise risky activities.

While AI may direct a subservient computer-guided machine to weigh, and then act on, the probabilities of various scenarios to determine the most rational course of action, a human is free to do otherwise, to ignore logically determined risk, act on impulse, take a less cautious approach and reap the relevant rewards.

Those rewards may be either success or failure, Cassandra mused, *but we, as humans, own them. They are ours, our responsibility and our prize. The thrill of a challenge, the flood of adrenalin, the racing heartbeat, the glow of pride, and the swell of love in our breasts ... these are the drivers that make us human.*

She wasn't characteristically susceptible to such bouts of sentiment, although such limitations on AI's logic did have some traction in her deliberations. What did appeal to her more persuasively was the notion that AI does not encourage innovation.

AI reflects logical conclusions drawn from the analysis of large amounts of data, thus representing a sort of average outcome, a consensus. *It is safe, but it is not innovative.* Genius doesn't flourish in an AI environment; rather, AI favours mediocrity.

Armed with such misgivings, Cassandra resolved to allow her creative imagination free rein, while assigning AI the role of fact-checker – a reality check designed to prevent innovation from straying into absurdity.

And her insights proved remarkable. A passion for history, a thorough knowledge of political science, an understanding of psychology and the discipline to adhere to proven analysis methodology enabled her to accurately predict many personal and public outcomes, when, to most others, such results initially appeared preposterous.

Cassandra's reputation for insight grew, based on her track record of accurate predictions. But her personality flaws appeared to limit her credibility. People simply wouldn't listen to her. Nobody wants to listen to the bearer of bad tidings – a Jonah, or in this case, a Cassandra.

Precognition – 2030

While Cassandra loved her work as a research officer on the staff of a federal senator, she was increasingly frustrated that few people would believe her predictions. In particular, the government had ignored all the warnings that, to her, were crystal clear. The recent bomb blast had shattered any confidence she had a truly meaningful role. *Was she just wasting her time?*

On the positive side, her involvement in the recent events had had an unexpected positive effect. Cassandra, the loner, till now focused only on her quest for power and climbing the ladder of success, had come to appreciate being part of a team. She'd shared intimate secrets with Aurora, the brilliantly successful celebrity whose private life was a disaster, wrecked by her own ambition. Cassandra realised if she wasn't careful, she was heading down the same path to destruction.

Yet Aurora's life had been turned around by the friend-ship and support offered by Marcus – her boss, whom she so admired. Dedicated, tempered, tough and committed, always willing to assist, counsel and, yes, even befriend her.

And then there was Digger, that rough diamond with whom she'd clashed in the early days of their working rela-tionship. Digger had suffered hardship and danger from many sources, including Cassandra's own disregard for his safety. Yet, he seemed not to bear any permanent malice towards her. Mas-culinity oozed from his presence, at times repulsive, but also alluring. Her initial dislike of Digger faded as guilt overtook her, to be eventually replaced by a kind of girlish admiration.

Cassandra sighed and put aside her papers. She must return to the reality of 2030 politics, albeit cast in a role like that of the ill-fated mythological Greek princess, predicting a dire future for her country that few would believe, and even fewer would act upon.

AURORA – THE WHITE QUEEN

White Queen – 2030

Like her three colleagues, Aurora had been stunned by the recent revelations of the bomb blast in Darwin. Each took the opportunity for some quiet time before meeting to discuss what to do next. Aurora decided she'd go through the two documents Cassandra had sent to her the week before.

Cassandra had briefly described each of the documents and had suggested the one of most interest to Aurora would be the longer one, *Journal of a Russian Patriot*. She'd warned Aurora it was a long document, but added it would help Aurora to understand her own Russian ancestry.

It had been written in the mid-1960s by Aurora's great-grandfather's brother, for his own son, outlining his life as a Russian naval officer and his journeys in the naval cruiser, the *Aurora*. His main concern had been to alert his country – and his own descendants – to the folly of war, based on his experience.

Aurora paused and reflected for a moment that the Russians must have been slow to learn that lesson, given the folly of Russian interference over the most recent sixty years in wars in Angola, Somalia, Afghanistan, Georgia, South Ossetia, Chechnya, Transdniestria, Tajikistan and, most devastating of all, Ukraine.

Cassandra also said Aurora would be fascinated by the 1917 letter written by the naval officer's brother, Aurora's own great-grandfather, from the Australian city of Newcastle shortly before his premature death at sea, and reproduced in full within the journal.

A long document, so Aurora decided to make herself comfortable on the sofa, with a cup of coffee at hand. She read ...

Journal of a Russian Patriot

Water ... clear, calm and cool, reflecting the distant peaks. This is my earliest memory. This vast expanse of Issyk-Kul Lake was my childhood playground, with the high Tian Shan Mountains of Central Asia rising in the background. From the earliest age, I would sail with my older brother, in our little boat, the fifteen kilometres from our home near the village of Karakol, to Oital on the northern shore.

Try as we might, we could not agree on a name for our little boat, until at last we implored Papa to decide for us. He set us both down and told us a strange story. Over two thousand years ago the Greek general, Alexander, invaded Central Asia, bringing Greek religion and mythology to this region. Eos (later known as Aurora) was the god of the dawn and mother of the wind and stars.

We would often set off at dawn, while wind was waxing and when stars were waning – so the obvious name was Eos ... or so I thought. But an eight-year-old rarely prevails over a ten-year-old, and my brother got his way. Aurora it would be.

From these journeys we derived our shared lifelong love of boats and adventure. Here, we would sleep under the stars, returning home the next day. Here, we would spend hours gazing across the lake at the glistening snow-capped peaks of the main Tian Shan Range, towering menacingly over the placid water. What strange people and places lay beyond?

Behind us, clusters of white yurts, the round tents of the Kyrgyz tribesmen, dotted the hills that gently swept up to define the lake's northern rim. These semi-nomadic horsemen were our friends. They were enthralled to be visited by the little blue-eyed Russian boat boys, so far from their home. Mama feared we would be abducted by bandits and sold in the Kashgar slave market, far to the south-east along the Silk Road. But Papa assured her that abducting little Russian boys would cause these Kyrgyz tribesmen more trouble than we were worth. So our early naval escapades continued unhindered.

Papa had ... I think ... an important job in the service of the Czar. I learned much later that he was some sort of military liaison – not an army man, but a civilian with the authority to sort out problems whenever the locals became rebellious. Papa told me that he was a sort of magistrate ... whatever that was. I thought he said "majesty". When I addressed him as "your majesty", I was severely scolded and told that he was "just the man who kept the peace on behalf of our beloved Czar".

There were many who would create problems for Russian administrators such as Papa ... Kyrgyz tribesmen (my friends) and the Chinese Dungans, who had also settled here. Twenty years earlier, these Muslim refugees had fled persecution on the other side of the Tian Shan, making their homes alongside the Kyrgyz.

My parents moved to Karakol in 1880, the year I was born, and they always joked that I was more Asian than Russian. Most of my childhood was spent outdoors, usually in our little Aurora. I was very close to my brother, who would often take me sailing and camping. In later years, he left to attend university in Saint Petersburg, and I did not see much of him after that. My two sisters were born much later, and, to my relief, did not much like doing boy things.

The outpost of Karakol was at the very edge of the czarist Russian Empire. In 1869, the Czar's army had established a military outpost here, to protect the south-eastern edge of the empire from the Mongols, the Chinese and the ever-threatening British, whom they believed to be advancing in a pincer movement from both mountainous Afghanistan and mysterious Tibet.

Early one brisk morning, my brother and I planned to set off in our little boat on our usual expedition. But this time, there was a great commotion down near the water's edge, and even I could sense that we should not venture out this day. Papa was there in his official capacity, and so too was the other man ... the important one, whom they had been expecting. We hung around at the back of the crowd, until Papa finally motioned for us to come forward. He introduced us both to the great explorer, Nicholay Przhevalsky.

Although I had never heard of him at the time, this man was destined to be my inspiration as I sought adventure in later years.

My early education was always a struggle, but later I was keen to learn more of Przhevalsky's five great expeditions, through Siberia, Mongolia, China, Tibet and Central Asia. Commencing in 1869 and suffering great hardships, Przhevalsky had explored the Ussuri River basin, crossed the Gobi Desert to Beijing, traversed the upper Yangtse River, and even crossed into the edge of Tibet. And now he was here with us, on the edge of civilisation, planning a further trip to Lhasa, the remote and mysterious capital of Tibet. But something was wrong. Przhevalsky was not well. His health deteriorated rapidly until, on 1 November 1888, the great explorer succumbed to typhus. To me he seemed old, but he was aged only 49 years.

We mourned Przhevalsky's passing, and Papa set about securing his possessions to be transported back to Saint Petersburg. Like all children, I was awestruck by a great hero, failing to recognise that there is a human heart behind every public persona. Przhevalsky had sacrificed all to his passion for exploration. He never married, his diary entry (dedicated to a mysterious young lady) betraying his priority,

> *"I will never betray the ideal, to which is dedicated all of my life. ... I will return to the desert ... where I will be much happier than in the gilded salons that can be acquired by marriage."*

But passion also leads to arrogance. To my dismay, I later learned also of the disdain that he assigned to those in whose lands he traversed. Przhevalsky had written:

> *"Here you can penetrate anywhere, only not with the Gospels under your arm, but with money in your pocket, a carbine in one hand and a whip in the other. Europeans must use these to come and bear away in the name of civilisation all these dregs of the human race. A thousand of our soldiers would be enough to subdue all Asia from Lake Baykal to the Himalayas ..."*

Today, such attitudes are considered appalling. Nicholay Przhevalsky failed in his ultimate goal of reaching Lhasa. The first European penetration of the Tibetan capital fell to the 1903–1904 British invasion led by the Englishman, Francis Younghusband. But this invasion resulted in up to 5,000 Tibetan deaths – a stark reminder of the brutality of the so-called "Great Game", played out in Central Asia between Britain and Russia in the late eighteen-hundreds.

The Russians re-named our town "Przhevalsk" in honour of the great explorer, although the locals later made such a fuss that in 1924 the name was changed, back to the original, "Karakol". But that was still in the future, and Nicholay Przhevalsky was my childhood hero ... the adventurer who had lived and died amongst us, for the glory of Mother Russia, beside my precious jewel, Issyk-Kul Lake.

Later ... much later, because my rudimentary education advanced at a snail's pace ... I became aware that Russia had been steadily growing for more than a millennium. In 865, the Viking war lord, Rurik, had established a fortified trading settlement at Novgorod, and, by so doing, assumed leadership over the local Slav tribe. Although momentarily checked between the 13th and 15th centuries by the Mongol Golden Horde, Russian expansion and consolidation continued, filling the power vacuum vacated by these retreating Tartars. Strength, the overarching feature of Russian leadership, gave rise to a series of powerful rulers, Ivan the Terrible being the best known. In 1613, following a prolonged period of instability, Michael Romanov was offered the crown, thus initiating a dynasty that became the envy of civilisation. Russian hearts swelled with pride at the mere mention of names such as Peter "the Great", Katherine "the Great", Alexander and Nicholas. Later, as I travelled through the empire and finally came to Saint Petersburg, I could but marvel at the wonders of the Romanov palaces and churches. The Winter Palace, the Peterhof, Katherine's Palace, Saint Isaac's Cathedral … just a few of the dazzling displays of Russian grandeur.

But I move too quickly. Papa was a good administrator and a loyal subject of the Czar. When I was twelve, we moved from Karakol to the major city of the Uzbeks – Tashkent, the "Stone City", down on the plain to the west of the Altai Mountains. For me, it was the end of my childhood freedom, wrenched as I was from the tranquillity of my beloved Issyk-Kul Lake. I missed the mountains, I missed the lake, I missed my boat, I missed my brother. I missed the fresh air and I missed my freedom. In short, I was miserable. But for Papa and for the family, it meant promotion and prosperity.

Although it took a long time, I eventually settled into our new home and our new way of life. Our governess took charge of my education, and she was very strict. In later life, I would be thankful for this thorough grounding in the history of glorious Russia, and the geography of our vast empire ... of course, along with a tenuous understanding of mathematics and the classics. But for the moment, I much preferred to be out and about, mixing with the local boys. Papa discouraged this fraternisation, but he was very busy in the Czar's service and was unable to devote the time necessary to restrict the movements of his rebellious second son. Despite our new prestige and prosperity, it was difficult not to notice the poverty of others around us. My rambling through the slums of Tashkent exposed me to the ubiquitous penury that others of my class did not, or chose not to, see.

Over the centuries, serfdom had evolved from its origin as a practical measure of "labour in exchange for protection" into the most unjust form of exploitation imaginable – little different from slavery. The lot of the peasants, these impoverished unfortunates, toiling endlessly on the estates of the landed nobility, had deteriorated markedly. In 1861, the well-intentioned Czar Alexander II had managed to emancipate the serfs, but it did not end well for either party. For his actions, the Czar was assassinated, and the serfs lost the security that had accompanied their previous enslavement. These unfortunate individuals were now transformed into dispossessed rural labourers, unable to afford the rents imposed on their occupation of the land that they had previously farmed without cost.

They became casual workers on the large estates, employed only when needed, and in constant fear of starvation.

At the tender age of thirteen, I accompanied Papa on one of his official visits, to ancient Samarkand, then west to Bukhara and finally to distant Khiva.

Samarkand had been the capital of the empire of the dreaded Timur, the fourteenth century Turkic warlord who invoked terror throughout Central Asia. With a fearsome reputation for cruelty, Timur was ruthlessly efficient in achieving his goals. For him, the ends always justified the means. Although Samarkand's enormous and beautiful mausoleums, madrassas and mosques were now in a state of ignominious dilapidation, they still testified to the wealth and prestige that had been generated during Timur's lifetime. Timur conquered ruthlessly in the tradition of his predecessor, the Mongol, Temujin (whom we now know as Genghis Khan), seeking to spread his empire from Türkiye to China.

Although initially successful, Timur died in 1405, without carrying out his planned invasion of Ming China. Over the next century, Timur's empire disintegrated into a number of independent khanates including Kokand, Khiva, Bukhara and Samarkand. Over time, a Central Asian power vacuum developed adjacent to the fabulously wealthy British-controlled India, just across the Hindu Kush and Himalaya barriers. This was the context of the inexorable southward czarist expansion towards Afghanistan, and the tableau for the nineteenth century Russian–British Great Game spy intrigues. Russia, of course, was ultimately successful here in Central Asia, although we did fail to take the Indian jewel, the centrepiece of the British Empire.

But at thirteen, I was more interested in adventure than in history. The ruins of Timur's capital afforded a myriad places to explore, and I did so with relish. Then it was over the mountains to Timur's birthplace, Shakhrisabz, and the long, uneventful journey to Bukhara. Like Samarkand, the ancient city of Bukhara was a major trading centre of the Silk Road, and it was here that one of the grisly incidents of the Great Game had been played out, just half a century before. I use that name "Great Game", which is a British term intended to romanticise the brutal intrigues and espionage that took place as the British interlopers sought to displace Mother Russia from Central Asia. In 1844, after a lengthy imprisonment, two British officers, Charles Stoddard and Arthur Conolly, who had been accused of spying, were publicly beheaded here in the main square.

Between Bukhara and Khiva, the traveller becomes painfully aware of the hardships that faced the trading caravans of yesteryear. The Kara Kum (Black Desert) and the Kyzyl Kum (Red Desert) demanded a passage by camel of three months, with oases providing periodic respite along the way. To the south flows the mighty Amu Darya, also known in history as the Oxus River.

With a history stretching back millennia, the walled city of Khiva was once a key trading centre on the Silk Road. But many of the mausoleums, madrassas, mosques and minarets are either unfinished or in ruins – Kunya-Ark Palace, the Madrassa of Muhammad Amin-Khan, the Juma Mosque, with its ornately carved forest of timber columns, the iconic unfinished Kalta Minor Minaret, and the recently constructed Islam Khoja Minaret. Here also is the Mausoleum of Pakhlavani Mahmoud Rubais, the 13th century Sufi teacher and professional wrestler who reputedly never suffered a defeat during his 79-year career. A man of both strong body and principle, he had written, "In the evening, I wiped my looking glass. When it was clean, I quickly cast a glance. I saw so many faults of mine in it, I forgot of other's faults at once". He had on one occasion disputed with the Emir of Samarkand, and was imprisoned for his stand, stating in a quatrain written for the occasion, "... to be left for ages in a dungeon is better than to have talks with [the] immature."

For a young Russian boy, the unexpected discovery that these places of ruin and poverty, at the edge of the Russian Empire, had once been the home of famous poets, teachers, thinkers and scientists was truly enlightening.

Khiva had been added to our empire in 1873, and Papa's work of consolidating Russian control over this region was (apparently) successful. Eventually, it came time for the long return journey back to Bukhara, Samarkand and on to our home in Tashkent. Again, we approached the Amu Darya (Oxus River) and Papa took the opportunity to give me a history lesson. In 329 BCE, Alexander the Great had crossed this same river, a little further upstream, thus bringing Central Asia under the control of ancient Greece. There have been many fateful river crossings in ancient history – Joshua crossing the Jordan, Caesar crossing the Rubicon and Alexander crossing the Amu Darya, to name a few.

This country has an ideal climate for growing cotton and has been producing it for over 2,000 years. All about us, the fields were dotted with labourers, forced by hunger into this backbreaking occupation. As we approached the outskirts of the city, I could see a boy, about my age, struggling to lift his stricken cart, which had lost a wheel and was now blocking the road. We dismounted, just as the loaded cart slipped from the boy's grasp, pinning his leg to the rutted road beneath. His shriek of pain tore at my heart ... I must help. I rushed forward to assist, as the combined weight of the cart and cotton bore down, crushing the boy's maimed limb. But, to my horror, my action was promptly arrested by a firm hand on my shoulder, and Papa's stern command, "Leave it. This is not our concern. The peasants will deal with it."

Had my ears betrayed me? My own sweet Papa, the kindest man in the world, was telling me that the pain of a fellow human was not my concern.

From this day onwards, I was consumed by an acute and increasing awareness of the inequity of Czarist Russia and its empire. There were two quite separate worlds – one of wealth and privilege, wedded to war and conquest, thriving on the labours of others; and the other, an underclass of peasants and urban proletariat, whose production funded the excesses of their overlords. While I sulked, our official party moved on ... but I had crossed my own Amu Darya, my Rubicon.

Aurora was fascinated. These were the words of her own great-uncle, the brother of her great-grandfather, written not long before his death, as he considered his life and the turbulent times in which he'd lived. How he must have suffered, both physically and mentally during this time. She continued with renewed interest.

I became very restless, longing to escape the insularity of Central Asia. I begged Papa to send me to Saint Petersburg, to continue my education at the naval academy, where my uncle was a senior officer. Finally, Papa relented, recognising that his unhappy second son needed to spread his wings and make his own way in the world. I left this outpost on the periphery of the empire to make a new life at the very heart of Russian civilisation. This was the best time of my life ... to be a man of importance (apparently older than my years), strutting about the very capital of the world's greatest empire. I took to my studies with gusto, and I did well – very well indeed. In fact, I quickly became the star student. My former governess had done her job well, and I now recalled, with a new fondness, the endless hours of instruction that I had previously resisted. Details of the glories and vast extent of our empire came flooding back.

Not all of the Saint Petersburg architecture was in the pursuit of luxury. The Peter and Paul Fortress, protector of the empire, frowned across the broad River Neva at the splendour of the Winter Palace opposite, and the huge edifice of Saint Isaac's Cathedral behind. The czars had created the greatest empire the world had seen. Nicholas II was invincible. The Russian Empire would last forever ... it must.

Unknown to me, great events were unfolding in the Pacific, east of Siberia. In 1854, an American naval squadron, under the command of Commodore Matthew Perry, attacked Tokyo, capital of Japan, forcing them to accept an inequitable and unjust trading arrangement. The Japanese never forgot this humiliating loss of face, and soon they had mastered the aggression, so ably demonstrated to them by the Americans. At this time a backward China was in political ruins, economically raped by Europeans and Americans alike, and the Japanese wanted their share. In 1904, the Japanese War – known to the world as the Russo-Japanese War – broke out. We Russians needed a year-round ice-free port in the Pacific. Our outpost, Vladivostok, did not meet this criterion, so the Czar's forces sought to establish a base in Harbin, known to us as Port Arthur, in northern China. But this clashed with Japanese aspirations in Korea and Manchuria, and conflict soon erupted. While our army battled in Manchuria, the navy was mobilised.

This was my opportunity to see the world. Although I was still young, my star status at the naval academy had established my credibility as a tangible asset. I harangued my uncle to use his influence and have me assigned to one of the ships of the Baltic Fleet, which was soon to set sail for the Pacific. "Papa will be proud. Mama will weep but then relent. I will bring glory to the whole family." At the last moment, I was assigned as a cadet attending the captain of the great cruiser Aurora (yes … the same name as my own little boat), and my great adventure had begun.

The Aurora was the pride of the Baltic fleet. It was one of the three modern Pallada-class cruisers built in the Saint Petersburg Admiralty Shipyards and intended for Pacific service. Commissioned in November 1903, it was virtually a brand-new ship! The Aurora had set sail for the Pacific immediately after her commissioning, but she had suffered numerous mechanical failures en route. When the war with Japan erupted, the Aurora, still stricken, was in Djibouti. Ordered back to Saint Petersburg, the ship was quickly refitted and then directed to join the newly formed Second Pacific Fleet, which was about to set sail.

My heart swelled in my breast with pride as I sauntered down the gangplank, saluted the quarter deck and reported to my new master, mentor and friend, Captain Yegoyev of the great cruiser Aurora. No longer in my little boat on my beloved Issyk-Kul Lake ... this was the real thing. On the fifteenth of October 1904, the great adventure began. The lines were slipped, the mighty engines throbbed, the helm guided the majestic vessel from its mooring and the bustle of the Russian capital yielded to the solitude of the Baltic. While the first part of the journey was uneventful, rumours of waiting Japanese warships rippled through the fleet, as we slipped out of the calm Baltic into the dangers of the North Sea. Torpedoes lurked in every wave, and every lightning flash signalled a volley of shells from a Japanese battleship.

Action! Call to battle stations! Adrenaline pumping! Enemy fire! Casualties! Enemy ships sunk! Or perhaps not. Fuelled by fear and rumour, the glorious Russian imperial navy had managed to negotiate a non-existent minefield, sink a British fishing trawler, damage four other trawlers, kill three British sailors, and wound five others. But even worse, our seven battleships had fired on the Dmitrii Donskoi and on the Aurora – us! … yes us. Our own warships had fired on us, killing a ship's priest and a sailor, while wounding several others. The damage would certainly have been worse had it not been for the inaccuracy of Russian battleship gunnery. I, along with many others of the crew, was appalled. The British, of course, demanded compensation, and only when this was granted could we proceed – but not via the British-controlled Suez Canal shortcut. Our inglorious baptism of fire, later known with infamy as the "Dogger Bank Incident", resulted in a long and tedious journey south, around the bottom of the great African continent.

Despite this humiliating setback, I settled into life at sea and started to thoroughly enjoy myself. Because of my privileged position, reporting directly to the captain, my routine was not too difficult. But my heart went out to those poor sailors whose stifling working conditions became almost unbearable. As we edged our way down the African coast approaching the equator, the heat below decks became hell. But what could I do?

In December 1904, we made landfall in the German southwest African port of Angra Pequena (Lüderitz), enabling the fleet to regroup. I was lucky to be granted the privilege of accompanying our captain ashore, my first experience of a land that was not controlled by our glorious Czar. I must say that I was not impressed. If the rest of the world is like this, I pondered, it is no wonder that we Russians are the envy of civilised society.

The fleet continued south until we were off the British port of Cape Town. Dominated by the brooding enormity of

Table Mountain, Cape Town seemed to symbolise the precarious nature of the British hold on southern Africa. Just two years earlier, the British had narrowly defeated the Dutch Boers of the Transvaal and Orange Free State in a ruthless and bloody guerrilla war, and it was difficult to see how British rule in southern Africa could last ... but I am sure that must be wrong. Surely, I thought, at the time, we Europeans have both the right and responsibility to bring civilisation to the world, just as Przhevalsky had written so many years before.

The Roaring Forties struck with a vengeance as the fleet rounded the Cape of Good Hope and ploughed through the freezing desolation towards the Indian Ocean. Again, the crew suffered appalling privations. Frustration, born of the powerlessness to correct terrible injustice, stalked my otherwise euphoric anticipation of historic greatness.

After a seven-month sea journey halfway around the world, we at last approached our enemy, Imperial Japan. Our fleet's task was simple – to engage and defeat the enemy, relieve our land forces at Port Arthur and rendezvous with the Russian First Pacific Fleet. But, as we learnt while in transit, Port Arthur had already fallen to the Japanese, and the First Fleet had been destroyed ... and now the Japanese fleet was stalking us.

Night-time, 27 May 1905, and the flagship of the cruiser detachment, Oleg, commanded by Rear Admiral Enkvist, led the cruisers through Tsushima Strait between Japan and Korea. Flashes ignited the horizon; shells screamed overhead, and explosions burst all around. Fear filled the breasts of all experienced crewmen as an awful truth dawned. The Japanese gunners had our range while we were still well short of returning effective fire.

Aurora suffered eighteen direct hits by 200-mm and 75-mm shells. The splinters of one 75-mm shell pierced the conning tower, wounding the officers and killing my beloved mentor, Captain Yegoyev. Fifteen brave shipmates were killed and 83 were wounded. But despite this carnage, we suffered only moderate hull and superstructure damage, destruction of five 75-mm guns and one 150-mm gun, and the disabling of our fire control system. But the Aurora, miraculously, remained afloat.

Others were not so lucky. One by one, our illustrious fighting ships and their brave crews, who had endured so many hardships during the eastern voyage, perished beneath the waves of the infamous Tsushima Strait. Water ... deep, dark and deadly.

It was the worst disaster ever to befall the Russian navy. Of our 38 fighting ships that departed Saint Petersburg, only a few were spared. Although wounded, Executive Officer Arkady Nebolsin took command of the Aurora, which assumed the role of flagship of the crippled maritime remnants. Together with the only two other surviving cruisers, we limped to the American colony of Manila, only to be interned there until the end of the war. Finally, after a humiliating imprisonment, we were repatriated to the Baltic.

So ended my first sea adventure, so ended my innocence and so ended the Czar's credibility. The Japanese had thoroughly defeated the Czar's forces, both on land and at sea. How could Czar Nicholas so betray his loyal soldiers and sailors? Chastened by the horrendous Tsushima Strait defeat, I vowed to never again be used in such a way. The suffering of the ordinary seamen, sacrificed to czarist ambition, sparked in me a growing revulsion towards Russia's rigid class system, the arrogance of the nobility, and the resulting exploitation of the masses. I began to study the reforming thinkers, Karl Marx, Friedrich Engels, Peter Kropotkin, Vladimir Lenin and others. So, too, was I drawn to the political intrigues that sprang from their writings.

But the crosscurrents of reform in Czarist Russia were much more treacherous than the dangers of the Tsushima Strait. The Czar's secret police were everywhere, routinely rounding up dissidents, destined for deportation or death. There were many political parties, some supporters of the Czar like the Octobrists, some liberal democrats such as the Kadets, and socialists including the Social Revolutionaries. I flirted with them all, but was secretly drawn to radical Marxist groups, including the Social Democrats, the Mensheviks and, in particular, the Bolsheviks. I decided that a radical violent overthrow of the Czar and all that he stood for – a complete break – was the only way to relieve the grinding poverty and suffering of my Russian comrades.

I thought long and hard about my current naval service but eventually concluded that remaining in the navy was the best way I could influence the course of future events. Because I was one of the few survivors of the disastrous Japanese naval engagement, and perhaps because of my family connections, I experienced rapid promotion and was soon assigned as a training officer on board the Aurora. The ship had been repaired, and continued service as a cadet training ship, travelling the world. In this role, I had the remarkable opportunity to advance my understanding of European and world politics, and the dangerous path currently being traversed.

I undertook many varied duties in the Czar's service ... study, promotion and travel following in quick succession. At first, I was engaged in the inspection of naval establishments in the disputed Baltic Sea, in the northern, often-frozen, White Sea, and in the far-eastern Pacific base of Vladivostok. But my most enjoyable travel experience was visiting my childhood home in the foothills of the Central Asian Tian Shan Mountains. I was sent there to assess the vulnerability of the mountain lakes and rivers on Russia's southern flank. My beloved Issyk-Kul Lake, now hosting a flourishing water-borne trade serviced by a wide variety of vessels, had assumed some considerable strategic importance to Russia. Sailing longboats and schooners were the first modern boats transporting cargo and passengers, principally to and from Rybachye and Karakol. It was there that I met and married my darling wife, and there, on that beautiful lake, that we spent our honeymoon.

I yearned to again be at one with the placid water, and I managed to convince my superiors that a two-week cruise in that idyllic setting was really a research project, aimed at determining the strategic importance of every bay and promontory around its periphery. We embarked on

*a three-masted schooner, which bore the name of the lake
itself, the Issyk-Kul, as if water and ship had become one.
Cargo, passengers and military strategy of the early twen-
tieth century defined the purpose of the lake, just as the lake
defined those that traversed it.*

Aurora reflected for a moment before resuming her reading. The lives of these people must have been torn apart by the
political intrigues and wars of the first half of the 20th century.
She wondered what they might have done if they could roll
back time. She turned again to the journal.

*Success in each of these assignments led my superiors to rec-
ognise that I was capable of more responsible tasks, and my
assignments became more varied both within the empire
and across the wider world. My new role was that of strategic advisor to the general staff on maritime matters – a
very important role indeed for a young man in his early
thirties. More travel, more prestige … and more insight
into the suffering that surrounded us.*

*Russia coveted British India. Britain feared a Russian
takeover of its worldwide empire, but was even more
alarmed by German expansion in Europe, Africa and
the Pacific. The Germans had thoroughly defeated the
French in the 1870s Franco-Prussian War, so now the
French sought to contain the Germans, through the British–French Entente Cordiale and, more recently, through
the British–French–Russian Triple Entente. In response,
the Germans allied with the Austrians, and courted the
Turks, who vacillated. It was the German promise to
replace two Turkish battleships that had been seized by*

the British while under construction in British shipyards that finally triggered the Turkish–German alliance. On the sidelines, the Americans and Japanese waited and watched. Nothing in international politics is as simple as it seems at the time.

In the early 1900s, most European countries except France were headed by hereditary monarchies – Romanovs in Russia, Hohenzollerns in Germany, Habsburgs in Austria–Hungary, Saxe-Coburg & Gotha in Britain (changed to Windsor in 1919), and the Ottomans in Türkiye. But pulling the strings of these marionette monarchs were the real powers – the landed aristocracy and wealthy industrialists. The schemers, the strategists, the capitalists, and the empire builders, all aided by their politician servants, and … trodden beneath their feet, the ever-docile exploited worker classes struggled for survival on the crumbs dropped by their masters.

Europe was ready to explode. Greed set the charges, and fear lit the fuse. The spark that ignited the conflagration came on 28 June 1914 in the obscure Serbian town of Sarajevo. Gavrilo Princip, a radicalised dissident Bosnian Serb from the Black Hand separatist movement, fired the fatal shots that ended the lives of the Austrian Habsburg Archduke Ferdinand and his wife, Sophie. The heir to the mighty and proud Austro–Hungarian Empire was dead – and this death must be avenged. Austria–Hungary demanded crippling reparations from Serbia, Russia sprang to the aid of their Orthodox Christian Slav kinsmen, Germany supported their Austrian allies, while France and Britain saw the opportunities for territorial gain at Türkiye's expense in the oil-rich Levant. The British dominions, naïve in the affairs of the world, dutifully followed their mother. Others were drawn in through a network of alliances and the scent of territorial expansion – Serbia, Montenegro, Greece, Japan and others joined with the British–French–Russian allies, while Bulgaria and other minor belligerents sided with the German, Austro–Hungarian and Turkish central powers. Finally, sensing commercial gain from a British–French–Russian victory, the United States of America eventually entered the fray as their ally.

None of us really understood the political intrigues that led to the outbreak of hostilities. What we did understand was that Kaiser Wilhelm's German fleet was far superior to Czar Nicholas's Russian fleet. But as officers and crew of the Czar's cruiser, Aurora, we dutifully set sail as ordered. I had been re-assigned to my old ship, and I enjoyed being back at sea. Our Baltic operations involved patrols and shore bombardment, but by February 1917 we were again in Saint Petersburg for repairs and a refit. Anchored in the River Neva, close to the Winter Palace, we waited. The plight of the army was a repeat of the 1904–1905 Japanese fiasco. Our defeated armies were retreating on all fronts. Morale evaporated and the suffering soldiers were mutinous. Czar Nicholas was useless, and finally the government had had enough. On 15 March 1917, the government of Prime Minister Kerensky forced Czar Nicholas to abdicate – the end of 300 years of Romanov rule and the end of the world as we had known it. But Kerensky refused to negotiate an armistice with the German–Austrian–Turkish alliance, instead persisting with the fruitless slaughter of many patriotic Russian comrades. The war dragged on, the deprivation worsened and the suffering of our gallant soldiers became intolerable.

News from the front was rare, and always bad. One of my cousins perished in the disastrous Battle of Tannenberg, and another two were horribly maimed. And then the worst news of all ... my closest cousin was killed in the meaningless defence of some obscure village outside Warsaw. And here was I, stuck on an obsolete ship, far from the action, guarding the obscenely ostentatious treasures of a deposed monarch on behalf of a heartless and ineffective government.

But events moved more quickly elsewhere. The extreme Marxist cell, the Bolsheviks, had split from the less-radical Menshevik wing, which now supported the Kerensky government. From his safe exile in Switzerland, the Bolshevik leader, Vladimir Lenin, was a vociferous and scathing opponent of Russian participation in the war. The Germans, cynically recognising this unique opportunity to neutralise their Russian enemy, acted decisively – they provided Lenin safe passage by train across Germany and smuggled him into Saint Petersburg on 16 April 1917 to join others of the Bolshevik leadership. Thus, the scene was set for a turning point in the Great War; indeed, as future events would prove, one of the most important events in modern history.

Mutiny and rebellion swept through both the army and the navy, and the Aurora was not immune. The seamen mutinied, Captain Nikolsky was murdered, and a new captain, Aleksandr Belyshev, who was sympathetic to the revolution, was elected. We were all compelled to declare our allegiance to the revolution. For me, of course, it was easy. From that day on the road to Tashkent, when I had first witnessed the pain inflicted by an unjust class system on a peasant boy carting cotton, I had been moving inexorably towards this moment. The injustice and suffering of the old system had persisted for too long and must be swept away.

At this time, the Kerensky government was meeting in the Czar's Winter Palace on the bank of the River Neva, just across from the Aurora. It had proven just as weak and heartless as the czarist regime so it, too, must be dispatched. At last, at 21:40 hours on 25 October (7 November in the western calendar) 1917, the order came: load a blank charge in the forward gun, point it in the direction of the Winter Palace and fire. Just one shot. And that Aurora shot resonated around the world – igniting the revolution.

Time passes so slowly, as if to mimic the stillness of the waters. Here I sit, 27 years later, gazing into the calmness of Lake Ladoga in southern Finland. It seems to reflect my innermost contemplation. Who am I? What am I doing? What has led me to this terrible situation?

I carried few personal effects when on active service, but one that never leaves my person was that letter from my beloved brother. Now, with a prisoner's freedom to contemplate such matters, I read his final words over and over again.

How different our lives have been. I, a warrior, an agent of destruction, and he, a man of peace. This is my brother's final letter.

Aurora paused. This must be a reference to her own direct ancestors, her great-grandparents. She began reading again.

Newcastle, Australia

20 June 1917

My dear brother,

I pray that you are safe from the ravages of the Great War that is consuming all of Europe and our beloved Russian motherland. It concerns me that I am here, on the other side of the world, while you bear arms in a struggle that involves such killing. Although I have devoted my life to working for peace, I fear that I, too, will in some way become ensnared in this vicious struggle.

But enough of such melancholy. I have a strange tale to tell. By coincidence, I too have embarked in a ship called Aurora and have experienced great adventure. My ship is the steam yacht, SY Aurora, a very different ship from that harbinger of destruction in which you sail. My SY Aurora is not an instrument of war, but an agent of peace and salvation. She was built as a whaler in 1876, but more recently has accrued a creditable record in Arctic and Antarctic humanitarian rescues. In 1884, SY Aurora participated in the attempted rescue of the stricken Greely Expedition, which was trapped for three years in the Canadian Arctic around Lady Franklin Bay. Together with three other vessels, SY

Aurora rescued seven of the explorers, although fifteen had already perished of starvation, hypothermia or drowning, and one had been executed for stealing food. But more shocking were the allegations of cannibalism. Life was tough in the polar regions in those days. Again in 1891, SY Aurora rescued the crew of the ill-fated Polynia, which had been crushed in sea ice. But these events were just a taste of her future role. In 1910, the Australasian Antarctic Expedition purchased the SY Aurora for Douglas Mawson's epic British expedition to the frozen waste of the southern continent. And this is when I joined her crew.

We departed Hobart, Australia, in December 1911 for Mawson's main Antarctic base at Cape Denison, calling first at the remote Southern Ocean radio relay station on Macquarie Island. We remained at Cape Denison for the construction of the main hut, and then embarked again for Hobart. When we later returned to Cape Denison in December 1912, we learned the distressing news that Douglas Mawson, Xavier Mertz and Belgrave Ninnis were overdue on a sled expedition. We waited for as long as we could, but when strong winds caused the anchor chains to break, we were forced to leave and return to Hobart via the Western Base.

Meanwhile, tragedy had struck the three-man sled expedition. First, Ninnis disappeared in a crevasse, together with one of the two sleds – the one carrying their food. Immediately after paying their respects to their departed colleague,

Mawson and Mertz turned back for Cape Denison. But they were desperately short of food and were forced to kill and eat some of their sled dogs. For Mertz this proved to be fatal. The high levels of Vitamin A in the husky liver that both men ingested eventually sent Mertz insane and, finally, into a lethal coma. Forced to continue the final 250-kilometre struggle to Cape Denison alone, Mawson was lucky to survive another crevasse fall. He was saved only through good fortune. His sled became wedged in the crevasse walls, thus enabling him to climb out. On he trudged, but in a bitter twist of fate, the SY Aurora had departed just a few hours before his arrival back at the base. The ship was unable to return, due to bad weather, so the emaciated and ailing Mawson, together with six colleagues who had remained at Cape Denison, was forced to winter there for a second year until being finally rescued in December 1913.

But our strange adventures in the SY Aurora were not over yet. We continued exploration during the summer months of 1914 and were then commissioned by Ernest Shackleton to set up supply depots for the Imperial Trans-Antarctic Expedition. Initially delayed by sea ice at McMurdo, SY Aurora despatched her supply teams to the depots and finally arrived in Discovery Bay. The delays had meant that SY Aurora was dangerously exposed to the encroaching winter, and in May 1915 we became ensnared in the pack ice. The ten men in the depots were stranded, and the eighteen of us who were still on the ship were trapped in a floating prison. For 312 days, the ship and the ice were locked together, drifting 3,000 kilometres across the Southern Ocean.

This was a time of hardship, but the biggest challenges were combating boredom and the closeness of our living conditions. Captain Stenhouse did his best to keep us active with games of cricket and football on the ice. Our final release came in February 1916, as the summer warmth finally disintegrated the softening pack ice, but we were lucky to escape sinking as the icy water poured into the hold between the timbers that had been squeezed, as in a vice, for nearly a year. After much pumping and judicious repairs, we were finally free. By April, the ship had reached the safety of Dunedin, in New Zealand.

Most of my shipmates took the opportunity to return to civilisation – New Zealand, that is – but a few of us signed on with a new captain, John King Davis, for yet another rescue mission. This time we were bound for Cape Evans to pick up the survivors of the Ross Sea shore party. We arrived on 10 January 1917, to find that only seven of the original ten had survived. Life in the Antarctic is fraught with danger. The sadness for departed colleagues was further compounded by the revelation that this was to be our final Antarctic trip.

The war had severely restricted funds for Antarctic exploration, so Shackleton was forced to sell the ship. The crew disbanded and went their separate ways. Perhaps it was sentiment, but I decided to stay with the ship. The SY Aurora has now returned to Australia and we are soon to embark with a cargo of coal from the port of Newcastle, bound for Iquique in Chile.

Oh, there is one more thing that I must share with you, my dear brother. For many years, I was resigned to a life of bachelorhood, wed only to the sea, so to speak. But on my last visit here in Australia, I met the most wonderful woman, a widow, whose younger brother now serves in the British forces somewhere in the eastern Mediterranean. She calls him Digger, but I think that might be a generic name given to all Australian soldiers. I must hasten to close now for time is short, but I will write again from the ship with all the wonderful news of my new love.

As always, dear brother, my thoughts and prayers are with you and our family. I suffer the remorse of knowing that I am here in the relative safety of this Southern Ocean, while you endure the northern peril of war. I fear for your safety in the conflagration that is destroying our homeland. I treasure our childhood adventures on Issy-Kul Lake in our own little Aurora. Keep safe.

Your affectionate brother …

I held his letter to my breast, as I had done so many times before. And so, my beloved brother's ship, the gallant Antarctic rescue vessel, SY Aurora, embarked on a voyage that she would never complete. Somewhere in the Tasman Sea, she disappeared forever. For the men of the SY Aurora, time had stood still. While they endured their frozen prison and their final destruction, we of the naval cruiser Aurora had been locked in a life-and-death European struggle that witnessed the deaths of millions around the world.

And so, the gallant man of peace perished, an innocent victim of war – while I, the man of war, live on, plagued by remorse for the destruction that my actions have wrought.

A long document, indeed, and Aurora needed more refreshment. A drink … no, not alcohol. Since her breakdown and illness, she'd sworn off the booze. Now her friends kept a close watch over her, and offered support whenever needed. A cup of tea would do nicely. She sipped the hot beverage, mulling over all she'd read so far then, feeling more alert, she picked up the journal again and continued reading.

But I have skipped ahead too far. As that single shot from the Aurora in 1917 resonated around the world, the Russian government collapsed and the city, initially known as Petrograd and, later, Leningrad, dissolved into chaos. Prime Minister Kerensky fled, the government fell, Soviet cells formed, while workers and peasants overthrew the ruling and moneyed classes and Comrade Lenin declared a new Russia based on the dictatorship of the proletariat. Russia withdrew from the conflict with the Germans and their allies, but the suffering did not end there. Everywhere there was violence, killing, starvation and retribution.

Within a year, the German armies had succumbed to the combined strength of France, Britain and its dominions, numerous smaller allies, and the belated contribution of the United States. On 11th November 1918 the guns fell silent. The armistice, signed in a railway carriage in the French Compiègne Forest, the subsequent Paris Peace Conference and resulting Treaty of Versailles, were supposed to mark the beginning of a new era of international cooperation. But the victorious allies were merciless and duplicitous in their demands on the defeated belligerents, as they ruthlessly carved up the spoils of war in their own interests. Germany was stripped of territory both within Europe and overseas.

Significantly, it lost the disputed Alsace–Lorraine region to the French, and eastern territory to a resurrected Poland and a newly created Czechoslovakia.

East Prussia became an isolated German enclave, separated from the rest of the country by the newly created Gdansk corridor, designed to give Poland Baltic access. Austria was stripped of its possessions, surviving only as a shadow of its former glory. Gone were Hungary, Serbia and Slovakia as well as the Balkan states, which combined to form Yugoslavia. Bulgaria was greatly diminished, and Türkiye, previously the greatest of the Islamic powers, was stripped of its possessions save its Anatolian heartland and the small European foothold adjacent to Istanbul. The victorious European allies established a string of new countries across central and eastern Europe, in the Balkans and in the Levant, to serve as buffer states preventing the expansion of Russia to the west or south. The British and French implemented the hitherto secret Sykes–Picot Agreement, which carved up the Middle East, such as to provide France hegemony in Syria and the Lebanon, and to protect British strategic interests from the Suez Canal to the Arabian Peninsula and Persian Gulf, to their precious jewel, India.

Of the major hereditary monarchies, only the innocuous British Windsors and the monarchs of a handful of minor states remained. Gone was the Hohenzollern Kaiser Wilhelm II from Germany, gone was the Habsburg Emperor Franz Joseph II from Austria–Hungary, gone was the Ottoman Sultan Mehmed VI from Türkiye and gone, at last, was our once revered Romanov Czar Nicholas II.

In-fighting within the Bolshevik Communist Party threatened the very power of the Bolshevik communist government. Lenin's death, on 21 January 1924, ushered in a ruthless power struggle between Leon Trotsky, champion of worldwide revolution, and Joseph Stalin, proponent of consolidation within the emergent Soviet Union. Stalin's victory saw two decades of purges, executions and deportations of dissidents to the Siberian gulags.

Violence begets violence. The overthrow of the Russian system led to another five years of civil war – Reds versus Whites. All over the empire, Red and White armies fought and pillaged. In Central Asia, our Red armies were initially successful, but then came the foreign intervention. British General Malleson assisted the Menshevik resistance in Ashkhabad in Turkmenistan and led an (unsuccessful) campaign north to Tashkent, Bukhara and Khiva. British Colonel Bailey participated in a mission to Tashkent, where my parents still lived and worked. The revolution pitted class against class, but it also split families. My father, the loyal servant of the Czar, and to the successor Kerensky government, "nailed his (white) colours to the mast", and publicly declared his support for the White army and its British allies. That declaration, honourable as it was, proved to be fatal. As the British withdrew, the White resistance collapsed and the Reds exacted their revenge.

In June 1918, the first regional congress of the Russian Communist Party was held in Tashkent. My honourable Papa, true to his beliefs and upbringing, refused to abandon the region and paid the ultimate price, execution. Of this I knew nothing until several years later, when I came across his final letter written from Bukhara. The Reds held Papa in the dungeons of the Bukhara Ark Fortress for several years because they thought he could prove useful, before finally executing him. My mother and my two sisters were only slightly more fortunate. Condemned to years of hardship in the tenement housing of communist Tashkent, mother survived in poverty and squalor until grief hastened her premature demise. Of my sisters, I only know that they continued to live somewhere in the far-flung Central Asian outposts of the Soviet Union. My brother, the companion of my youth, had already perished in a watery grave in the Tasman Sea as the SY Aurora slipped silently beneath the waves. And so, I was alone.

And for my part in the revolution, I was rewarded with promotion. I spent many years at the naval academy in Leningrad. Finally, in the 1930s, as the dark clouds of war reappeared in Europe, I returned to my old ship, the cruiser Aurora, this time as the political liaison officer.

Life was harsh in Stalin's Soviet Union, but it was also intolerable in those countries that had been defeated during the Great War. In particular, post-war German hyperinflation, staggering unemployment and grinding poverty fuelled an unfettered resentment of the crippling reparations imposed by the victorious allies. The German people struggled for an escape, and to many the national syndicalism policies of Adolf Hitler's Nazi party seemed to provide the solution. But there was a dark side to this path that many could not (or would not) recognise in the 1930s. Europe was again sinking into the mire of extreme nationalism, which leads inevitably to rearmament. Industrialists thrive on arms production. German rearmament relieved the unemployment problem, while salving a wounded national pride. But the inevitable outcome of rearmament is war.

As a keen student of international politics, with experience in the black arts of war, I read with dismay classified reports detailing the 1930s manoeuvring of Hitler, Stalin, Chamberlain and Daladier as they played their dangerous games of intrigue and brinkmanship that would ultimately result in the deaths of millions and the ruin of their homelands. The secret Molotov–Ribbentrop Pact of 23 August 1939, whereby Russia and Germany agreed mutual non-aggression, was the green light for the dismembering of Poland and the commencement of the next deadly phase of European warfare. Confident that his eastern flank was secure, Hitler launched the western German blitzkrieg, overrunning the Low Countries, France and Norway in a matter of weeks.

But the Russian–German rapport did not last long. As the British navy enforced a trade blockade, Hitler's Germany became desperate for the grains and the oil of the western Soviet Union republics. On 22 June 1941, an over-confident Hitler launched Operation Barbarossa, which struck eastwards with lightning speed at the Soviet homeland. German preparation had been meticulous and the Soviet armies were taken by surprise, initially falling back on all fronts. But the German planning had not properly accounted for the logistics of extended supply lines, the bitter weather, the lack of locally sourced food and the sheer determination of the Soviet resistance. Battles for Moscow, near the upper Volga, and Stalingrad, on the lower Volga, finally meant the onslaught ground to a halt. During Operation Barbarossa, over a million Germans soldiers perished, while Russia suffered nearly five million military casualties. On top of these staggering military losses, millions of others died of starvation or the effects of exposure.

By 8 September 1941, Leningrad was surrounded, but our gallant soldiers fought desperately to secure and defend the perimeter, determined to yield not a single metre. Again, the naval cruiser Aurora played its part in defending the city, although this time suffering the humiliation of partial dismemberment. The great guns were removed to the city perimeter and used to shell the advancing German horde. Virtually undefended, the ship was fortunate to survive several German bombing raids. The Siege of Leningrad dragged on through two merciless winters, as hunger and cold competed with bombs and bullets to claim the most lives. Food was drastically rationed and ammunition ran critically short, as the Grim Reaper stalked every part of the beleaguered city.

By late 1941, the Nazi German armies had almost completely cut off Leningrad, except for one route across Lake Ladoga. During the warmer months, a trickle of supplies had to be transported by watercraft. But as winter took hold, the lake froze and this provided a hard surface, the Ice Road, upon which our supply trucks might travel. At first the meagre provisions that trickled in made scant difference, but even so, they immeasurably boosted morale.

My years in Leningrad and my love of the water had pre-destined me for this time and place. As a naval officer and an intimate of the lake, I was ordered to command a convoy of relief boats. Running the gauntlet of Luftwaffe attacks was dangerous, but I was in my element. As summer water hardened to winter ice, my boat convoys were transformed into motor vehicles, trundling by night across the frozen sur-face. Subject to constant German bombing and negotiating ice of variable thickness, the risks multiplied exponentially. Bombs explode, the shattered ice yields to the lake beneath and the deadly water swallows many who traversed that treacherous highway.

Aurora had drifted off to sleep, but woke with a start to the sound of her phone buzzing. A quick check showed an incoming email from Marcus, arranging a meeting to discuss the current situation. That man must never sleep. She dashed off a quick acceptance, then resumed reading from the last paragraph that she could recall – something about bombs, ice and water. Yes, there it was …

Floating … drifting … darkness … suspended in time and space. I do not know how long I remained in this condition, but I got colder … and colder … until I was freezing. Was I dying? Was I already dead? I had entered this world beside the tranquil waters of Issyk-Kul Lake, at the very edge of the Russian Empire, and now I would depart amidst the cold chaos of Lake Ladoga, at the centre of the Russian Soviet Republic. They say that your whole life passes before your eyes at such a time ... my childhood in Central Asia, my little boat, the companionship of my beloved brother, the shocking poverty of the peasants, my adventures in the naval cruiser Aurora during that disastrous Japanese war, and that fateful shot from the Aurora that signalled the start of the revolution ... But no more.

Light again ... breathe again ... live again ... Now I remember!

Bombs exploded, the shattered ice yielded to the depths beneath and the deadly water swallowed those of us who traverse that treacherous highway. The Russian soldiers snatched me from a watery grave moments before drowning, but had to abandon me on Ladoga's frozen surface as a probing Finnish patrol drew dangerously close. And so, I became a prisoner of the Finns. My enemy's enemy is my friend – or so they say. The Finns had long fought us Russians for control of the Baltic coastline, and so the current hostilities between Germany and Russia had forced an uneasy Finnish–German cooperation. But who needs a friend like Nazi Germany? For the Finns it was a mixed blessing, but at least it preserved their independence.

The brutality of this war was such that a captured Russian officer had few privileges. The conditions of the Finnish POW (prisoner of war) Camp were so severe that a quarter of the Russian prisoners died of malnutrition. On the other hand, perhaps being a prisoner saved me from the slaughter of the battlefield. Convalescence seemed to take forever, but slowly I returned to normal health. Many times, I would retrieve that torn and faded letter that I always kept close to my heart: the letter my brother had sent from that far antipodean shore.

I learnt during these intervening years that the fate of the mercy ship SY Aurora had been sealed by the Great War German raider, the SMS Wolf. During this conflict, much damage had been inflicted by vessels such as the Wolf, designed specifically for subterfuge. Launched in March 1913, this armed merchant cruiser was one of several German raiders that wrought havoc south of the equator. With a displacement of only 11,400 tonnes, a length of just 135 metres and a mere 20 kilometres per hour top speed, she was by no means a great warship. But she was lethal. The Wolf bristled with six 150-mm guns, three 52-mm guns, four torpedo tubes, a seaplane and in excess of 450 mines. Her real tactical advantage lay in the ability to disguise her identity with a false funnel, masts and sides, and thus lure her unsuspecting prey to their doom.

Leaving her home port of Keil in November 1916, the Wolf threaded her way down the Atlantic, across the Indian Ocean and into the Pacific. It was in these southern climes that she wrought the most destruction. Hers was the longest voyage by any warship during the Great War. On returning to Kiel in February 1918, after a record 451 days at sea, the Wolf disgorged 467 prisoners, together with a significant cargo of hijacked zinc, brass, copper, rubber, silk, cocoa and copra. During the 15 months of the voyage she had despatched to the depths over 110,000 tonnes of enemy shipping – fourteen captured and sunk in addition to at least thirteen that fell victim to its mines.

A deadly legacy of the voyage lurked undetected in those perilous waters off the east coast of Australia, where the Wolf had deposited many of the mines. Although there is no formal record, there can be little doubt that my brother's ship, SY Aurora, fell victim to this hazard. But in a strange twist of fate, even the depths of the Tasman Sea could not silence the SY Aurora. A colleague, charged with gathering intelligence on foreign shipping, obtained, and then passed on to me, a newspaper cutting from twenty years earlier. It reported that an Australian – a Mr Bressingdon – while strolling on the sand of Tuggerah Beach on Australia's east coast, had discovered an old wine bottle. Exhibited on the bottle was an engraving of the SY Aurora and a message that read, "Midwinter's Day, 1912, Shackleton Glacier, Antarctica. Frank Wild, A. L. Kennedy, S. Evan Jones, C. Arch. Hoadley, Charles T. Harrisson, George Dovers, A. L. Watson and Morton H. Moyes". It was a fitting tribute bearing witness to the valiant rescue missions, and the men who owed their lives to this ship and its courageous crew. The bottle was believed to be still on board the SY Aurora when she vanished with all hands in 1917.

My brother's legacy was a faded letter and a newspaper clipping. But what of my legacy? Four decades of naval and political experience had placed me in the thick of violent struggle – the Japanese War, the Great War, the Revolution, the Civil War and now the Second World War. The Russian people's quest for survival had been fraught with a history of greed and violence. We had replaced the self-serving aristocracy and a useless Czar with the ruthless ideologues of a dictatorship that had now led us to destruction in the most violent war known to humanity. How could we so blindly follow those who dispensed death so casually?

I spent the remainder of the war as a prisoner of the Finns … disillusioned, dispirited and debilitated. Thankfully, the conflict did not last forever and I was finally repatriated, in 1945, to the ruin that was Leningrad. By now I was 65 and in poor health, the privation and humiliation of being a prisoner of war having taken its toll. I was excused from further military service and permitted to retire quietly to one of those boxes they call an apartment. My darling wife had perished in the barbarous Siege of Leningrad … I miss her beyond all comprehension … but you, my son, thankfully have survived your military service and have now returned to me. As I approach the winter of my life, I weary of my daily task of recording the vicissitudes of my ongoing being. I therefore entrust this journal to you, confident that you will preserve it and in turn pass it on to your son, and so on down the generations.

Ever your loving father.

Canberra – 2030

Aurora put down the journal. It had been a lot to take in, but while she had struggled a little with the detail, the writings had, as Cassandra had predicted, provided her with considerable previously unknown knowledge of, and insight into, the lives of her ancestors.

She took some time to mull over what she had learnt. So, the journal had been recorded by her great-grandfather's brother, a Russian naval hero, who saw action in the Tsushima Strait in 1905 aboard the naval cruiser *Aurora*, witnessed the shot that sparked the Russian Revolution in 1917, and participated in the defence of Leningrad in the dark depths of World War 2.

His brother, Aurora's great-grandfather, had sailed the Antarctic waters in the rescue ship, SY *Aurora*, been trapped in sea ice for a year, engaged in a brief but passionate relationship with an Australian woman, and ultimately departed Newcastle to a watery grave in the Tasman Sea.

Aurora's mind went into overdrive. This was family history of which she knew nothing. The exploits and fate of her own great-grandfather now became crystal clear. So, too, the origin of her middle name, Aurora, now made more sense. No longer was it just a family tradition. It constituted history, personalised through loss and family tragedy, handed down through the generations.

In addition to the copy of the journal, Cassandra had provided a commentary, summarising her own interpretation of the document. In Cassandra's opinion, the naval officer had served the Bolsheviks faithfully, but the fog of war had clouded his judgement. As that fog slowly lifted, he had sought to redeem himself, to undo the harm his military adventures had wrought, and to follow peaceful pursuits, as his older brother had done. But life had been precarious in the USSR, Cassandra believed, and he had had to be careful what he wrote. So, she believed, he wrote using metaphors.

The *Wolf*, that notorious World War 1 German raider, was meant to symbolise the far-reaching devastation of war, indiscriminately destroying all it encounters, she proposed. This evil leads down the path to extinction and must be avoided at all costs. The Russian schooner *Issyk-Kul* spent its whole service in peaceful but self-indulgent seclusion, trading in splendid isolation on the tranquil lake whose name it bore, while the whole world fell apart around it.

We cannot turn our back on a bleeding world, opt out and ignore the suffering of those around us, Cassandra believed. *But we should use what peaceful times are available to us to gather our thoughts and reflect on how best to serve our fellow humans.* The most famous (or infamous) of the ships was the Russian naval cruiser, *Aurora*, the ship that, earlier, blindly participated in fruitless imperialist adventures, immersed itself in the carnage of two world conflicts, and ushered in the death and destruction of violent revolution. It represented, therefore, the folly of youthful spontaneity, and the suffering it can bring if it's directed towards violence. Cassandra referred to his exhortation to *resist the war hawks, those who would consume the carrion of their own creation.* The mercy ship, SY *Aurora*, offered our best hope for our future, standing as a stark reminder that ongoing and valiant self-sacrifice make the world a better place.

Aurora pondered Cassandra's observations as she glanced through the journal a second time, her eyes lingering on the sentence, *How could we so blindly follow those who dispensed death so casually?".*

Then she noticed a comment. Barely legible at the bottom of the last page, the old man had scrawled a short postscript.

A long-lost letter, written to me in 1922 by my own Papa from his prison in Bukhara, has recently come into my possession. I will enclose it with this journal.

Danger approaching on all sides – 2030

Aurora explored the portfolio for further information. There was the final letter from her great-great-grandfather, the Czarist White-Russian bureaucrat caught up amid chaos and hardship of the great upheaval in Central Asia, from the Bukhara Ark Fortress in June 1922. Aurora had first read this letter in the company of Cassandra, when she had learned she and Digger most likely shared a common ancestry. The letter described in detail the incarceration of Digger's great-grandfather, and his suffering and final days in the "bug-pit".

But tiredness was now relentlessly stalking Aurora and her eyelids were refusing to remain open. She decided to read this letter again later, although she did take one quick look at some closing passages before she slept. As she drifted off, the old Russian's words, recorded in his letter from the Bukhara Ark Prison, echoed through her fatigued brain.

> *I sense danger approaching on all sides. From the north, a huge bear bounds across the steppe, from the south a ravenous lion descends from the mountains, in the western sky I see an eagle circling and, in the east a fiery dragon is stirring.*

Aurora was moved by the tragedy of her ancestors … her great-great-grandfather's futile loyalty to a doomed aristocracy, and her great-grandmother's devastating sense of loss as her fiancé disappeared in the murky depths of the Southern Ocean in

1917. Their family had suffered much, frustrated by the greed of tyrants and an ignorance of their place in history.

But, of course, the real tragedy of any war, she reflected, *is the young soldiers, sailors and airmen who give their lives to a violence from which nobody benefits.* Although she accepted we have a responsibility to resist intimidation by thugs and bullies, we also have a responsibility to temper our reactions and must clearly understand the likely long-term outcomes of any violence to which we might be tempted.

Much had happened to Aurora during the past sixteen years since her own southern adventure on the *Aurora Australis* in the Southern Ocean – most significantly, a meteoric rise up the TV journalistic ladder, accompanied by an equally spectacular crash in personal relationships. Thinly disguised alcohol addiction had fuelled argument, rift, formal separation and, ultimately, divorce from her husband. With this marital breakdown came estrangement from her own children and, worst of all, from her grandchildren. *But*, she reflected, *she had been rescued from the abyss by the respect and friendship extended by friends and colleagues who cared for her wellbeing.* A calmness settled over her, the reassurance that fraught personal relationships could, and would, be repaired.

Was it possible, she wondered, *that international relationships, just like personal relationships, could also be repaired through national attitudinal change? Or are we so irrevocably wedded to past bias, fear and xenophobia that we would prefer to simply be consumed by changes that we neither understand nor resist? Are we able to simply push a reset button?*

Aurora was aware that, while she and her newly discovered distant cousin, Digger, shared common ancestry, their experiences were quite different. How would Digger react to this new information of his forebear's past experiences?

DIGGER – THE QUEEN'S PAWN

Queen's Pawn – 2030

Crux is a Latin name, given centuries ago to the most easily recognisable constellation of the southern sky, the Southern Cross. Many dreamtime stories of Indigenous Australians owe their origin to the Crux. It guided the Lapita ancestors of the Polynesians, the Māori and others, as they populated the South Pacific Islands, half a millennium before the Europeans rounded Cape Horn or the Cape of Good Hope. The Crux also steered the course of the European explorers, including Magellan, Torres and de Quiros as they traversed the Pacific, the "peaceful" ocean. And so too, the Crux watched over a later generation, Hartog, Janszoon, Dampier and Cook, as they charted the great south land, *Terra Australis*.

Digger was not normally moved to philosophy, or even anything close to it, but in the light of recent events he took time to reflect on his country's history, his family's history and the intertwining of the two. The Crux, for generations part of our flag, had both inspired and watched over country and family as the decades slipped by.

Digger's grandfather had been … well, wise. Yes, that's the correct word. We never fully appreciate the wisdom of our grandparents – the kind of wisdom that only accrues through a lifetime of experience.

Grandad would often speak of the Crux, although he used its colloquial name, the Southern Cross. To him, it symbolised the crossroads of life and the many choices we make between foolishness and wisdom. He'd sit with Digger for hours, nurturing his eldest grandchild through the love only grandparents can give. He'd speak of the adventures of his own childhood, the excitement of the Roaring Twenties, the hard times of the 1930s Depression, and the dark days of the 1940s as warfare overwhelmed the world again.

Grandad often spoke fondly of his own father, Great-Grandad, also known as Digger, who'd been a loving and affectionate parent. He'd become a father late in life, after the traumatic and violent decade of World War 1 and its aftermath.

But as young Digger grew older, he recognised a gap in the narrative. What had his great-grandfather done during that war, the *Great War*, as the old folk preferred to call it, and in the following years? And, for that matter, what had his own grandfather done during World War 2?

Enquire as he might, Digger remained in the dark all through his teenage years as to what his great-grandfather and his grandfather had experienced during those two conflicts. As he approached manhood, however, the spectre of new global conflicts loomed large. Perhaps, for Grandad, the prospect that his eldest grandson could soon be sent to some new killing field finally prompted him into sharing stories of his and his father's wartime activities.

The Great War

Digger's great-grandfather (Great-Grandad, also known as *Digger* to his friends) had enlisted in the Australian Imperial Force in late 1914 at eighteen. He and his fellow soldiers trained in Egypt, shipped out to Lemnos in the Aegean Sea, and then plunged into the thick of the invasion of Gallipoli.

Here was his baptism of fire, struggling ashore with the first wave before dawn on 25 April 1915. He lost many good friends that first morning. He told of one mate, a sergeant killed by friendly fire from the beach as he struggled up the first line of hills, even before sunrise. That death, during those first few hours, almost drove him mad; perhaps it did rob him of his sanity.

The invasion dragged on until the troops were withdrawn after eight months. Later, he served in the desert campaigns of the Light Horse, including the famous charge on Beersheba. Eventually, the war came to an end, not due to advances in the east, but as the carnage of the French and Belgian killing fields began to foreshadow a victory for the western allies. The elder Digger had survived, but the killing and carnage had rendered him unable to cope with civilian life, at least for a few years.

Central Asia, a Crucible of Violence

In 1919 came a real surprise for his Australian family. Instead of returning home with his fellow soldiers who'd survived, Digger's great-grandad joined the British forces, embarking on yet another foreign invasion.

Again, in the service of the British, he participated in the invasion of Central Asia, fighting the communist forces of the Red Army. Captured during the retreat of the British troops, he was cast into prison, or the Bukhara "bug-pit" as he called it.

But he also spoke fondly of his fellow prisoner, an old Russian who'd helped him to understand and, ultimately, survive the ordeal. It was a terrible time during which he was in constant fear of execution.

Then, unexpectedly, came his release. He didn't know why he'd been freed, but assumed it was probably part of a prisoner exchange. He knew nothing of the fate of the old Russian cellmate, his friend and mentor.

Freed from his incarceration into the custody of a Russian intelligence officer, Great-Grandad had been secreted south, across the Amu Darya (known in the west as the Oxus River), and delivered into the care of British agents, still operating in the region. Transported west to Ashkhabad, and thence through the Elburz Mountains to Tehran, he was at length taken down to Basra, below the marshes at the confluence of the great Tigris and Euphrates Rivers. At this time, in 1922, the British had moved to establish a "protectorate" in Persia, which afforded them undisputed access to the vast oilfields of the region.

After interrogation by British intelligence officers, Great-Grandad was repatriated by sea via the Persian Gulf, through the Strait of Hormuz, passing through the Indian Ocean, until he was back to the safety of his native Australia.

Grandad spoke to Digger of his father's disillusionment. For eight years, Great-Grandad had been the puppet of the imperialists, condemned to unspeakable hardship and killing, simply to enrich the rulers of a far-away empire that had banished his forebears to the other side of the world. Time and time again, he'd repeat the words of his aged Russian mentor: *This foreign Central Asian civil war offers no credible threat to your antipodean homeland, yet you are here. You are again blindly following your bungling imperialist masters, and yet again you are betrayed. Perhaps you Australians are incapable of thinking for yourselves. As I said, I do not understand you people.*

Family

It took a long time and much loving care by his family before Great-Grandad emerged from the depths of depression. His sister was particularly supportive.

She, too, had known loss during the Great War – not of an Australian serviceman, like so many of her friends, but a Russian sailor. It had been the briefest of romances, while his ship was being refitted in Newcastle in preparation for a voyage across the South Pacific to Chile. But it was passionate. Her Russian sailor promised to return, make Australia his home and marry her. With a heavy heart, she wished him *bon voyage* and watched as his ship cleared the Hunter breakwater, beyond Fort Scratchley.

That was the last she ever saw of her Russian sailor. Some years later, she noticed a newspaper article about a man who'd discovered some flotsam on Tuggerah Beach: an engraved bottle that turned out to be from her sailor's ship. The closure helped her to move on.

Digger, his father and grandfather had long since lost contact with these distant cousins. *Somewhere in Australia,* he reflected, *must be relatives descended from Great-Grandad's sister and her Russian sailor consort. Whoever they might be, it would be interesting to contact them to exchange histories and learn from each other.*

Repair

Determined to build a new life, Digger's great-grandfather eventually emerged from his chasm of despair and immersed himself in work and study.

By the time he re-entered the mainstream of the Australian workforce, the grandiose soldier-settlement schemes of the 1920s (whereby returning servicemen were settled on rural landholdings) had proved a dismal failure. Undercapitalised and under-skilled, most of these would-be farmers had succumbed to financial pressures and been forced to leave their precious farms and return to the cities.

Arriving half a decade too late, Great-Grandad was fortunately spared this angst. Instead, he sought trade qualifications and employment in the newly emerging motor vehicle assembly industry. In 1925, Ford Motors Australia was established, followed in 1926 by General Motors Australia, the latter merging with Holden Motors in 1931 to form General Motors Holden Limited.

As the years rolled by, Great-Grandad would frequently predict: "Take it from me, Australia has a great future in manufacturing. We will always have a vibrant manufacturing industry, and our vehicle manufacturing will lead the world, well into the next millennium!".

Our ancestors may have been wise, but they certainly weren't clairvoyant[18] .

Lessons Lost

The completion of the Sydney Harbour Bridge in 1932, spanning gracefully from Dawes Point to Milsons Point, symbolised the unification not only of the previously disparate parts of this burgeoning metropolis but also the country as a whole – north and south would be joined in perfect harmony. But beneath this apparent unity lay division and hostility.

On 19 March 1932, Captain Francis de Groot, mounted on a borrowed horse and wielding a ceremonial sword, charged through the crowd at the official Harbour Bridge opening and slashed the ribbon before the New South Wales Premier, Jack Lang, could claim that honour.

This was no childish prank, but rather a symbolic declaration of political defiance. It was in the same spirit as the shot from the *Aurora* that had signalled the beginning of the Russian Revolution and the advent of world communism some sixteen years earlier.

Across the world, factory workers and rural labourers worked in appalling conditions. The post-war boom of the 1920s had cemented the differences between capital and labour, while the looming Depression of the 1930s cast fear into both rich and poor. Marxism emerged, championing the cause of the proletariat, and led to the formation of ultra-left communist parties and violent revolution.

Capitalists, along with other forces of conservatism, feared this movement, and thus reactionary ultra-right fascist movements also gained momentum.

Australia wasn't immune to these extremes, although the political players were aligned differently. Captain de Groot was a member of the New Guard, a fascist paramilitary group founded by Eric Campbell and boasting, at its peak, a membership of 50,000 predominantly monarchist, Protestant and anticommunist ex-servicemen.

Opposed to the New Guard were the left-leaning Labor, led in Sydney by Premier Lang, while further to the left were the Communists. This was a period of ugly street violence by paramilitary groups, when Australia edged closer to civil war and coup d'état than at any other time in its history.

As Grandad told of these events from his youth, he became increasingly agitated. His father had personally witnessed the outcome of such intransigence elsewhere in the world.

In the depths of his "bug-pit" prison, Great-Grandad's aged Russian mentor had carefully explained how such intolerance had brought about suffering and death in his own country. Greed and selfishness fostered poverty and despair, leading inevitably to violence, revolution and civil war. And, he had stressed, *nobody wins*.

His mentor's advice? "Show compassion for your fellow humans, always seek the middle ground, look for the 'win-win' solution, and never resort to violence".

As Digger listened to his grandfather and observed his agitation, it occurred to him perhaps all generations experience periods when they're tempted to resort to violence to resolve those issues they can neither understand nor control.

Although Australian commonsense prevailed in domestic politics in the 1930s, and support for both ultra-right-wing fascists and ultra-left-wing Communists melted away, it wasn't the case in other parts of the world.

Fascism or neo-fascism rose to ascendency in Germany, Italy and Spain, but it also had a strong following in other European and American countries.

Communism prevailed in Russia and gained solid support in most other industrialised countries.

Europe was perched on a powder keg. The Molotov-Ribbentrop non-aggression pact of 1939 between Russia and Germany gave Adolf Hitler confidence Russia wouldn't intervene if Germany expanded westwards. Germany soon overran the Low Countries and France, followed in quick succession by Norway. Soon, most of western Europe was allied with, or under the control of, the Axis Powers.

Despite the creation of the Commonwealth of Australia in 1901, the Australians of 1939 were still very "British", and Australia was an integral outpost of the British Empire. In the words of then-Prime Minister Robert Menzies: ... *Great Britain has declared war on [Germany] and ..., as a result, Australia is also at war ....*

Soon after, the folly of rashly committing Australian troops to yet another European entanglement became apparent.

Japan took the predictable step of breaking out of the economic straitjacket imposed on it by the imperialist western powers, thus initiating the Pacific War.

Australia was caught flat-footed. The bulk of its armed forces was engaged in defending the European and Asian imperial interests of Britain. Of the four divisions of the

Second Australian Imperial Force (2nd AIF), the 6th Division was attacking Greece, the 7th and 9th Divisions were fighting in north Africa, and the 8th Division was defending British imperial interests in Malaya. Most of our principal naval ships were deployed by the British Admiralty, and our RAAF (Royal Australian Air Force) squadrons were participating in the Battle of Britain, or under British command in north Africa. Just who was defending Australia?

When the inevitable Japanese attack did eventuate, British Prime Minister Winston Churchill was reluctant to release these Australian forces. American General Douglas MacArthur, acknowledging the resulting difficulty in defending northern Australia, reputedly coined the term, the *Brisbane Line*, the concept of temporarily ceding northern Australia to the advancing Japanese forces, while conducting a strategic withdrawal towards the south.

The minority of mature-minded Australians were appalled. They'd seen it all before, and, no doubt, would see it all again. But, like obedient schoolchildren, Australians had rushed off to the other side of the world, eager to defend the imperial ambitions of powerful "friends", with barely a thought for where our own geopolitical interests lay.

Much later, Digger's grandfather would relay to him the wisdom handed down through the family, supposedly from the aged Russian sage, veteran of the Bukhara bug-pit, *You are again blindly following your bungling imperialist masters, and yet again you are betrayed ...*

War came to Australia, and Digger's grandfather, barely 18 years old, enlisted in the hastily reorganised army. A volunteer in one of Australia's prestige independent commando companies, he participated in the seaborne invasion of Timor Leste.

When their situation became untenable, they were evacuated by sea. After suffering malaria, and following some leave and further training, he saw action in New Guinea and Borneo[19].

After the war, in 1945, he took the opportunity to see a bit more of the world, volunteering for the Australian contingent of the allied occupation forces in Japan. Here, he visited the site of one of the world's most horrific war crimes, the American atomic bombing of Hiroshima.

He was reticent to talk much of these exploits, but eventually a complete picture emerged. On reflection, a mature Digger would ask himself: *How cruel are we to hand an immature 18-year-old a gun and tell him to go off and kill other human beings, for reasons that he does not understand?*

Grandad survived, returned, married and settled down to make a home in the suburbs. After the war, the entire family moved across the notorious Brisbane Line into Queensland, the deep north.

In 1959, Digger's father was born, followed by a couple of siblings, so-called baby-boomers, the generation that would accelerate through life with new freedoms and no boundaries. For a child of the 1960s and a teenager of the 1970s, life was good, full of fun, adventure and friends. In the early 1980s, he too would marry and start his own family, Digger being the first-born.

Little did Digger's parents know the Australia their son was born into, the so-called lucky country, would boom economically in the short term but, before long, stagnate under short-sighted political and economic policies.

Desiccation

The optimism of previous generations for a brilliant Australian manufacturing future was understandable, but misguided.

Following the Depression of the 1930s and the warfare of the 1940s, the 1950s heralded a period of unprecedented stability and growth in Australia. Conservative governments of the 1960s reaped the benefits of previous Labor post-war reconstruction, subsequent economic booms generated by global demand for pastoral, agricultural and mining products, and local demand fuelled by steady immigration.

But this increased wealth fostered over-confidence and complacency. From the 1930s to the 1960s, Australia manufactured cars, aeroplanes, ships, heavy equipment, radios, television sets, electrical goods, household white goods, clothing, specialised building materials and more.

But by the end of the millennium, Australia had ceased production of virtually all of these, in any significant quantity. The Australian people, led by conservative governments, failed to anticipate or prepare for changing world trade patterns.

The "protection versus free trade" arguments of the previous century resurfaced, under the guise of "wet" versus "dry" economics. But both these extremes of economic ideology failed to recognise the need for nuanced moderate economic management. During the following half-century, "free trade" would kill "protection", "dry" would desiccate "wet", and Australia would lose its manufacturing ability.

As the ultimate decline and demise of his beloved manufacturing industries occurred, Digger's grandfather's faith was shattered. The slow death of these enterprises, devoured by short-term greed and complacency, was eventually mirrored by his own slow decline as his body was relentlessly consumed by cancer.

But that was in the future.

Now married with a young family, Grandad had settled down into northern Brisbane suburban life and was establishing a career to support them.

Manual labour, being "on the tools" in a workshop or construction site, or time on the front desk, are invaluable in a person's working life. While a career-oriented young person may rightly aspire to employment as a captain of industry or an expert in their chosen profession, this sort of hands-on experience, particularly in the company of work colleagues, help to develop not just work skills but social skills as well.

A late entry to the trade, Grandad served his time as a fitter, then progressed steadily into a management role. Further part-time study equipped him with an engineering degree and a pathway to more responsible roles in the company.

But he never forgot those with whom he'd initially laboured, and perhaps this enlightenment blunted the aggression many saw as a prerequisite for those at the pinnacle of management.

Grandad eventually quit the corporate world to establish his own consulting practice, using his wealth of expertise to service the industry he knew so well. Like the stock market collapse of 1929 and the Depression of the '30s, the 2008 Global Financial Crisis and the COVID19 pandemic of the 2020s would plunge many into unemployment, devastating their families. Conversely, it's at such times of business crisis that experts in their fields survive, because their skills are in such high demand.

And so it was with Grandad … his consultancy thrived.

Learning Experiences

Digger was blessed with a close and loving family, responsible, hard-working parents and affectionate, nurturing grandparents. They all took a close interest in his school activities, and he was encouraged to study hard and enjoy his childhood and teenage years.

He was close to his grandparents on both sides of the family, but age eventually claimed them, one by one. Grandad was the last to succumb, although not until he reached the age of 70, at that time considered by a teenager to be old, but perhaps not today. One of Digger's last memories of Grandad was the day he came to the high school to watch him play in a rugby league match …

Thump … that hurt!

Digger spat out the dirt as he dragged himself to his feet again. He'd brought the opposing player down, but the ball still went out along the enemy back line. The opposition five-eighth flicked to the inside centre, then onto the outside centre. No need to send the ball any further to their wing.

The centres had neatly side-stepped Digger's team's entire back line and had scored yet another try. That must make it twenty-something to nil! They were being slaughtered!

But that was no surprise. The opposition were their school's elite, the first-grade rugby league team. And worse still, they were the best team in the Brisbane high school competition. Later in the season, they'd take the city's schoolboy premiership. In contrast, Digger's team were just the reserve-grade team, the guys not good enough to play first-grade, but they played for fun.

This game was a so-called "friendly", a chance for both teams to get in some pre-season practice, but turned out to be no ordinary footy game. It was open warfare – and Digger's team was losing badly. Of course, they'd known they would, but they played anyway.

Most of the first-grade team were decent kids. Digger had known many of them since Year 9. But a few of them were bullies, thugs who spent too much time beating up other kids and not enough time studying. Now they were repeating Year 12.

They were older, bigger and stronger than Digger and the other mere mortals on his team, and they made school life precarious for anyone who would not suck up to them.

Stop dreaming … here they come again. Tackle low and … thump! … that hurt again.

This was suburban Brisbane of the early 21st century, a middle-class municipality on the northern fringe of the city with its burgeoning population of baby-boomers' kids crowding into the local high school. The school boasted a population of well over a thousand, drawn from half-a-dozen feeder primary schools. School life was raw, rough and riotous … certainly never dull.

Look out!

The kick went deep into Digger's team's backline, the fullback fumbled it, and they were all over him. Another scrum.

Well, that's a joke.

Digger played in the forwards, second row. As they packed down, they well understood the futility of this exercise. The collective weight of the opposition pack was at least 50% greater than their own. No chance Digger's pack could push them back, even if their hooker *had* been lucky enough to claim possession. Out came the ball, the opposition half-back flicked it to blind, and their wing crossed for yet another try.

Despite the bullying, senior school life was pretty good. Most of all, Digger enjoyed the comradeship of good mates, some lined up here beside him now in this team. They, too, were suffering the targeted onslaught from the opposition bullies, determined to pursue vendettas that couldn't be fought so easily in the classroom. This was their opportunity to bring Digger and his friends to heel, to make them kowtow to so-called "superiors".

Digger, fully aware of the scores to be settled, had been apprehensive going into the game, but buoyed by the solidarity of their collective resolve and a camaraderie in the true Aussie spirit, none of them buckled. They just kept playing – fronting up, tackle after tackle after tackle.

Thump … more pain!

But school life is not all football. There is, believe it or not, study, too. Despite appalling classroom discipline – *ha-ha, that was a joke* – a few of them managed to scrape through the Year 12 finals with a university matriculation.

Thump … But let's get back to the important things in life – surviving the brutality of this slaughter. Too late, another opposition try.

One particularly unfortunate Year 12 classmate had been subjected to excessive bullying all year. Although this poor boy wasn't particularly likeable, he didn't deserve the excesses heaped on him by the "cool" group.

To befriend him was deemed social suicide, but that's exactly what Digger and his mates did, to their credit. He was never a close friend, and he wasn't the sporty type, so he certainly wasn't a member of Digger's rugby team, but at least in their company he was safe. (Digger met him briefly a few years later. Just an ordinary guy who seemed to have survived a horrendous Year 12 without too much personality damage).

Thump ... Hey, that one wasn't so bad!

The ball went loose, and Digger's team managed to grab it. Although they still couldn't cross the line, they were now playing better than anyone had expected.

Thump ... thump ... thump.

And so it dragged on. Digger's team never did score, but at least they'd fronted up and played the game to the best of their ability.

At last, the whistle blew and it was over. The score – oh, never mind, that's best forgotten. But they'd achieved something more important. As they limped off the field, they could hold their heads high. They'd stood up to the bullies, against the odds, and they'd survived.

After the game, Grandad and Digger called in at one of the local coffee shops. Grandad was never reticent in equating life's hard knocks to what he liked to call "learning experiences". His advice, as they waited for their lunch, was profound.

"Be loyal to your friends," he'd said. "Be passionate in sharing your love and show generosity and compassion to those less fortunate than yourself. And above all, don't be cowed by the bullies.

"You know, boy, Australia's now playing a football match, one in which the stakes are the very survival of our independence and our way of life. We are, by far, the weaker team. We face some formidable opposition – the bullies of the world. Those large countries that dominate world affairs, the superpowers. We have no choice but to play the game, and we must play by the rules. But we must never be bullied into abandoning what we know to be right."

Digger had simply nodded as their order arrived. He was starving hungry, and didn't fully understand what his grandfather was telling him, not yet, anyway. But he never forgot it.

Canberra – 2030

In the serenity of his Canberra office, Digger was reminiscing about happier times with his family, and particularly with his beloved Grandad from whom he'd learned so many of life's lessons. He recalled that Year 12 rugby game, the visit to the coffee shop afterwards, and what his grandfather had told him.

Realisation dawned as he reflected on the political theatre currently playing out. We defend a fair go for our weaker Pacific neighbours. The Chinese place embargos on Australian barley, beef, wine and coal, because we dare to publicly help our neighbours.

Thump ... that hurt!

We aspire to promote international peace. The Americans demand we dispatch armed forces to invade yet another country on their behalf, even though there's no threat to us or to our way of life. Korea, Viet Nam, Afghanistan, Iraq ...

Thump ... that hurt again!

We resist the commercial pressures of greed and exploitation that conspire to rob us of our independence and desiccate our planet.

Thump ... the most painful of all!

Corporations and politicians threaten us with lower living standards, if we baulk at sacrificing our natural resources to foreign investors.

We are now approaching the full-time whistle and the game is reaching its climax, Digger mused. *So, just when will we stand up to these bullies?*

A little later on the afternoon of the football match, Grandad had continued his story, this time conveying some of the wisdom he'd learned from his own father.

"You know," he'd said. "My father , your great-grandfather, spent some time with an old Russian bloke once, who helped him to think through how we should act in the world. Although my father understood none of his language, and the Russian's English wasn't so good, I think he got the gist of what the Russian was trying to say.

"Up until he met him, he'd been oblivious to the damage he'd been causing in the world. He was just an impetuous teenager, rather than a mature adult. Sometimes the old Russian would talk in riddles, sometimes representing the countries of his day by animals like bears and lions, eagles and dragons. He tried to warn my father that small countries, like Australia, should be very careful of the superpowers, the bullies."

Very careful, indeed, thought Digger now.

Sadly, that was the last time Digger and his grandfather talked. Grandad died just a few days later, suddenly, but peacefully. Active throughout his whole life, he was mourned by all who knew and loved him.

His funeral was well attended by his family: his sons and his daughter, their spouses, his ten grandchildren, a handful of other close relatives, many friends from his church, and several work colleagues from his consultancy office and others from his charity work. Also a couple of older men, perhaps ex-army buddies, who placed a small floral tribute on his coffin with a card that simply read, "Goodbye".

The unexpectedness of Grandad's death shocked Digger, but the more he reflected, the more he came to understand how fortunate his grandfather had been. Despite the early disruption of World War 2, he'd been able to live a good and productive life, happy and in relatively good health, and to pass on these virtues to a loving family.

What more can any person ask?

Shared Legacy

Through their shared diversity, Cassandra had warmed sufficiently to Digger to pass on to him the same documents she had given to Aurora. Until then, Digger had been unaware Aurora and he shared a family relationship, albeit a distant one. Aurora's great-grandmother, who had the liaison with the Russian sailor, and Digger's great-grandfather, the soldier in the bug-pit, were sister and brother.

After reading the documents Cassandra provided, and considering his own family history, Digger was left with a myriad questions.

Is it nature or nurture, heredity or environment, that shapes our personalities? This question, of course, is as old as recorded history. It invites us to consider the drivers that move ordinary people either towards or away from war. *To what extent are citizens driven to take up arms by their innate nature, goodness or evil, or by nurture, the circumstances in which they were raised and live?*

There's no doubt we are genetically hard-wired for survival, to take actions that will preserve and protect our progeny – nature, he mused. *But the form of those actions, fight or flight, surely varies with the circumstances in which we are placed – nurture.*

We are neither innately violent nor innately pacifist. Rather, we will adopt either violence or pacificism in response to how we have been nurtured – our upbringing – and as the circumstances dictate.

Digger pondered further questions the documents had raised in his mind.

What environmental factor is most likely to lead us to war? Is it fear? Is it greed? Is it poverty? Or is it ignorance? Or perhaps a search for relevance? What part do loyalty and honour play?

And what drives us away from war? Is it altruism? Is it compassion? Is it fear? Self-preservation?

How are each of these factors influenced by our culture, religion, education or financial status?

How are the attitudes of ordinary people to politics, warfare and international relationships influenced by the actions of the state? How does a sense of loyalty to the state tempt them into actions that they would have otherwise considered unacceptable? Put more simply, what leads the "hawks" to war and the "doves" to peace?

Digger considered how his own family, and Aurora's, could be characterised for posterity as hawk, dove, martyr or penitent.

The hawk: The naval officer had been born in a peaceful setting on the shores of Issyk-Kul Lake, in idyllic surrounds. But

this situation had been cut short, and he spent his later childhood exposed to the poverty of Tashkent. Born the second son
of the local magistrate, he had idolised his father and his older
brother. But then, as he grew older, he had also become more
rebellious and independent, yearning to leave the family home
for the adventure of a naval career on the cruiser *Aurora*. This
career had ultimately consumed him. The violence of warfare,
into which he was thrust, had honed his skills and propelled his
advancement through the ranks. Only in later life did he take
the time to reflect on the folly of this pathway.

The dove: The rescue-ship officer had been the first-born of
the magistrate and had also spent a privileged, carefree childhood in the outdoors of a rural paradise. Free to roam the foothills of the Tian Shan mountains and sail the placid waters of
Issyk-Kul Lake, he'd grown strong, healthy, independent and
confident. Imbued with a sense of compassion inherited from
both his parents, he, too, had sought overseas adventure – but
he did so with a conscience, convinced the future of a turbulent world could be best assured through peaceful scientific
endeavour.

Unfortunately, fate had intervened, and his life was cut
short as his ship, the SY *Aurora*, sank in the Tasman Sea in
1917. But the rescue-ship officer's influence didn't die with
him. Clearly, his younger brother had been eventually moved
to remorse by his self-sacrificing altruism.

The martyr: The magistrate himself had been a product of
his time and place. In 19th-century Russia, class was pervasive
and people knew their allotted position in society. Loyalty was
the most valued attribute one could display. Obedience was
more esteemed than enquiry, faith was more important than
scepticism, and conservatism trumped revolution. When the

system was overturned in 1917, the magistrate could not – and, more to the point, would not – change with it. What was right was right and what was wrong was wrong. Black was black and white was white; no grey area. We're tempted to applaud such blind devotion, but his martyrdom had achieved little. Perhaps, with the benefit of hindsight, he could have been more flexible. The magistrate had been a martyr, a true tragic hero.

The penitent: The "digger", Digger's own great-grandfather, had been the most enigmatic of all. Born and raised in relative obscurity in a remote and harsh country, living by his wits and ingenuity, he'd grown up tough.

But this had been just a façade. Deep down, the digger was insecure, afraid and immature. As such, he was easily led, and prone to coercion by those whom he assumed to be more powerful. That is why he had so readily followed his British masters, first into the Great War and then into the Central Asian conflict.

Like so many of his compatriots, the digger could have perished. But he'd been lucky. He got a second chance. He returned to his homeland, a chastened and wiser man. The suffering he'd witnessed changed him, and after a time in an emotional wilderness he emerged with new insight and renewed vigour.

The penitent digger devoted his life to helping others, to lovingly raising a family and dispensing compassionate care to those less fortunate. He'd demonstrated that all of us can be, at different times in our lives, both the beneficiary and the donor of sacrificial giving.

These thoughts solidified in Digger's mind as he continued to mull over all he'd read.

Those of us who are given an opportunity for repentance and redemption should embrace it enthusiastically.

WHITEHORSE – THE WHITE KNIGHT

White Knight – Canberra, 2030

Marcus paused to consider the recent turn of events, and how international history, geopolitics and his own experiences had converged on this intersection of circumstances – how he'd reached, through an adult lifetime of travel and study, the conclusion that Australia must undertake a seismic shift in foreign policy.

During a happy but unremarkable childhood, Marcus did sufficiently well at primary school to consider an academic stream in high school, heading towards a profession. High school was his great awakening, as childhood morphed into the excitement and adventure of adolescence and on to the cusp of adulthood. Matriculation led to graduation from university with undergraduate and masters' degrees in engineering and international development. He travelled widely overseas, experienced much, learned much.

He spent many years working in environmental research institutions before being head-hunted by the manufacturing industry, then rounding out his career as the principal of a successful consulting firm and, then entering politics. He'd married and he and his wife had been blessed with both children and grandchildren. His parents had lived long and fruitful lives. Such is the circle of life. Now, he too had entered his senior years, although he refused to admit it.

Sitting in his comfortable Canberra office, Marcus reflected on how fortunate he'd been to live during the second half of the 20th century and the early decades of the 21st century, a period when Australia had managed to prosper, albeit at the expense of a once-viable manufacturing industry.

Along with fellow baby-boomers, he'd been born into the relative affluence and abundance enjoyed universally within the western democracies. Good health, low-cost travel and comparative peace gave young Australians opportunities no previous generation had experienced.

During the 1970s, international air travel became accessible to almost all. Where a previous generation would have spent several weeks on a Europe-bound ship, Boeing 747 flights took only an uncomfortable thirty hours.

Initially, travel to and within Asia was not so easy. The region was impoverished and emerging from colonialism, with anti-communist wars in Viet Nam, Cambodia and Laos, communist insurgencies and violence in Malaysia and Indonesia.

Singapore, Thailand and the Philippines were still poverty-stricken and China was a closed communist society in the grip of the violent Cultural Revolution.

India, Pakistan, Bangladesh, Sri Lanka and Myanmar, then known as Burma, were desperately poor. So too were the South Pacific Islands, which were yet to discover tourism.

Understandably, in these circumstances, most Australians feared Asia. Therefore, like most young Australians venturing overseas, Marcus and his wife were drawn initially to

Europe, only later travelling in Africa, Asia, the Pacific and the Americas.

At that time, Australians in general stayed at home and remained insular in focus, whereas Marcus and his wife's experiences abroad changed the way they approached and participated in world events and international relations.

It had seemed almost like a golden age for young Australians. But there was also a dark side. During this period, Australia hid behind the military might of an increasingly belligerent and arrogant United States, relying on the ANZUS (Australia, New Zealand and the United States of America) Treaty for protection from the international threats lurking on its doorstep, some perhaps real, but most imagined.

Even then, Marcus knew there was no such thing as a free lunch, but always a quid pro quo. The price of our "protection" had been our active engagement in foreign wars that didn't present any credible threat to us.

Since federation, a short century-and-a-quarter previously, Australia had participated in the South African Boer War, World War 1, the European theatre of World War 2, the Korean War, the Malayan conflict, the Viet Nam War, two Iraq Wars, the Afghan War, the blockade of Iran and Russia, and a host of smaller conflicts – all at the behest, and for the benefit of, British or American interests – and to the detriment of the ordinary people living in the countries where these wars had been fought.

Unlike the others, only the Pacific theatre of World War 2 had been a defensive war.

Although Marcus's career had been in engineering, his passion was for history and the broad sweep of geopolitics. This was his motivation for recording his annotated memoirs. His proposition was that ordinary citizens, himself included, tend to become blinded by a sense of loyalty to the state, which encourages them to actions they'd have otherwise considered unacceptable.

This had been witnessed in many of the world empires considered to be the flowering of civilisation of their time. The ancient empires of Egypt, Persia, Greece, China, Rome, Arabia, Mongolia, Turkey, Aztec and Inca had all exhibited the same characteristics: the subjugation of the weak by the strong, who demand and receive blind obedience from armies of ordinary citizens seduced by their association with the "winning side".

Modern empires exhibit the same characteristics, although they are presented differently, Marcus mused. *In turn, the Scandinavians, Venetians, Spanish, Portuguese, Dutch, British, Russians, Germans, Japanese and Americans have all sought to impose their politics, religion and economics on others. The patterns are the same in every case. An oppressed proletariat ... plebians ... working-class ... common people ... the third estate – whatever you want to call them – seeks the overthrow of its oppressors by lending support to sympathetic strong leaders. But those leaders then grow fat on the fruits of their success and, in turn, become the oppressors. Thus, the cycle repeats.*

Marcus opened his laptop and called up his electronic copy of *2025 Reflections – The Journal of a Concerned Australian*, his 2025 autobiography of fifty years of world travel. He'd been encouraged by his wife, his constant companion and confidante, to take time away from his busy schedule to write a travel memoir. Decades of travel, study and thought provided the source material for this literary challenge.

While other aspects of his life, family, friends, work, both paid and voluntary, were important to Marcus, he'd resolved to concentrate this writing endeavour on the intersection of international travel, history and foreign affairs.

The choice of genre and style had been difficult. How could he impart his accumulated knowledge and wisdom without succumbing to the temptations of embellishment and bias, yet maintain sufficient intrigue and interest to prevent a reader from abandoning the book through boredom?

The final choice was an autobiography, to be entirely factual, without exaggeration or distortion.

Although logic dictates an autobiographical memoir should flow chronologically, Marcus considered that tracing a thematic thread from adventure to adventure would serve his purpose better. Consequently, this decision led to the exclusion of those travels that didn't contribute significantly to the overall theme.

For example, although he'd travelled widely in the Americas, both north and south, the experience hadn't offered many lessons pertinent to the point he wanted to make, so weren't included in any detail. To protect other people who'd feature in the manuscript, Marcus also decided not to use real names, but refer to these characters as his wife, friend, colleague, confidant, or companion, or refer to them by their occupation (councillor, bishop, president, CEO and the like).

He acknowledged this work wasn't intended to be a learned treatise or academic dissertation, but simply a travel memoir, including only sufficient referencing to other publications necessary to explain the origin of some of the more controversial historical and demographic comments. Above all, this document would record his own opinion, based on his lifetime of travel, study and contemplation.

Having settled on these principles, Marcus, with his characteristic enthusiasm and perseverance, had completed the task within twelve months. Most likely he'd never publish his memoir, but it served its purpose of focusing his thinking on matters of importance to Australia. His writings would reveal his innermost thoughts on our place in the world, his journey through life progressing – he would hope – from ignorance to wisdom and would lay bare his deepest concerns for our country.

Towards Maturity

Marcus would've preferred to relax for a couple of hours with the tattered hard copy of his chronicle, but such luxury wasn't appropriate in these perilous times. Instead, he decided to be content with simply skimming through the soft copy, pausing at his favourite passages and devoting some time to reconsidering his original conclusions. He'd read the whole document in more detail when the current crisis had passed. And so he read, concentrating only on the critical parts and skipping the rest ...

2025 Reflections –
The Journal of a Concerned Australian

Introduction

It is 2025. I write this journal, knowing that it may never be read in full by others. But I undertake this task to clarify my own thoughts on Australia's role in the Indo-Pacific region. My home is Australia, the country of my birth.

Marcus paused for a moment, before skipping to the section describing his travels in western China.

China, 2016

Ürümqi is a large modern city, capital of the Xinjiang Uyghur Autonomous Region in the far west of the country, and is populated mostly by Han Chinese, who have migrated from the east. The demographic data is telling.

In Ürümqi, 75% of the 3 million population is Han Chinese, 13% is Indigenous Uyghur ... The 2005 Tulip Revolution, in neighbouring Kyrgyzstan, ushered in a period of political instability throughout the region, with China's Xinjiang region suffering increasing Uyghur militancy and acts of violence.

Chinese authorities have clamped down on separatism. Recent reports from human rights organisations indicate the severity of the Chinese government reaction (to what is claimed to be Uyghur terrorism) has increased dramatically ...

We were not part of any organised tour (you could say we were quite disorganised), and we believe this attracted the attention (assistance) of the Chinese security service. A well-dressed gentleman (at first introducing himself as part of the hotel management ... although we are now convinced otherwise) insisted on "helping" us to join an organised day trip to Heavenly Lake. That he could command the immediate cooperation of the hotel staff was not in doubt, but later enquiries revealed that he was indeed not part of their staff.

A day excursion to Heavenly Lake is the highlight of any visit to Ürümqi, popular with the many tourists from eastern China. The spectacular natural scenery of the eastern Tian Shan Range, and the serene mountain lake, were augmented by the kind of spectacular open-air show of cultural and gymnastic prowess that only the Chinese can perfect ... a most enjoyable day.

The following morning, the same gentleman kindly organised our trip to the Xinjiang Regional Museum. He also arranged for us to be accompanied by an athletic young man, who (although he spoke no English) kept a close eye on us to ensure we did not stray too far, and that we returned safely to our hotel.

"Guide", "companion" or "minder" ... what is the difference? None of the extra security service attention involved us in any expense, and no money changed hands. Even our offer to pay for the taxi to the museum was rejected. But the close supervision did ensure that we did not get up to any mischief ...

As if to reflect the security concerns in the city, airport security at Ürümqi was the strictest we have encountered. Your phone goes one way, while you go another, only to be reunited after each has undergone the closest of scrutiny. Not only must you remove all items from your pockets, your belt and your shoes, but you must also expose the soles of your feet to the metal detector.

Journalists have been known to hide SD (secure digital) cards in the strangest of places. But perhaps these security precautions were not without justification. While we did not witness any violence in China, we were in Bishkek (capital of neighbouring Kyrgyzstan) a week later, when the nearby Chinese embassy was bombed by Uyghur separatists.

In his 2024 book, Great Game On, former Australian ambassador to China Geoff Raby confirms that, due to remoteness and political sensitivity, travelling in Xinjiang is now challenging unless you are part of an official tour. More important, he comments on the wealth of the natural resources of Xinjiang, its attraction to other countries such as Russia and its strategic importance to China. [20]

Again, Marcus paused to reflect on the events just described. After a few moments of contemplation, he flicked forward a couple of pages to that part of his memoir dealing with pro bono assistance to communities devastated by natural disasters and man-made violence.

Sri Lanka, 2005

On 26th December 2004, a massive magnitude 9.1 earthquake occurred off the Indonesian coast near Banda Aceh, triggering the Indian Ocean tsunami. The resulting waves rose up to 30 metres, the height of a six-storey building. Over 223,000 people perished, over 600,000 homes were destroyed and approximately 1.8 million people were displaced. Through no fault of their own, these unfortunate people were just in the wrong place at the wrong time ... A huge rebuilding program then mushroomed across the region, instituted by many NGOs.

By mid-2005, one such large NGO had identified a need for technical auditing of their house construction, and management auditing of their program execution. I undertook two pro bono auditing assignments for this

NGO ... to Thailand and Indonesia, and to Sri Lanka and India. The extent of the devastation I witnessed was overwhelming, but so, too, was the intensity of the rebuilding programs.

But not all parts of this region were peaceful. ... The road approaching Trincomalee, in eastern Sri Lanka, was at that time lined with military watchtowers spaced strategically about a kilometre apart, to provide desperately needed security against night-time raids by the Tamil Tiger (LTTE) separatist terrorist group. ... Our driver, a Muslim man, was prevented from entering one of the refugee camps for fear of sparking a riot among the displaced Hindu Tamil residents.

It is difficult for us, from peaceful, tolerant Australia, to gauge the extent to which sectarian hostility clouds the judgement of many people whose interests would be better served by compassion, cooperation and tolerance ...

The realisation of this intolerance had served as one of the key motivators for Marcus to record his memoirs. Next, he zeroed in on those events that had first sparked and then fanned the flames of an awakening awareness of the need to actively resist the violence of war.

Viet Nam, 2011

By 1975, Australia had been embroiled for over a decade in the Viet Nam War. "All the way with LBJ", Australian Prime Minister Harold Holt had proclaimed back in 1966 to United States President Lyndon Baines Johnson. And so it was. Australia blindly followed its US master. Although the war became increasingly unpopular, our involvement dragged on.

Over 500 Australians died, with more than 2,000 wounded, and the war ended up costing Australia a staggering $218 million. But even worse, Australians had contributed to the death of an estimated two million Vietnamese.

In 2011, we visited Vietnam as tourists, eventually reaching Ho Chi Minh City. In our travels, we have been to some very confronting places – places that scream evil: Hiroshima, obliterated in 1945 by one of the two atomic bombs dropped by the Americans in the closing days of World War 2; the Jerusalem World Holocaust Remembrance Centre; and the Nazi death camps of Auschwitz and Dachau.

But the knowledge we Australians (whether we served in the armed forces or not) were complicit in inflicting the horror, depicted so vividly in the Ho Chi Minh City War Remnants Museum, still claws at our conscience. Millions of innocent men, women and children were slaughtered simply for the commercial gain of the political class of a remote superpower. I pray we will never again allow such evil. And yet, in the 21st century it is still happening ...

Türkiye, 1975

Our first visit to Gallipoli [Türkiye] was on 7 April 1975, almost 60 years after those fateful ANZAC dawn landings. Ironically, less than three weeks later, North

Vietnamese troops dramatically entered Saigon (now called Ho Chi Minh City) defeating the South Vietnamese (and by association, the United States and Australia).

Gallipoli had been repeated; Australia had been defeated ... again. Gallipoli's Lone Pine Cemetery in 1975 was, for me, a turning point, the first time and the first place I had really been confronted by the futility of war. The poignancy of the juxtaposition of our visit to Gallipoli and the fall of Saigon (Ho Chi Minh City) kickstarted our lifelong anti-war sentiment.

From that point on, the retreat from Gallipoli became symbolic of a necessary paradigm shift – a retreat from evil, when we pull back from the brink, turn our back on war, and set a new course in the direction of peace. But so far, that goal has proved elusive.

Marcus skimmed the rest of the memoir, before settling on the final chapters. These dealt with his political activities, which had brought his conclusions into sharp focus.

Australia, 2025

From the time we started our travels, I had a passion for the intersection of history, foreign affairs and politics. While one must account for modern context, the ancient relationships between countries tend to reflect the vanities, greed and ruthlessness of individuals, and they are a constant that transcends time and place.

Lessons from the past can help us understand the present. In 1984, well over 40 years ago, I presented a discussion paper to the local federal electorate conference of one of the leading political parties. The synopsis of my paper, Australia's Place in World History [21] reads as follows:

The Australian Government must carefully consider our place in world history when determining foreign policy. What is our long-term contribution to humanity? Can we best achieve it by close alignment with our traditional European and American friends, or should we draw closer to Asia and Africa?

This paper recommends:

1. *Australia must provide a cultural bridge between the traditions of Europe and America, on one hand, and Africa and Asia, on the other.*

2. *We must specialise in several key high-technology industries in a range of disciplines demanded by our neighbours.*

3. *Most importantly, Australia must adopt enthusiastically the role of regional peacemaker. We must develop a genuine friendship with the people of many differing countries." [22]*

Unfortunately, not until the upheaval of the 2020s, the Chinese trade tariffs and Donald Trump's catastrophic second United States presidency did such considerations began to permeate mainstream Australian political thinking.

History tells of the cruel and indifferent exploitation by nations who believed themselves to be culturally or religiously superior. These have justified appalling atrocities, committed in the name of civilisation or religion – just a smoke screen for self-interest.

But this realisation is just a beginning, not the end. A new vision for a cooperative, compassionate and caring world can emerge, one in which small and middle-sized countries are instrumental as peacemakers – but only if we, the ordinary citizens, recognise and exercise our responsibilities. We must adopt a new paradigm.

A Call to Action

Marcus lowered the laptop lid. The publication of *2025 Reflections – The Journal of a Concerned Australian* had alienated many, but had also attracted the attention of several progressive politicians. This had led to his recruitment as a policy writer for the new Paradigm Party. Many of his ideas had been developed into policy statements, and he eventually allowed his name to go forward as a Senate candidate in what was thought to be an unwinnable position on the election ballot paper.

Despite his age, and against all odds, Marcus had been narrowly elected. Now part-way through a six-year Senate term, he was settled comfortably in his role – that of exercising the balance of power – a "kingmaker", as some liked to characterise him.

Marcus sighed. The period of quiet reflection had been cathartic, but he must now return to the present, to the 2030 political and diplomatic debacle that Australia had arrived at through previous governments' blindness and arrogance.

PART 3

The End Game

WHAT JUST HAPPENED?

To see a carefully considered strategy falter is a blow for any chess player. In such circumstances a seasoned player will calmly consider what just happened, before devising a new plan for recovery and resumption of play.

7:00 pm, 9 July 2030, Parliament House Studios, Canberra

Her face uncharacteristically grim, Aurora faltered as she attempted to regain her composure. But the teleprompter was merciless. This broadcast must proceed no matter what, without delay and devoid of emotion, no matter how the news of this incident had affected her.

Gathering herself, she focused on the camera.

"Prime Minister, can you advise the cause of the explosion that has just ripped through Port Darwin?"

Aurora waited for an answer, but the Prime Minister was tight-lipped.

"It's too early to comment on the details of this explosion, apart from saying that my government extends its heartfelt sympathy to the families of those deceased or injured, and that we are doing all that we possibly can to assist the local police and emergency services. Now, unfortunately, I must terminate this interview in order to make preparations for practical aid and arrange for a full enquiry as soon as possible."

And that was that.

The planned interview, the one exposing the truth behind the secret "Queen's Pawn to D4" file, was now old news, relegated to the dustbin for stories that would never be told, truths mothballed in the realms of myth, and documentaries destined to remain journalistic fantasies.

The Port Darwin explosion had occurred a week ago. Since then, each of the four key players, involved in the bid to expose the truth of the event, had retreated into the solitude of their own consciousness, to evaluate the recent turn of events and consider their next steps. Now they were together again, in the privacy of Senator Marcus Whitehorse's parliamentary office.

Aurora had been initially stunned into silence by the suddenness of the changed circumstances: an obscure explosion in remote Cape York surpassed by a spectacular explosion in Port Darwin.

During the past week she had examined her life and some of her forebears', scrutinising documents explaining her own ancestry, the follies and triumphs of her predecessors, and their ultimate commitment to world peace.

With the help of family and friends, she'd struggled with her own personal demons and risen above them.

She'd entered the Senator's office committed to helping to guide Australia towards a secure and responsible future.

Digger sat silently, chastened by the revelation of the most recent explosion. He'd worked closely with Aurora to expose the secret of the "Queen's Pawn to D4" file. His narrow escapes from danger while researching in the rural remoteness of Timor Leste, Papua New Guinea and the Solomon Islands had been harrowing enough, yet insignificant compared to his recent lucky escape from abduction in Darwin Harbour.

Darwin had been his home for many years. He had good friends who still lived there. Were they safe? Was there an ongoing threat? Was this explosion somehow linked to the previous one near Torres Strait, the one he'd first reported to Aurora and to the network, the incident that had ultimately led to his temporary employment on Senator Whitehorse's staff?

Across from Digger sat Cassandra, the Senator's assistant, similarly shocked into uncharacteristic silence. She and Digger had moved on from their mutual hostility, first through ambivalence, and then respect. She'd grown to appreciate Digger's bravery, resilience and can-do resourcefulness in life-threatening situations, while he now had a deeper understanding of her commitment to in-depth analysis, that nit-picking persistence that could uncover hidden truths in innocuous (or seemingly innocuous) data, be they official statistics, government reports or purloined top-secret documents.

Senator Marcus Whitehorse swung into action, addressing his three companions.

"Right!" he said. "We have a lot to do. I have no doubt whatsoever that this explosion in Port Darwin is somehow linked to the previous explosion near Torres Strait, and that both have something to do with the American Queen's Pawn to D4 file. So just what is our government hiding?"

XIANGQI

Xiangqi is the name of a board game originating (in a primitive form) around 2,000 years ago, the Chinese equivalent of chess.[23]

The Australian Federal Police had quickly established a task force to investigate the Port Darwin explosion. The Australian authorities were initially all over the inquiry, making good progress right up to the point where they were instructed "in the national interest" to step down in favour of a parallel American investigation, coordinated by security professionals at the American Cedar Valley establishment.

While the so-called joint report remained confidential, available to only a select few in government, the powers-that-be did issue a short press release, a transcript of this brief statement Cassandra now studied.

The massive explosion had, fortunately, caused little loss of life. According to the preliminary report findings, an aged Chinese general cargo ship had spontaneously blown up. Fortunately, the entire crew were ashore at the time, apparently in response to an anonymous tip-off that the ship represented some sort of safety threat.

A faint smile crept across Cassandra's countenance as she marvelled at the security service's talent for understatement. She read on, pausing only as she reached the final paragraph. The name of the ship was the *Xiangqi*. Her heart missed a beat as she stared incredulously at the report. The United States Consul in Darwin had only recently blurted out a rather odd response to taunts by peace demonstrators:

> *"You should thank us for being here. Chess is still a better game than xiangqi ..."*

Cassandra swung into action, downloading much available public data via the internet: registers of shipping movements in Port Darwin, records of ship registrations and ownership, and did a broad web-search of the word *Xiangqi*. She also contacted her Darwin-based journalist friend to help her ferret out details of any rumours regarding what had transpired in the port. As the incoming data rolled across her computer screen, she mentally recorded anything that appeared unusual.

Although Cassandra regularly made full use of the readily available AI technology, she fully appreciated its limitations. By their very nature, AI algorithms search for, and present, the "normal". AI could, therefore, serve a purpose of providing a useful benchmark of normality.

But in this case, she was searching for the *abnormal* – behaviour patterns and reported occurrences that, to her acute sensibility, stood out as unexpected. This was her strength, the skill that gave her an uncanny insight into otherwise unpredictable future happenings. In times past, she might have been called a seer, a sybil, a prophet, or even a witch. But today, she was simply Cassandra, carrying out important research as part of a team committed to shaping a peaceful and equitable Australian future – a new paradigm.

As suggested by the joint press release, the *Xiangqi* was registered in China, confirmed by a check of the Chinese Classification Society website[24] and augmented by follow-up through other ship-registry links. But it was a very old ship, not part of the extensive fleet of modern bulk carriers, container ships, tankers or general cargo vessels that flew the familiar red flag with its five golden stars.

Further in-depth scouring of some less-frequently visited websites indicated the ship had been sold several times in the past decade, with the current owners apparently an "exempt" private company registered in the Cayman Islands.

No further meaningful information was available. Local enquiries by her journalist contact revealed the crew had been recruited in the bars of the Philippines' Metro Manila and, as reported, were all (fortuitously) ashore at the time.

So, what was an ancient tramp cargo vessel, registered in China but owned by a shady Cayman Islands private company, with a Filipino crew, doing in Port Darwin, packed with explosives?

Cassandra collated the rapidly increasing mountain of electronic data into several cross-referenced files. All this new data was publicly available, albeit from numerous diverse sources , and none of it was confidential classified information.

She then created a simple, yet comprehensive, executive summary, and copied it all to several secure back-up folders on different servers, each with different passwords known only to her and to Marcus. Cassandra sent the summary, together with a few key source documents, as a final report to the Senator's parliamentary email address.

Later, all four – Marcus, Cassandra, Digger and Aurora – met for a brief discussion. What should they do next? The outstanding question was how to get evidence of the suspected American involvement, from the formulation of the hitherto secret Queen's Pawn to D4 strategy, through to the *Xiangqi* explosion. They agreed Digger should immediately travel to Darwin to pay a courtesy call on his nemesis.

TEXAS HOLD'EM IS NOT A CHESS MOVE

Texas Hold'em is a popular form of the card game, poker, involving a high degree of chance. A skilful player requires a canny combination of risk awareness and luck.

I t was good to be back in Darwin, even though this was not a pleasure trip. Flanked by two of his burly mates, Digger sauntered into the Alamo Bar and approached a lone, slouching drinker from behind.

"Howdy, Tex," he drawled, placing a firm hand on the drinker's shoulder. "Been fishing recently, mate?"

Cassandra had worked her magic again, using her contacts to track down the off-duty American agent, then informing Digger, who'd flown up from Canberra that morning.

"What the …" the bewildered Texan exclaimed as he spun around to be confronted by three muscular Australians. Then, recognising Digger from their previous encounter, he stammered, "I thought you was dead. I'll kill you myself next time I get the chance!"

"Afraid not, Tex. Remember what you said last time … 'This cat has at least nine lives.' We thought you might like to go fishing."

Before he knew what was happening, the three Aussies bundled the protesting American out the door and into a waiting van, while the obliging bartender turned a blind eye and counted the bank notes that were thrust into his hand. A searing pain surged through Tex's brain as he, unfortunately, "bumped" his head on something. Then, all went dark and he felt nothing more.

When Tex awoke, it was pitch black and he was in a small boat … a leaky dinghy devoid of motor and oars, with water seeping in through the seams.

"See? We brought you to your favourite fishing spot, Tex … you know, the place where you brought me a month ago," Digger called from the deck of the cruiser close by.

"What do you want?" Tex mumbled. "I'm an American. You can't do this!"

"Don't worry, Tex. We'll have you back home safe and sound, just as soon as you sign this little piece of paper I have here. Or … if you would prefer not to sign it, we could just leave you here to do some nice peaceful fishing on the mudflats over there. But just be careful of the salties. They're a bit more aggressive than your alligators, and I believe they just love nibbling on plump Americans."

"You can't do this!" Tex shouted again.

"But I can … and I will," Digger responded, motioning to his colleagues to push the dinghy away from the cruiser.

"No, wait! I'll sign!" Tex screamed. "What is it?"

And with that, they hauled Tex back alongside, handed him the pen and the document and, by the feeble light of a torch, photographed him signing a confession to his part in organising a former Chinese ship to enter Port Darwin.

When the signed document was checked and the video filed, Digger looked down at Tex, still in the dinghy.

"Thanks, pardner," he drawled in mock Texan. "I just got a couple of final questions. Have you ever been in Timor Leste?"

"Tin Lizzie? What's that? Is it some bar in Darwin?" the Texan responded, demonstrating his lack of geographical awareness.

"Well, I guess, if you say so, you weren't there," Digger responded. "How about Hela Province in the Papua New Guinea Highlands?"

Tex shook his head. "I heard about your little accident with the truck, but hey, that wasn't us. Go ask your Chinese mates."

Then Digger posed his final question.

"I know you were staying at the Gizo Hotel in the Solomon Islands at the same time as I was. I saw you and some of your rowdy mates in the upstairs bar. What do you know about my boating accident near Kennedy Island?"

"Well, Digger ... mate ... cobber ... whatever you want to be called. That one *was* us – and we did a pretty good job of it too. With the wonders of modern computer and drone technology, we can use a simple laptop to lob a bomb or fire a projectile anywhere we want. And all the time you thought it was the Chinese. Don't fool yourself, mate. We Americans can outsmart them any day. And we'll do it again. But I won't sign for that one. You've got what you want. Now let me go."

But instead of hauling Tex back into the cruiser, Digger cast off the line of the dinghy with the parting comment: "Don't worry, Tex. If you just wade to the shore, you will find that the main road back to Darwin is just 50 metres beyond the mangroves. Enjoy the walk. *Mate*."

PIECE COORDINATION

Piece coordination is a term that describes how various chess pieces work together to achieve a particular strategy, and how they cooperate to repel a threat. Pieces must support and protect each other to ensure proper piece coordination.

Just after dark that same evening, a young boy walked out the back door of his rundown Nightcliff home on the outskirts of Darwin. He carried an empty beer bottle, a box of matches and a skyrocket. Fireworks were still legal in the Northern Territory, and the boy had been waiting a long time for permission to ignite this one, the last of several rockets purchased by his parents for the annual celebration of Territory Day.

He stood the bottle on the concrete path, placed the stick of the rocket in the open neck, lit the wick and stood back. *Whoosh!* The rocket soared up into the blackness of the night sky, leaving a fiery trail, before disappearing into the distance.

A few moments later, the boy's neighbour telephoned the Nightcliff police station to report she'd witnessed "some sort of rocket, or something" flying towards the city. Her call was duly logged by the duty officer, but no further action was taken.

The boy was one of several who received a scholarship from the not-for-profit charity, the Whitehorse Foundation, to defray their education costs. The neighbour was one of the local trustees. Both were good friends of Marcus Whitehorse.

Around the same time, the bartender from the Alamo Bar in central Darwin had telephoned his local police station to report a disturbance, during which a drunken American had been arguing with three other men and threatened to … *kill one of them the next time he got the chance.*

After wading through the mangroves, Tex would have had a very long walk ahead of him along a meandering bush track, before he eventually got back to his Darwin apartment. Meanwhile, the cruiser skimmed across the harbour, transporting Digger back to Darwin.

No time to lose. Marcus and Cassandra inspected the emailed confession and the accompanying video, and were satisfied. However, they'd need more evidence directly linking the American Consul to the port explosion.

From Canberra, Marcus telephoned some of his senior contacts in the Northern Territory Police, and the duty magistrate, requesting an urgent interview with his colleague, Douglas, aka Digger. It was 03:00 by the time the interview was granted.

Digger requested an urgent warrant to *search the apartment of an American, known as Tex, for evidence of his involvement in past and possible imminent bomb attacks in Darwin.*

Marcus, meanwhile, advised Digger not to declare everything they knew about the American involvement, but to simply say there was evidence Tex represented a risk to public safety.

Consequently, when asked to provide said evidence, Digger played only that part of the recorded interview in which

Tex had stated: ...*With the wonders of modern computer and drone technology, we can use a simple laptop to lob a bomb or fire a projectile anywhere we want. And all the time you thought it was the Chinese. Don't fool yourself, mate. We Americans can outsmart them any day. And we'll do it again ...*

When the magistrate, with sensible caution, asked for further proof, Digger suggested there may be other independent evidence of Tex's intent, and perhaps even corroboration of unusual drone or similar activity.

The magistrate instructed the police inspector to make further enquiries, and he reported back that a bartender had called in suspicious behaviour by a drunken American – presumably Tex. Independently of this, someone else had reported an unidentified rocket, or similar, flying towards Darwin earlier in the evening. This was enough to satisfy the magistrate, who granted a limited warrant to the police to search Tex's apartment for "anything suspicious".

In response to a request by Marcus, the police inspector permitted Digger to accompany them because of his "unique knowledge" of the American's habits. On entering the apartment, the police scoured rooms for anything incriminating. They quickly located Tex's laptop, tried to gain access, but were thwarted by the password requirement.

Digger thought for a moment. Tex was not very bright and would have trouble remembering a complex password. More than likely, there'd be a reminder somewhere in the apartment. It was spartan, except for a huge poster of the American football team, the Dallas Cowboys. That had to be it.

"Try *Cowboys*," Digger suggested. And they were in.

They quickly scanned the email activity, paying particular attention to incoming emails.

Yes ... there it was. The smoking gun. A short email from the American Consul to Tex, ordering: *Initiate the contingency option of Queen's Pawn to D4 without delay. You are authorised to deploy and activate the Xiangqi immediately.*

As soon as he saw it, Digger recognised its significance. He whipped out his mobile phone, photographed the email, and sent copies to Marcus and Cassandra. By the time the unsuspecting constable realised what had happened, the photograph had been sent.

"Nothing to see here," the constable reported to the inspector, as he handed over the laptop to his superior.

I'll bet that's the last we will see of that computer, Digger thought.

END GAME

The End Game, as the name implies, is the closing stage of the chess game, when each player consolidates their position before undertaking those moves that will achieve their goal.

Once again, the four met in the Senator's office to consider Cassandra's report in more detail, and Tex's confession, which Digger had gently persuaded him to sign.

By now, Tex and the consul would be safely ensconced on a military transport plane bound for some obscure base in the backblocks of an American mid-west desert.

At Marcus's request, Cassandra ran through the implication of Tex's confessions and laptop disclosure, which had confirmed her own suspicions derived from her research.

After a while, Aurora ventured a question.

"OK, I understand the long-term American strategy, Queens Pawn to D4, was for Australia to goad the Chinese into taking action against Australia. So why did the Americans initiate both the Torres Strait and Port Darwin explosions?"

Marcus nodded to Cassandra to respond.

"Well, the Americans did not detonate both explosions, only the one in Port Darwin. The Torres Strait explosion was the result of a missile fired from a Chinese submarine sailing out of Betano Bay in Timor Leste, as originally suspected. It was in response to a string of provocations, over many years, by the Australian military, politicians and press, just as the Americans intended in their Queen's Pawn to D4 strategy.

"However, to its credit, the Australian Government wasn't as impetuous as the Americans had hoped. The Australians, quite rightly, carefully considered the trade implications before committing to any rash diplomatic or military response. And it was the Americans who eventually got impatient."

Cassandra paused, then continued.

"If the Australian Government wouldn't respond to an attack on a remote secret Torres Strait communications base, perhaps they, and the Australian public, might be angered by an explosion in Port Darwin. But such an explosion would need to be convincingly portrayed as being of Chinese origin. Hence, the use of the *Xiangqi*, and the appropriation of the investigation by the American Cedar Valley security service.

For their plan to work, the Americans had to convince the Australian population – and the government – that China was their enemy, not their friend. They'd been attempting this for many years, with some considerable degree of success, although not to the extent they'd hoped."

And with that explanation, the four started the formulation of a plan to extricate Australia from the "no-win zero-sum" game – the trap into which it had fallen.

They now set about devising an end game.

STALEMATE

There comes a time when a weaker player must face up to the fact that they cannot win, that they cannot achieve a checkmate. Their only option, apart from being thoroughly beaten, is to force a stalemate. This is the realisation that neither of the opposing players can achieve a decisive win, a checkmate, and both must concede a truce.

In war there are no winners … only losers[25]. Even the so-called winners eventually lose all. Successive Chinese dynasties rose, only to fall. For a while, the Indian kingdoms of history achieved some degree of unity, only to ultimately fragment. European unity, the goal of a succession of kings and dictators, has proven illusory.

And what of the most recent hegemons, the United States of America and its arch rivals, Russia and China? Each has a chequered past, and each will experience meteoric rise, followed by a catastrophic fall.

So where should Australia stand amid the swirling currents of international politics and diplomacy? This question taxed the minds of Senator Marcus Whitehorse and his three colleagues during the spring of 2030, as each pondered the events that had been unfolding.

Aurora, veteran journalist and broadcaster, the public face of informed enquiry, had, during the past twelve months, faced down her personal demons to emerge a stronger, more committed advocate for informed debate and political transparency. She would shortly be able to deploy her skills and talent in the most important interview of her career.

Digger, the fearless, practical, can-do Aussie, had escaped unscathed from several life-threatening situations, both in Australia and overseas. He now acted with determined focus and purpose, confident he, like all of us, has an important role to play at the coal-face of life.

Cassandra, intelligent, articulate, methodical and clinical, able to deploy logic and reason, with a flair for in-depth research, had now learned both empathy and humility. She'd grown in maturity, accepting that (true to her name) the good advice of a "Cassandra" is not always followed by those with the power to do so. Yet she, like others in a similar advisory position, realised she must continue to present her research findings clearly and promote her conclusions logically. The cause is always greater than the career, and the consequence more important than the credit. She now recognised she was part of a team, a cog in the machine, albeit a critical cog.

And Marcus himself. He reflected on a lifetime of commitment and service to his fellow humans, both in Australia and across the world. From an early age, he had recognised the potential trainwreck of Australian foreign policy, one driven by a paranoid fear of imagined enemies, a fear whipped up by a self-serving media. With the help of his three colleagues, he'd assumed the task of shining a light on recent international developments with a view to changing the direction of government policy.

Together, in the past few days, these four had achieved an unbelievable outcome critical for the future of Australia. They'd forced the sitting Prime Minister and his government to commit to reversing Australia's previous international policy. They'd successfully argued Australia's subservience to stronger overlord countries must cease.

The critical meeting two days ago had been tense. For many years, the Senator and the Prime Minister had shared a mutual respect; indeed, a friendship. The older man had previously acted as supporter, advisor and, arguably, mentor for his younger contemporary, while the younger man skilfully played party politics until he finally rose to the pinnacle of political power.

But friendship aside, each now owed allegiance to opposing political parties, the PM (prime minister) leading his government from the House of Representatives, and Marcus making his not-inconsequential contribution from the Senate crossbench.

Marcus was accompanied to the meeting by Cassandra, the research wizard, and Digger (introduced, of course, as *Douglas*), the on-the-ground eyewitness. Aurora's pivotal role in making the public aware of the behind-the-scenes intrigues must remain undisclosed for the moment. Her time to act would come.

The Prime Minister was flanked by a bevy of senior public servants and political advisors, each glowering at the Senator and his two companions.

After the requisite brief introductions and pleasantries, Senator Marcus Whitehorse spoke.

"Thank you, Prime Minister, for this opportunity to present previously unknown information regarding the origin of two recent unexplained explosions in Australia – one close to Injinoo near Torres Strait, and the other a few days ago in Port Darwin.

"We acknowledge that your senior public servants keep you well advised, based on information provided by Australian and allied security services, but our information results from careful analysis of historical data – by my colleague here, Cassandra, and on-the-ground observation by my other colleague, Douglas."

Marcus gestured towards both parties, and the Prime Minister politely acknowledged their contribution.

Marcus continued: "Cassandra will present documentary evidence for your assistants to examine. Since the early 2020s the American security services have systematically sought to coerce Australia into covertly initiating a military conflict with China.

"The purpose of such a conflict was to provoke a military reaction from China, which would be interpreted by global public opinion as the big Chinese bully victimising an innocent little peace-loving Pacific country ... that is, Australia. This top-secret American strategy was known as Queen's Pawn to D4.

"As you no doubt know, Prime Minister, in chess the Queen's Pawn is the foot-soldier piece, stationed immediately in front of, and protecting, the Queen. D4 is a position on the chess board two spaces in front of the White Queen's Pawn, and a common opening move is to advance the Queen's Pawn to this position. Here it can threaten the opposing side, although it is also very vulnerable, normally not surviving very long. You might well ask, 'What do these terms, these chess moves. mean for Australia's international policy?'"

He paused, cleared his throat, then went on.

"The American strategy was devised in the early 2020s, at a time when the English Queen Elizabeth II was the reigning monarch of Australia. I suppose the American strategists thought they could highlight our national backwardness and immaturity by identifying Australia as the Queen's Pawn.

"And where, or what, was the real D4? This was a geographical position, most likely the Taiwan Strait, but possibly anywhere in the South China Sea, within the 9-dash boundary designated by China as its own protective zone. The strategy called for Australia to secretly sail one of its warships, even a proposed new nuclear submarine into the disputed area and covertly cause a disruption to the passage of one or more Chinese military vessels. The Americans would then, unknown to Australia, leak to the Chinese that the intruder was in fact Australian, not American.

We believe that late last year this disruption occurred. You will recall there were Chinese accusations and indignant denials by an outraged Australia. We cannot prove an Australian incursion occurred, or if it did, what actually took place. But that's not what's important.

"What does matter is the Chinese – with good cause – believe Australia *did* carry out a hostile action inside their region … a sort of Cuban missile crisis in reverse. And this belief provoked a Chinese reaction.

"Just a few weeks ago, Prime Minister, you participated in a television interview on *Australasian Focus* on this subject. May I play you a recording of the opening part of that interview?"

The Prime Minister winced, but indicated his consent to the inclusion of the television recording in the formal meeting transcript.

For the record, he had said, it has now been revealed by reliable sources that the explosion which occurred six months ago close to the gas terminal near Torres Strait was, in fact, at a secret submarine communications facility on an adjacent property. Not just the location, but the very existence of this communication base, has been vehemently denied by the Australian Government for years.

It has further been revealed that the base was destroyed by a missile, fired from a Chinese submarine, which sailed from Betano Bay in Timor Leste, a week earlier.

We have it on good authority the attack was retaliation for a similar attack in the Taiwan Strait, launched from an Australian warship, under American orders.

We understand the purpose of the attack near Torres Strait was a warning ... intended to indicate to the Americans that China is prepared to take drastic action to protect their claim to Greater China ... to Taiwan, in other words.

The recently discovered Pentagon Leaks revealed that since the beginning of the 21st century, the Americans have referred to Australia as the Queen's Pawn – a reference to the fact that Australia, under our previous monarch, failed to become a republic when we had the opportunity.

Apparently, the Chinese and the Americans both view Australia as a mere pawn in the bigger game of international politics ... an expendable pawn. The Chinese, wisely, are reluctant to attack any part of the United States for fear of massive nuclear retaliation. But they, quite correctly, have assumed that attacking Australia can provide a potent demonstration of their resolve without the risk of starting World War 3.

The American strategy of Queen's Pawn to D4, formulated at a time just before the AUKUS agreement, was a calculated

American risk of advancing an Australian vessel, in preference to an American one, into the Taiwan Strait disputed zone.

It is clear the Australian defence planners, politicians and public all failed to understand the enormous relational damage the repeated taunts and provocations inflicted on China by Australia, and the hypocrisy of blindly obeying American instructions to escalate any and all conflicts they deemed to be in their interest, would cause. For decades, the Chinese repeatedly warned Australia not to meddle in their affairs ...

At this point, Cassandra handed over a file containing a copy of the executive summary of the Queen's Pawn to D4 strategy, the document photographed and transmitted by Digger from Darwin Harbour immediately before his abduction.

"My colleague, Douglas, obtained this document at considerable risk to his own life, and can vouch for its origin and veracity," she interjected.

Digger nodded his agreement, secretly thinking, *very considerable risk to my life.*

The Prime Minister, now struggling to restrain his fury, muttered, "OK, Marcus, all this stuff is already on the public record. But we're here to talk about the Port Darwin explosion, not some past event up there in the Torres Strait."

"Oh, I'm coming to Port Darwin," Marcus said. "Obviously, we don't have the formal transcripts of the dialogue between the Chinese and Australian security agencies, either before or after the Torres Strait explosion, but we do have it on good authority there were intense discussions at the highest level between the two governments, in both Beijing and in Canberra.

"Both governments have been tight-lipped, but the media, even the commercial media, have speculated something was very wrong with the relationship. So wrong, in fact, it transcended the tit-for-tat trade restrictions that normally accompany a disagreement. And then, of course, came the explosion near Torres Strait, more calls for explanations by ambassadors, and more denials all round.

"During the last few days, Douglas has been active pursuing the most reliable of sources. He can confirm, by statutory declaration, he was told by an American security operative, now in transit back to the US, that the American Consul in Darwin was aware that the *Xiangqi* was carrying explosives, and that the consul's comment some weeks ago that *chess is still a better game than xiangqi* ... was a not-too-subtle threat for the Australian Government to remain wedded to American allegiance.

"While we don't know for sure who detonated the explosives on the *Xiangqi*, we can be certain of the following ...

"First, the Australian navy carried out some sort of subversive act in the Taiwan Strait or in the South China Sea in response to instructions by the Americans. The Chinese then retaliated with a missile strike on a secret Australian communications base near Torres Strait, intended to be a warning against Australian meddling. The subsequent negotiations between Australia and China were unsuccessful.

"The Americans then purchased the old Chinese ship, put the explosives on board, and sailed it into Port Darwin. Someone, almost certainly American, detonated the explosives, after first ensuring the crew weren't on board."

Marcus paused and gazed around the table. The Prime Minister and his advisors sat quietly, apparently stunned into silence. It wasn't clear to Marcus what had shocked them the most – the actual disclosures, or the fact Marcus and his team had uncovered them.

The Prime Minister lifted his gaze and spoke quietly, directing his response to the Senator.

"OK, Marcus … let us suppose you are right, that both countries have treated Australia as a pawn in a giant global chess game. Where do we go from here?"

Whitehorse, the White Knight, deliberate and methodical, patient as a marathon runner, renowned for his dispassionate dissection of any problem and his analysis of the possibilities in the minutest detail before devising and implementing a strategy with deadly precision and ruthlessness, now articulated his boldest plan.

"Of course we have taken precautions. All the information we've just handed over to you and your advisors has been copied multiple times, and those copies are stored in various safe locations. They'll only be exposed to the public if the following suggestions are not implemented.

"Both the House of Representatives and the Senate are finely balanced. You govern only by the grace of a couple of independents and members of minor parties. I have briefed a few key senators and lower-house MPs, although not with the full details. Nevertheless, they support the proposal that I'm about to put to you.

As a first step, Prime Minister, may I suggest you contact the Leader of the Opposition, and invite her to a meeting involving the three of us in which I'll explain, as I just have to you, the situation as it currently stands. If she agrees, you'll both put the following brief statement to your respective party rooms and, hopefully, get their endorsement.

"Once that's achieved, I suggest you make a public announcement, on a prime-time current affairs television program – something like *Australasian Focus*. I'm sure if we approach her nicely, our mutual friend Aurora will oblige with a special interview.

"The following – in your own words, of course – could be considered a reasonable address to the public:

> My fellow Australians,
>
> Many of you are still in deep shock and bewilderment on learning of the recent explosions in northern Australia, the first near Torres Strait and the second in Port Darwin. The Australian Federal Police are continuing to investigate both incidents, and I cannot go into detail tonight. However, I can say that preliminary indications suggest that these incursions into our sovereignty are at least partly attributable to our own previous foreign policy attitudes, and the resulting actions by my government, and by previous Australian governments, over a long period of time.
>
> Put simply, we have spent too much effort in making enemies and have not paid enough attention to maximising friendship. We need to shift our focus to friendship, understanding and cooperation with ALL the countries in our region, be they large or small, rich or poor, distant or close.
>
> There is no doubt the actions of some other countries, particularly the larger ones, are making the world a more dangerous place. But Australia must avoid, at all costs, being drawn into a global conflict.
>
> The events of the past few months have clearly demonstrated the dangers of Australia immersing itself

in conflicts that, first, we don't understand, second, we are powerless to influence and, third, have no immediate impact on the welfare of our country.

I have had lengthy discussions with the Leader of the Opposition, and we agree on the need for a return to a bipartisan approach to foreign affairs. We must place less emphasis on countering imaginary threats, in favour of promoting improved friendly relationships with all countries in the Indo-Pacific region.

I will be raising this matter in Parliament, and I look forward to support from the Opposition and from the crossbench.

Thank you.

The Prime Minister nodded a tentative agreement. At least such a statement would allow him to save face, while also ensuring a pivot toward a new paradigm, one that he, like most intelligent, informed people, could see was a better direction for Australia. The meeting closed with a shaking of hands and an undertaking by the Prime Minister to take up the proposals.

PREPARING A NEW GAME

No matter how a chess game ends, whether checkmate by one side or the other, or in stalemate, there is always an opportunity for a new game, a chance to clear away the pieces and set them in place for a new challenge.

Marcus, Digger and Cassandra stared anxiously at the monitor in Aurora's office. Aurora herself was downstairs in the studio preparing to do her job – impassively, the way she'd been conditioned to do it by her thirty years of journalistic experience.

Marcus had briefed her thoroughly with the details of his verbal agreement with the Prime Minister, outlining the questions she must put to him. She must ensure that the PM answer clearly, succinctly and with conviction, committing Australia to a new position in international politics, one in which it would take a principled role as a peacemaker rather than as a belligerent. There must be no prevarication, no waffle, and no equivocation.

Aurora entered the studio and took her place. The Prime Minister entered and took his seat facing her. He was obviously not happy about the situation, vociferously berating the staff, his own assistants and anyone else within earshot. He clearly preferred to resist any policy change, despite the undertaking he'd given verbally to Marcus. His hostility momentarily unnerved her, but she was not to be deterred.

And then the bombshell.

Just as the cameramen were ready to roll, but before Aurora could even greet him, the PM announced that he'd changed his mind and wouldn't proceed with the interview. Instead, he declared bitterly, he'd call a general election to resolve the matter. And with that, he stormed out of the studio.

Aurora quickly swallowed her dismay. She must improvise. She must move to Plan B.

7:00 pm, 26 September 2030, Parliament House Studios, Canberra

Her face uncharacteristically grim, Aurora faltered as she attempted to regain her composure. But the teleprompter was merciless. This broadcast must proceed, no matter what, without delay and devoid of emotion, no matter how this incident had affected her. Gathering herself, she focused on the camera.

"Good evening, and welcome to *Australasian Focus*. The Prime Minister has just announced off-camera that he's calling a general election, to obtain a clear mandate for what he believes are the steps necessary to avoid Australia being drawn further into the imminent world conflict.

"He has declined, at short notice, to elaborate on air. However, we at *Australasian Focus* believe the Australian people deserve to know how successive governments have led our country to the brink of participation in World War 3. We're calling for the following fundamental paradigm shift ..."

Marcus, Digger and Cassandra were still watching the scene play out from the privacy of Aurora's office. They glanced at each other, then back at the screen, as Aurora continued to improvise, calmly and with true professionalism, a "Call to the Australian People".

A Call to the Australian People

"As I speak, the new Australian flag of the Southern Cross flutters on many flagpoles across the nation. Its green and gold are the colours of the Australian bush on a misty mountain morning, the colours of the wattle in the springtime. They are also the colours of our sporting prowess.

"This flag features flowers of the Australian golden wattle, symbol of a flowering society, stylised in the shape of the Southern Cross to signify our southern hemisphere home. Its most important symbols are the single leaf, depicting one people of many ethnicities, on a single branch, following a united destiny, against the dark green background that symbolises the Australian bush that we know and love.

"This flag represents our aspirations … non-confronting, non-violent, non-racist, post-colonial, fauna-friendly and eco-friendly. The validity of those symbols will depend not on what we say, but on what we do. The use of them is not a birthright; it must be earned.

"Previous generations of Australians dutifully followed Britain into a series of remote conflicts, such as China's Boxer

Uprising, the South African Boer War, the disastrous European World War 1 and the European theatre of World War 2.

"Australia's lack of preparedness for a Pacific conflict with Japan, in 1941, is largely attributable to the fact that most of Australia's regular armed forces were engaged in a war in support of British masters on the other side of the world.

"Our 'rescue' from Japanese invasion by the United States and the post-war decline of Britain heralded an altogether unhealthy reliance on US 'protection'. This reliance was consummated through the ANZUS Treaty of 1951, which has led directly to Australia's involvement in the Korean War, the Viet Nam War, two Iraq Wars, the Afghanistan War and several other lesser conflicts.

"In 2001, Australia committed to supporting the American invasion of Afghanistan in retaliation for the 9/11 terrorist attacks on the New York World Trade Centre buildings. Prime Minister John Howard effectively committed Australia to 20 years of continuous war, stating: '... [I have] expressed our resolute support for the United States ... our steadfast commitment to work with the United States ... in support of the US response to these attacks.'

"Consider the similarities to Prime Minister Harold Holt's 1966 statement committing Australia to the Viet Nam War: '... All the way with LBJ ...'; Prime Minister Robert Menzies' 1939 pledge which launched Australia into World War 2: '... Great Britain has declared war on [Germany] and ... as a result, Australia is also at war ...'; and Prime Minister Andrew Fisher's 1914 declaration to send the flower of Australian youth to the killing fields of the Great War: '... Australians will stand beside ... [Britain] ... to help and defend her to the last man and the last shilling'.

"As the debacle of the Afghanistan conflict hit home, many asked, 'Is Australia really addicted to war?' Perhaps the Australian wars of a century-and-a-half should be more wisely remembered as tragedies, when an immature country sacrificed its impetuous youth for the benefit of nobody except its avaricious overlords.

"So, when will we learn from our history, rather than continuing to live in blissful ignorance? When will we befriend our neighbours, rather than habitually insulting and belittling them? When will we seek a balanced media rather than believing the biases that the moguls serve us? When will we reform our political institutions rather than succumbing to the same hollow promises every three (or is it two-and-a-half?) years? When will we act compassionately rather than only in our own self-interest, and when will we refuse to partake of international violence rather than mindlessly following our so-called allies into their hegemonic wars?

"In short, when will we grow up?

"As the world superpowers duel for economic and military supremacy, they move their chess pieces, their so-called 'allies', about the board – about the world, that is – trying to seek military and economic advantage. But such allies are expendable.

"Australia is in grave danger of succumbing to such manipulation. Just as in chess, two opposing sides each seek to demolish and dominate the opposition. As the game progresses, pawns attack and defend, always at risk of their own capture and removal from the board. The carnage is widespread, with few pawns surviving.

"But ... what if a pawn refuses to take its allotted place on the board, refuses to advance, and refuses to attack?

"What if that pawn can broker a solution where none of the pieces, from both sides of the board, threaten each other, but instead live in cooperative harmony? The pawn would no longer be expendable. It would not be 'chess', but it would certainly be a more productive game.

"We are joining with caring and compassionate people throughout the world as they cry out for a paradigm shift – a new vision of a cooperative, compassionate and caring world, where self-interest is subservient to mutual interest – a new vision in which countries of the Southern Cross may emerge as the world's peacemakers.

"It is time for Australia to renounce state-promoted violence and to promote respect, cooperation and assistance throughout the region and the wider world. Australia must step up, not as a belligerent protagonist, but as a peacemaker.

"This is the only sustainable means of international interaction ... our last chance for survival."

2025 Reflections – The Journal of a Concerned Australian

Introduction

I t is 2025. I write this journal knowing it may never be read in full by others. But I undertake this task as an exercise in clarifying my own thoughts on Australia's role in the Indo-Pacific region. This journal deals with the intersection of international travel, history and foreign affairs. It is an autobiography, entirely factual, without exaggeration or distortion.

My home is Australia, the country of my birth. My profession is engineer, although I'm now retired from a full-time professional career. I've been fortunate to have the time, resources and opportunity to devote much of my energies to pro bono work for NGOs serving our neighbours in the Asia–Pacific region. And finally, I have a long-term interest in international affairs and politics. Who knows what the future will bring?

As a '50s baby-boomer, I'm old enough to have witnessed the death-throes of the ailing British Empire as it conceded world dominance to American global hegemony, and young enough to anticipate the next change. For a time, the Soviets challenged American ascendency, but the USSR has long since disintegrated. Russia has been sidelined, and now China and the United States compete in a not-so-subtle struggle for Asian ascendency.

But so much for international politics. Let's begin ...

We are, indeed, blessed to live in an age where international travel is relatively easy, safe, fast and affordable. Consider the hardships of the journeys of yesteryear – the 13th-century Chinese adventures of Italian Marco Polo and his uncles; Moroccan explorer, Ibn Battuta, travelling through Africa and Asia to China in the 14th century; or the 15th and 16th-century sea voyages of da Gama, Columbus, Magellan and others.

In comparison, our modern inconveniences of delayed flights and poor room service pale into insignificance. This blessing of modern travel opportunities must be cherished, nurtured and, above all, exercised.

For five decades, my wife and I travelled the world. I've journeyed through six continents, lived on three of them and visited eighty-four countries, many of them multiple times. We're fortunate to have formed international friendships that span two-thirds of a lifetime.

China, 2016

It is 2016, and my wife and I are about to embark on a travelling holiday in China, before proceeding through three of the former Central Asian Soviet socialist republics – Kazakhstan, Kyrgyzstan and Uzbekistan. Next year, we'll continue through China, followed by Estonia, Latvia, Lithuania, Poland, Czech Republic and Russia.

These two consecutive adventures trace the great Silk Roads from China, through Central Asia, to Russia. I've selected these two journeys to provide the overall theme for this narrative, because of the extraordinary experiences and insights they presented. I'll deviate to describe other journeys, but I'll always return to our China, Central Asia and Russia travels.

In the Silk Road network, many highways were used for intercontinental trade when Han Chinese goods found their way into aristocratic Roman households 2,000 years ago. Most of the land trade routes passed through the region now encompassing western China, Xinjiang, and modern Kyrgyzstan, Uzbekistan, Kazakhstan and Russia, which were our intended destinations.

These land routes were in constant use until eventually displaced by sea trade, which increased progressively from the early 16th century following the Ottoman expansion in Western Asia.

The sea route between India and western Europe, via the Indian Ocean and southern Africa, was pioneered by the Portuguese, building on Vasco da Gama's 1497 to 1499 voyage to India. A competing sea route from the Philippines to Europe, via the Pacific, Panama (land trans-shipment) and the Atlantic, was developed by the Spanish in the mid-1500s in the wake of Ferdinand Magellan's epic world-circumnavigation 1519 to 1522 voyage.

For millennia, China's Great Walls proved a bulwark against barbarism, and preserved Chinese civilisation.

But "building a wall" isn't always beneficial. When the Mongols ultimately breached the barrier, ushering in Kublai Khan's Yuan Dynasty in 1279, Chinese culture regenerated and boomed. This was the fabulous civilisation reported by Marco Polo.

To truly understand the world we live in, it's first necessary to understand the world of our forebears and the trade routes they traversed. We first went to China in 1999 as tourists, visiting Beijing, the Great Wall, the Forbidden City, the Ming Tombs, Tiananmen Square – the whole tourist bit.

At this time, the economic reform process initiated by Deng Xiaoping had been under way for about twenty years, but tourism in China was still in its infancy. In 2013, I returned to China on business visiting Beijing, Tianjin, Hebei, Shanghai, Nanjing and Foshan – six days in six cities – in and out of factories, all testifying that political firmness, foresight, investment in modern technology and a penchant for hard work can combine to make a modern, manufacturing-based prosperous society.

Guangzhou was but a staging post on our 2016 journey to the Silk Road, although we lingered long enough for two nights of good sleep, bookending an enlightening city tour. I suppose all city tours are the same … a couple of aged religious buildings (churches, temples or mosques, depending on whether you travel the Occident, the Orient, or in between), ancient forts and battlements (usually spruced up in response to a service life of hardship and a retirement of neglect), and the inevitable dose of local craft and souvenir shops.

But on closer examination, Guangzhou was more relevant to the Silk Road than it first appeared. The Silk Road initially comprised the land routes that connected China and Europe for almost two millennia, the trading corridors along which the camel caravans dispensed goods, wealth and ideas.

When Portuguese caravels, those small sea-going fighting and trading ships used from the mid-15th century to the early 17th century, eventually displaced the overland caravans, it was to seaports such as Guangzhou that these ships journeyed.

Since the late-15th century, the Chinese Ming dynasty had been in inexorable decline, the bureaucracy systematically stifling the international inquisitiveness of Chinese maritime traders. Just when Europe was expanding, China was contracting.

The Qing Dynasty appropriation of power in 1644 failed to arrest this decline, and by the time the Europeans appeared in force, China was ripe for exploitation.

Malacca (in present-day Malaysia), which had until then been a Chinese vassal, was conquered in 1511 by the Portuguese, who established a trading post there. In 1516, Rafael Perestrello journeyed from Malacca to Guangzhou, followed a year later by an eight-ship expedition led by Fernão Pires de Andrade.

However, Andrade was defeated by the Chinese Ming forces. It wasn't until 1554 that Leonel de Sousa bribed the Chinese admiral Wang Bo, facilitating the Luso-Chinese Accord. Portuguese trade with China was thus secured and relocated to nearby Macau, first as a trading post and then, in 1887, as a colony, a status it retained until reverting to Chinese sovereignty as late as 1999[26].

With the Portuguese traders diverted to Macau, Guangzhou attracted the attention of other European powers, principally the British. The prized commodity was Chinese tea – but how could the British pay for it?

The solution … wage two wars: the First Opium War (1839–1842) and the Second Opium War (1856–1860), to force the Chinese to accept Indian-grown opium as payment for Chinese-grown tea[27]. Tea for free! Drug trafficking has a long pedigree[28] .

One sure way to combat the boredom of a long flight from the Chinese Pacific seaboard to the far west of the country is to read the in-flight magazine. But to an air traveller unschooled in interpreting the Chinese script, negotiating the in-flight publication of the Chinese domestic airlines can be a challenge.

Fortunately, one article appeared in both Chinese and English, a sort of modern Chinese Rosetta Stone. Look for a commonly occurring word in the English text and find the corresponding Chinese symbols. The article in question was about the great museums of the world, and their role as the oracles through which the lessons of civilisation are conveyed down the millennia.

In the English version, the words *China* and *civilisation* appeared in many places, but in the Chinese version they appeared to be almost interchangeable. The most common Sinitic name for China is Zhongguo, denoted by the characters 中国, the symbols meaning *middle* and *state* respectively, and differentiating between the cultural central region of the Yellow River valley and the barbarous periphery.

During the Zhou and Han dynasties, which spanned the period 1046 BCE to 220 CE, Zhongguo was accepted as the "centre of civilisation" or "centre of the world". Pride is admirable ... but arrogance is fatal and there is but a fine line between the two.

While China's proud cultural heritage was (and is) the envy of the civilised world, the growing arrogance of the recent Ming and Qing dynasties fuelled the introspection that witnessed their decline from the 17th to 20th centuries. Perhaps we should ask: "Which countries are following suit in the 21st century?"

The four-hour morning flight, from Guangzhou to Ürümqi in the far west Xinjiang Uygur Autonomous Region, is a reminder of the vastness of modern China. Unlike other large countries, China has only a single time zone, resulting in long western afternoons of brilliant daylight.

With plenty of time to spare, we decided to try our luck with the airport bus rather than catch a taxi to our Ürümqi hotel. Although this may have seemed like a good idea at the time, the execution was less than ideal.

We do not speak Mandarin, and few ordinary people in Xinjiang speak English. We failed to exit the bus at the appropriate stop, and it finally dawned on us when the bus pulled into the central station terminus that we should alight.

My failure to identify the location of our hotel on a map – any map – resulted in a four-hour "unguided walking tour" of this large, modern city. Perhaps with uncharacteristic foresight, we'd opted to take carry-on luggage only, which provided some relief. After a belated lunch and some directions at a friendly fast-food chicken shop, we surrendered to the inevitable and summoned a taxi. Five minutes later we were at the hotel.

The north-eastern Dzungaria region, inhabited by Tibetan-Buddhist Dzungar[29] nomads, and the south-western Tarim Basin, inhabited by Turkic-speaking Muslim Uyghur sedentary farmers, existed separately before being united by the Qing Dynasty in 1884 to form Xinjiang. This effectively reinstated the Chinese political control that had previously existed under the Tang dynasty between the 7th and 10th centuries of the modern era.

The Tarim Basin is rich in oil and gas, and China seeks to supply approximately a fifth of the country's consumption from this region[30]. One cannot fail to be impressed by the abundance of power stations, factories and blast furnaces along the nearby freeways.

Ürümqi is a large, modern city, capital of the Xinjiang Uyghur Autonomous Region in the far west of the country, and is populated mostly by Han Chinese, who have migrated from the east.

The demographic data is telling. In Ürümqi, 75% of the three million population is Han Chinese, while only 13% is Indigenous Uyghur. However, in Xinjiang as a whole, only 41% of the 22 million population is Han Chinese, while 44% is Uyghur.

This, together with the presence of the vast energy resources, has given rise to an acute separatist problem, and, consequently, the police, army and security are omnipresent. The Uyghur separatist movement claims the region was invaded by China in 1949 and has been under subsequent Chinese occupation. The Chinese government, on the other hand, states Chinese control dates back to the Tang era.

While the Uyghurs of Xinjiang are linguistically and culturally Turkic and Muslim, the Han Chinese speak Mandarin and mainly adhere to Buddhism, Confucianism, Taoism or no religion at all. Although devotional practice is tolerated, the government of the People's Republic of China does not formally endorse or support any religion.

The 2005 Tulip Revolution in neighbouring Kyrgyzstan ushered in a period of political instability throughout the region, with China's Xinjiang region suffering increasing Uyghur militancy and acts of violence. Chinese authorities have clamped down on separatism.

Recent reports, from human rights organisations, indicate the severity of the Chinese government reaction to what's claimed to be Uyghur terrorism has increased dramatically[31] [32].

Although our movements around Ürümqi were in no way restricted, and we were not prevented from walking unaccompanied about the streets, one does become quite conscious of the military convoys moving down the highway and through the city.

The hotel was a high-rise upmarket modern building, but with hardly any guests ... we counted only three other diners in the breakfast room the next morning. Perhaps tourists had been discouraged by the army post (with guns bristling) erected just outside the main entrance to the hotel. Or were they put off by the army personnel in the lobby, who periodically patrolled the residential floors?

The ubiquitous presence of army patrols in the streets suggests a general crackdown on the populace at large, but the military concentration in, and around, our tourist hotel is more indicative of targeted terrorism against tourists. There are two sides to every story.

We were not part of any organised tour (you could say we were quite disorganised), and we believe this attracted the attention (assistance) of the Chinese security service.

A well-dressed gentleman (at first introducing himself as part of the hotel management ... although we're now convinced otherwise) insisted on "helping" us to join an organised day trip to Heavenly Lake. That he could command the immediate cooperation of the hotel staff was not in doubt, but later enquiries revealed he was indeed not part of their staff.

A day excursion to Heavenly Lake is the highlight of any visit to Ürümqi, popular with many tourists from eastern China. The spectacular natural scenery of the eastern Tian Shan Range, and the serene mountain lake, were augmented by the kind of spectacular open-air show of cultural and gymnastic prowess that only the Chinese can perfect – a most enjoyable day.

The following morning, the same gentleman kindly organised our trip to the Xinjiang Regional Museum. He also arranged for us to be accompanied by an athletic young man, who (although he spoke no English) kept a very close eye on us to ensure we didn't stray too far, and that we returned safely to our hotel.

"Guide", "companion" or "minder" ... what is the difference? None of the extra security service attention involved us in any expense, and no money changed hands. Even our offer to pay for the taxi to the museum was rejected. But the close supervision did ensure we didn't get up to any mischief.

The highlight of this museum is its display of twenty-one ancient mummies[33] dating back approximately 4,000 years. Preserved by the extremely dry conditions of the Tarim Basin, the mummies, their burial practices and their woven clothing point to an origin quite unexpected in this region. The evidence suggests that these Tokharian people were Indo-European (not Asian), related to the Celts who settled in western Europe.

A related Indo-European nomadic people, the Yuezhi, were pushed westward into the Tarim Basin following their defeat in 170 BCE by the Xiongnu (Altaic nomads)[34]. Subsequent invasions by Han Chinese were followed by the Uyghurs (a Turkic people) in the 7th century CE, and more recently by the Chinese Tang, Ming and Qing dynasties[35].

That these peoples were successively victorious, and then displaced, testifies to the volatility of the region and to the historical fragility of land claims in general. Perhaps none of us can legitimately claim exclusive land rights. Is history simply telling us to use it or lose it?

As if to reflect the security concerns in the city, airport security at Ürümqi was the strictest we've encountered. Your phone goes one way while you go another, only to be reunited after each has undergone the closest of scrutiny. Not only must you remove all items from your pockets, your belt and your shoes; you must also expose the soles of your feet to the metal detector. Journalists have been known to hide digital SD cards in the strangest of places.

But perhaps these security precautions were not without justification. While we didn't witness any violence in China, we were in Bishkek (capital of neighbouring Kyrgyzstan) a week later, when the nearby Chinese embassy was bombed by Uyghur separatists.

In his 2024 book, *Great Game On*, former Australian ambassador to China, Geoff Raby, confirms that, due to remoteness and political sensitivity, travelling in Xinjiang is now challenging unless you're part of an official tour. More importantly, he comments on the wealth of the natural resources of Xinjiang, its attraction to other countries such as Russia and its strategic importance to China."[36]

In days of old, Silk Road traders would pay enormous sums for luxury items. Today, coffee is the life-blood of the modern traveller, but in a region where tea is ubiquitous, coffee must be considered a luxury. In our case, each cup of coffee at Ürümqi International Airport cost the same as the taxi fare from the city.

Zambia, 1975

Our 2016 flight from Ürümqi to Almaty in *Kazakhstan* was relatively short, although it was long enough to reflect on the rapid development of China and the consequences of this over the past three decades.

But China's 21st century Belt and Road Initiatives were not its first foray into international development. We'd first become aware of China's impact five decades earlier, in southern Africa.

Just as European colonial powers were retreating from Asia in the decades following World War 2, so too they were exiting Africa, leaving in their wake a poor, undeveloped, tribally heterogenous and violent continent and a score of new countries.

Zambia, in the heart of central-southern Africa, is landlocked by Zimbabwe, Botswana, Namibia, Angola, Congo, Tanzania, Malawi and Mozambique. In the mid-1970s, violence, poverty and corruption surrounded this isolated country.

In 1975, Angola and Mozambique were abandoned by their colonial overlord, Portugal, resulting in violent civil wars as left and right factions, puppets of the superpowers, battled for control.

Namibia, or South-West Africa as it was then known, was firmly controlled by the apartheid South African regime, which used it as a base for the invasion of Angola.

Zimbabwe, then known as Rhodesia, had declared a UDI (Unilateral Declaration of Independence) from Britain, with a white-minority government prosecuting a violent, but ultimately unsuccessful, war against its neighbours.

The Democratic Republic of Congo was renowned for the corruption and violence that besets it to this day, while Tanzania, Malawi and Botswana were, at that time, desperately poor.

But Zambia was relatively stable, and life for ex-pat professionals was reasonably comfortable.

As the 1960s faded into the 1970s, Zambia's economy approached a perilous situation. Although rich in copper, which at that time commanded a good price, Zambia relied entirely on railways through hostile neighbouring countries for the export of this valuable metal.

The Benguela Railway to the west was blocked by civil war in Angola and corruption in Congo. The eastern railway across the Zambezi River to the Indian Ocean ports of Beira and Maputo (previously Lourenço Marques) were blocked by violence in Mozambique, and by a hostile Rhodesia. So, too, the option of transporting the copper to the south was prevented by the war with Rhodesia and the hostile apartheid regime in South Africa.

In such circumstances, communist China offered to construct a lifeline to the north, the TAZARA Railway, linking Kapiri Mposhi, near the Zambian Copperbelt, to the Tanzanian Indian Ocean port of Dar-es-Salaam.

Built between 1970 and 1975 by up to 50,000 Chinese and 60,000 Africans, the TAZARA Railway traverses 1,860 kilometres of Africa's most forbidding terrain. Financed by the Chinese at a staggering estimated equivalent cost of nearly $3 billion (2020 US dollars), it represented an enormous foreign commitment, particularly given the parlous state of Chinese domestic politics at the time.

In 1966, Mao Zedong had plunged his country into the turmoil of the disastrous Cultural Revolution from which it hadn't yet emerged. But on 24 October 1975, the first passenger train arrived at Dar-es-Salaam terminus and the railway service was ready to start.

Two months previously, we'd arrived in Zambia. Conscious of the poverty that crippled many parts of the world and the need for educated people (such as us) to share their skills, I obtained a two-year contract, subsequently shortened to one year, with an Italian consulting engineering firm. Three days in the capital, Lusaka, were enough for us to meet my new work colleagues and deposit our meagre possessions in a company townhouse.

Then we were off again, on a 1,000-kilometre road trip to Nakonde, a village on the remote northern border, where the brand-new (still not in regular service) TAZARA Railway crosses the Zambia–Tanzania border.

We were in Nakonde for the first of two two-week visits to survey an existing dam, a proposed 15-kilometre pipeline and water treatment works. My boss, who stayed with us for only one day before returning to Lusaka, left instructions to "hire a boat and survey the dam".

No boat? No worries. A hastily constructed raft consisting of three 200-litre oil drums, lashed to a makeshift frame of steel pipes, was sufficient to support three of the Indigenous Zambians hired to assist – one to hold the surveyor's staff, one to paddle the raft, and the third (a policeman equipped with a rifle) to stand guard against the "crocodile". Some days later, I met the "crocodile" face-to-face … a very large monitor lizard.

True to our shared love of adventure, my wife accompanied me to this remote outpost, and her support and assistance were invaluable. Despite being a relatively inexperienced driver at the time, she drove work teams in the ute to various sites. For most of this period, we were the only non-Indigenous ex-pats in the region. Communication with Lusaka was by two-way radio and occurred only once during our two trips.

My boss had stayed long enough to define the job and hire far too many locals, about forty in all, including some who were from across the Tanzanian border.

Needing to reduce this workforce to a manageable six, at the end of the first week I found that dismissing so many workers, engaged at different times and from both sides of the border, proved not to be simple. The biblical parable of the vineyard workers, each hired at different times, in *Holy Bible*,

Matthew Chapter 20 Verses 1 to 16, provides the best explanation of my dilemma.

On our second trip to Nakonde, we were much more self-sufficient. Equipped with a portable fuel stove, we'd drive off into the African bush to cook evening meals more suited to our delicate western palates, before returning to the sort-of safety of the rough and raucous resthouse.

No more nshima (mealie glue) or kapenta (minuscule fish eaten whole). The internet says: "There is not much that I can say about nshima ... and there's not a lot that can be done with it; it's hardly a chef's dream"[37].

Because we didn't bring a driver or any colleagues on this second trip, we were able to detour for some sightseeing on the return journey. We drove west to the spectacular Kalambo Falls, where the river plunges 235 metres before draining into the vast expanse of Lake Tanganyika.

We ate a "proper" meal in Mbala's Grasshopper Inn dining room, and slept in a comfortable bed, replete with clean sheets and devoid of bed bugs, in the Arms Hotel. Such luxury, compared to the Nakonde government resthouse that had been our home for the past fortnight. Then south to Kasama and Mpika.

We were now in the region, stretching from the Victoria Falls on the Zambezi up to Lake Tanganyika, made famous by Dr David Livingstone a century earlier. Dr Livingstone dedicated his life to evangelising, exploring and evolving the economy in the heart of Africa. Here he battled Arab slave-traders, hostile tribesmen and malaria.

Although unsuccessful in each of these endeavours during his own lifetime, Livingstone's sacrificial single-minded dedication inspired many others to follow in his footsteps.

On 1 May 1873, he died of malaria and dysentery near Lake Bangweulu, close to where we were now travelling. Although his body was transported back to London to be interred in Westminster Abbey, Livingstone's heart was buried under a tree in this country that he loved[38].

That we could travel here in relative safety just three generations later, a short 102 years, was nothing short of a miracle[39]. Realising our efforts are never in vain sustains us through the most difficult of life's circumstances. Although commitment and dedication might appear at times to be wasted, once a seed is planted, tended and nurtured, it will eventually grow to a strong tree and bear nourishing fruit.

Many caring and compassionate people are moved to help those less fortunate than ourselves, but they lack the opportunity. When an opportunity does present itself, we should seize it with gratitude.

Our year in Lusaka presented my wife with one such unique opportunity. While I was off designing water schemes, she wasn't permitted to engage in paid work. Instead, she volunteered to teach basic English, maths and craft to children in the Lusaka Hospital paediatric ward. Often, their parents slept under their beds and had to bring food for themselves and their children. Families were always wailing in the outdoors areas, as quite often the children died.

She also volunteered to teach sewing to young girls at the YWCA (Young Women's Christian Association), so they could make their own clothes and learn skills to help them gain employment later in life. This dedication to helping others, developed in Zambia, continues throughout her life.

Making good use of our year in Zambia, we visited most corners of the country: the Copperbelt (Ndola, through the mining towns and out to Solwezi), Northern Province (Kalambo Falls, Mbala and Nakonde), Kafue Game Park, and south to the Kariba Dam, unaware this area was gradually becoming a guerrilla hotspot in the escalating war with Rhodesia.

We also visited the magnificent Victoria Falls, Mosi-oa-Tunya, or "The Smoke That Thunders". It didn't disappoint. Unfortunately, at the time, we couldn't cross into Rhodesia via the iconic arch bridge spanning the mighty Zambezi River.

Many years later, in 2002, we visited Cape Town, Johannesburg and Pretoria (in South Africa), and Harare in Zimbabwe, as part of a holiday, lecture tour and inspection of micro-credit projects.

But not until 2019 did another southern African trip – this time to South Africa, Mozambique, Namibia, Botswana, Zimbabwe and Zambia – at last give us the opportunity to stride across the Zambezi Arch Bridge from Victoria Falls in Zimbabwe into Zambia. That journey continued by taxi to nearby Livingstone, and then by local bus for the full-day trip to Lusaka, the city where we'd made so many good friends over four decades earlier.

Back in September 1976, after a year of fruitful work, we departed Zambia for our home in Australia, taking the opportunity to drive through Malawi to Blantyre, Zomba and Lake Malawi, and to visit friends in Kenya, Mombasa and Nairobi.

Isolated back in Australia, we didn't get much meaningful news from Africa. By 1978, the war between the Rhodesian minority government and the various guerrilla organisations (Robert Mugabe's Mozambique-based ZANU (Zimbabwe African National Union), Joshua Nkomo's Zambian-based ZAPU (Zimbabwe African People's Union), and others was reaching a climax, with cross-border incursions by both sides to and from Mozambique and Zambia.

On 3 September 1978, cadres of ZIPRA, the armed wing of ZAPU, used surface-to-air missiles to shoot down an Air Rhodesia civilian passenger plane. Thirty-eight passengers were killed in the crash, and another ten men, women and children, who initially survived, were machine-gunned to death. Only eight of the original passengers survived to tell the story. The barbarity and brutality are beyond belief[40].

Rhodesian retribution was swift and coordinated, with the launch of Operation Gatling. On 19 October 1978, the Rhodesian Air Force's "Green Leader Raid" bombed the ZIPRA base at Westlands Farm, the helicopter-borne Rhodesian Light Infantry attacked the nearby Chikumbi base, and the Rhodesian SAS (Special Air Service) struck the ZIPRA base at Mkushi. Well over 1,500 people died that day.

Despite this violent retribution, Operation Gatling didn't prevent a recurrence of civilian planes being targeted. On 12 February 1979, a second civilian plane was shot down, killing all fifty-nine on board near Kariba[41].

It's truly chilling, half a century later, to listen to the original recording of the Green Leader's voice, supercharged with testosterone and oozing adrenalin, as he released the bombs that would kill hundreds of his fellow humans at Westlands Farm.

... I'm going to get them ... f-ing beautiful ... bombs gone. They're running. Beautiful. Jesus Christ, you ought to see them f-ers, them bombs are beautiful ... f-ing beautiful ... f-ing magnificent ... they're like f-ing ants running around there. [42]

War makes men into monsters, no matter which side they're on.

While there have been many atrocities and genocides since that time, this one struck a chilling chord for us. We'd left Zambia just two years earlier. In isolated Australia, we remained oblivious to these events.

Westlands Farm, the target of the "Green Leader" raid, was only a short 16 kilometres from our Lusaka townhouse.

Kazakhstan, 2016

Almaty is the largest city and former capital of Kazakhstan. Here we joined our formal three-week tour of three of the "stans" (Kazakhstan, Kyrgyzstan and Uzbekistan); here we met two travelling companions; and here we met the first of our two very professional guides. Travel in the company of friendly and adventurous companions is always fun, and we were blessed with the best.

Almaty is a clean, contemporary city with an impressive mountain backdrop on the northern edge of the Tian Shan Range. What impresses visitors most is the unexpected modernity of the place, with its tall buildings, moderate but well-disciplined traffic, and the apparent affluence of the people. The wealthy have homes nestling above the city in the foothills of the Tian Shan, while the less affluent have homes below the township on the edge of the vast Central Asian steppe.

As a tourist, some aspects of a country are always difficult to gauge. For example, Kazakhstan is considered by the World Bank and the World Economic forum to have a severe corruption problem, although we were oblivious of such concerns[43]. The city boasts a diversity of attractions, including the Green Market, the renovated Russian Orthodox Cathedral, the historical museum, the music museum and the war memorial. No ex-Soviet republic would be complete without one.

The highlights of this introductory tour included the skating rink, enfolded within the Tian Shan slopes, and the lookout, replete with entertainment area, overlooking the city. During our visit, an open-air opera rehearsal was being conducted at the lookout as the sun set over the city below, a timely reminder of the cultural diversity and richness of this region.

Leaving Almaty, we headed north-east by road, skirting the northern edge of the Tian Shan along the old Northern Silk Road. Although geographically the simplest route, this road was the least favoured by the traders of old, because it exposed the travellers to the onslaughts of marauding nomadic Mongols, sweeping down from the north, across the broad Asian steppe.

To avoid these attacks, the caravans often turned south, crossing the Tian Shan through a series of passes such as Charyn Canyon. This canyon is a 150-kilometre-long series of slashes of spectacular grandeur in the red sandstone plateau[44].

Today, the grasslands of the steppe are peaceful, and the northern corridor is currently favoured for the burgeoning east–west rail and road trade between Europe and China, rather than the canyon shortcut into the remote mountain region of north-eastern Kyrgyzstan.

Kyrgyzstan, 2016

Entry into Kyrgyzstan by this route is a gentle reminder that this mountainous republic is still very much a rural-based society, in which pastoralists venture into the hills each summer to tend their flocks. While modern caravans and trucks are in evidence, the yurt (the antecedent of the modern dome tent) is still the preferred accommodation option, while the horse is still the most effective means of managing the migrating flocks.

But it would be wrong to assume all rural activities are stuck in the past. We were warmly welcomed to dinner at a modern horse-stud, owned and operated by a proud husband-and-wife team who'd built a flourishing business during the twenty-five years since independence. With three horses entered in the second World Nomad Games in nearby Cholpon-Ata, this couple had much justification for pride.

The northern Kyrgyzstan area boasts many attractions, including the Jeti Oguz Valley and Chon-Kemin National Park, and we enjoyed a couple of laid-back days of sight-seeing.

But my fondest memory of this holiday was our visit to Issyk-Kul Lake, with its clear, calm and cool waters. This vast aquatic expanse, set high in the northern Tian Shan Mountains of Central Asian Kyrgyzstan, gives weary travellers an opportunity to pause for a few days in an idyllic setting and reflect on the travel experiences of previous decades. Stepping back in time is a luxury busy modern Australians rarely indulge in, but the serenity of this place affords both time and location to reflect on the past, as it surely must have done for travellers and traders for millennia.

United Kingdom, 1974

I was a child of the '50s, as was my wife, both baby-boomers and the eldest offspring of hard-working middle-class parents from Brisbane's burgeoning northern suburbs. Skip forward two decades to our wedding, plus a couple of months to adjust to married life, and we started a life peppered with world travel and adventure.

Like many other boomers, we took advantage of the affordable and fast international air travel of the 1970s. Thirty hours in a jet (no matter how uncomfortable) was more convenient than the slow voyage by ship experienced by previous generations. Travel in many parts of Asia was neither comfortable nor safe at this time, so we travelled initially to Europe, only later exploring other parts of the globe, including Africa, Asia, Pacific and the Americas.

Within one week of arriving in London, we'd rented a flat, purchased a new Kombi van and had full-time jobs ... too easy! Although travel in the 1970s was simpler than today, it had its challenges.

Mobile phones didn't exist. Telecommunications with Australia were expensive and, therefore, rare. Normal communication was by aerogram, a lightweight sheet of paper that folded into a pre-stamped envelope, whose delivery took up to a month. Credit cards weren't in common use, which meant travellers' cheques had to suffice. Passports were required at every border, and each country had its own (pre-Euro) currency.

The normal tool for engineering calculations was the slide rule. Personal computers hadn't yet been invented and handheld calculators were only just becoming affordable. In fact, I bought my first simple hand-held calculator in London and purchased a manual typewriter, which served me reliably for the next decade.

But travel was our passion. Although we were living and working in London, our weekends and holidays of 1974 were spent driving and camping in all parts of the United Kingdom.

Belfast at the height of The Troubles was our first taste of sectarian violence ... barricades, bomb checks and armoured cars ... but it was all requisite experience for future travels.

Spain, 1975

The summer of 1975, the open road and 100 days to "do" Europe. We crossed the Channel on March 1, headed south through France, across the Pyrenees at Andorra and into Spain. Then through Barcelona and around the coast

– Tarragona, the 13th century Knights Templar castle of Peñiscola, Sagunto, Valencia, Benidorm and Murcia.

Here we left the coast and headed towards Granada. As you rise, first into the hill country and then into the mountains, the orange orchards yield to the sparse tufts of grass reminiscent of the drier parts of our homeland. The beauty of the snow-capped Sierra Nevada, framed by the pretty pink of the peach orchards, dominates the landscape.

Venturing onto smaller side-roads brings its own rewards, with sights and experiences not encountered elsewhere. In 1975, this part of Spain was still very poor, the first of our many glimpses of rural poverty. In the small villages where houses nestled in caves, donkeys laboured under produce-laden wicker baskets and elderly, black-clad women were similarly laden with heavy loads balanced dexterously atop their heads.

The 15th century was a turning point in world history. During the 1430s, the Chinese repudiated the outward expansion of earlier Ming emperors, leading ultimately to their humiliating subjugation in the 19th century by expansive European powers.

The fall of Constantinople in 1453 to the Ottoman Sultan Mehmed II sealed the Muslim domination of Asia Minor and beyond. The European Renaissance flowered, proclaiming the victory of arts and science over superstition, and the fall of Spanish Granada to Christian forces secured Europe's southern flank.

Here in Granada in 1492, Emir Muhammad XII, the last Muslim ruler in the Iberian Peninsula, surrendered to the Catholic monarchs, Queen Isabella and King Ferdinand, confirming Christian domination of a united Spain, which would conquer the New World in the same year.

This, in turn, led to the spread of European culture through-out the world, and European domination for the next 500 years. Not until the devastation of the 20th-century world wars and the accelerated growth in technology would so many changes occur in such a short period.

Belying the optimism of a tolerant transfer of power from Muslim to Christian rulers, which should have guaranteed freedom of religion to the Muslim and Jewish residents of Granada, Christian intolerance took hold.

Just ten years later, the Muslims and Jews were forced, under threat of violence, to convert or to emigrate[45].

Notwithstanding its violent past, the beauty of Granada surpassed all our expectations. The Alhambra fortress, with its Moorish architecture unknown in Gothic Europe, towered over the township crouching in the shadows below. The tranquillity of the Generalife Gardens sprang to life as a sprinkling of snow enhanced its natural beauty. Falling snow may seem no big deal to residents of colder climes, but for us, a couple of young Queenslanders who'd never witnessed snow falling, it was simply magic.

Next, we made our way to Seville, made wealthy by the New World plunder of 16th-century conquistadors, and then further west towards the Portuguese border. But here our plans came unstuck.

On 11 March 1975 (the day before we were due to cross), the Portuguese Carnations Revolution came to a head. Army supporters of General Spinola attempted a coup, which collapsed within hours, as armed workers and soldiers united to hunt down the coup plotters[46].

Uncharacteristically, wisdom overruled the impulsiveness of our normal travel plans, and we hastily deviated from the

Portuguese border back towards Madrid. A lucky escape, perhaps. But this 1975 Portuguese revolution would also affect our future, in ways that we couldn't yet anticipate.

Timor Leste, 2004

As Portugal dissolved into chaos, it abandoned its colonies around the world. Mozambique and Angola, wracked by civil war, would become the haven for Zimbabwe terrorists/freedom-fighters, complicating our future time in Zambia. Not until 2019 could we visit Mozambique as part of our return to South Africa, Namibia, Botswana, Zimbabwe and our old haunts in Zambia.

The former Portuguese colony of Timor Leste (half of a small island within the Indonesian archipelago) also sank into violence before being occupied by the Indonesian military.

The Timor Gap, that area of open sea between Timor and Australia, is rich in oil and natural gas. So, when Australia and Indonesia couldn't agree on the location of the sea-bed boundary, the separatist aspirations of a significant proportion of the local population suited Australia's purpose very well, and Australia enthusiastically provided political and then military support for their independence. Thus, Timor Leste was born as the poorest country in South-East Asia, a more "satisfactory" sea-bed boundary was negotiated, and Australian companies began "pumping gas".

But when revelations of Australian espionage later surfaced, relations soured and Timor Leste launched successful litigation in the Permanent Court of Arbitration in The Hague to have the treaty overturned. Not quite the outcome most Australians had expected!

In 2004, between the bouts of sporadic violence, I visited Timor Leste to observe Australian-funded microfinance projects and village construction. My father had served in this part of Timor in the war in 1942, as a commando in the 2/4th Commando Squadron. They had been set ashore from the naval destroyer *Voyager*, to reinforce remnants of the 2/2nd Commando Squadron, the famous Sparrow Force, and to continue their guerrilla operations in the hills behind Japanese-occupied Dili.

But such operations don't always run to plan. During the landing, the ship ran aground, was bombed and subsequently scuttled.[47] The joint commando forces then carried on their clandestine operations for another four months before being evacuated. This retreat required the commandos who were sufficiently fit, including my father, to swim out through the surf of Betano Bay to waiting boats for the final escape on the naval destroyer *Arunta*.

Now I wandered about the quiet little village of Aileu, high in the Timor hills behind Dili, the same area where my father had served, sixty-two years previously. But I was here not to commit sabotage, but to witness the rebuilding of communities. How times change, and how fortunate are we modern Australians to have the opportunity to carry out acts of construction rather than acts of destruction.

Southern Europe, 1975

I have strayed too far from the narrative of our 1975 European road trip. By now we were used to free camping, but this is not such a smart practice in a region frequented by Basque terrorists.

A late-night visit by the military was the first of several such encounters with police or military during the next three months, but hey ... when you're in your twenties, you're bullet-proof.

Next came a loop through Italy and a run down the Dalmatian coast into sunny Greece. Here, among the ruins of ancient Greece, my newly acquired infatuation with history bloomed into a full-blown passion that would last the rest of my days.

During the remainder of this trip, we visited most European countries, many of which we'd revisit multiple times during the following decades. History on more history; I couldn't get enough. But for now, we were about to cross the border from Greece into Türkiye.

Türkiye, 1975

The year before, in 1974, a Greek-backed coup in Cyprus had drawn Greece and Türkiye into a brief war during which Turkish troops occupied a significant proportion of the island. Now the two countries faced off over a Cypriot cease-fire line. The temperature on the Greek–Turkish border was also rather frosty.

But cross we did and, eventually, we made our way down the peninsula to Gallipoli (Gelibolu), that place so sacred to the memory of fallen Australians. Although 1975 was well before the era when a "visit to Anzac Cove" was a popular rite-of-passage for young Aussies, the magnetism of mystique, history and calamity of the peninsula were still irresistible[48].

The serenity of Lone Pine Cemetery helps soothe the rawness of this location's violent history. But it's a place of great tragedy and suffering for many Australian families, including my own. My great-uncle[49], the only son of my great-grandparents, and the only brother of my grandmother and her three sisters, was a twenty-three-year-old schoolteacher from Brisbane who'd volunteered as a private in the 9ᵗʰ Infantry Battalion, sent first to Egypt and then to Gallipoli.

Military tradition was strong in our family, his father having risen to the rank of major through the Boer War in the early 1900s. Although the average age of sergeants was twenty-eight years (only three years older than their charges), my great-uncle's military background and teaching experience ensured he rose quickly from private on enlistment, to corporal before the month's end. He was subsequently promoted to sergeant by mid-January 1915, a model of military merit.

Just eight months after enlisting, in the cold darkness of the pre-dawn of 25 April 1915, my great-uncle was among the first wave of Australian soldiers who struggled ashore at Anzac Cove and up the steep cliffs fronting the beach. Although the soldiers had been instructed not to fire from the beach for fear of hitting others already scaling the cliffs of Plugges Plateau immediately inland, my great-uncle was hit in the back by a shot fired by an Australian on the beach, just 20 minutes after landing. [50] [51]

My great-grandparents lost their eldest child, their only son, while my grandmother and her sisters lost their only brother.

After a bitter eight-month campaign, the invading allied troops withdrew without achieving their objective. In 1975, we were on the very spot where these Australians had invaded and subsequently retreated, where they'd fought, died and been defeated.

World War 1 marked a decisive moment in Australian history, and to this day the ANZAC legend is promoted as the coming-of-age of a young nation. But contrary to popular Australian mythology, Australian deaths (although high) were only 8% of the total Gallipoli campaign deaths, which numbered well over one hundred thousand.

Yet the Gallipoli legend has lured generations of Australian youth into more than 100 years of almost continual warfare.

Türkiye, 2024

After an interval of nearly 50 years, we returned to Türkiye in late 2024 for a brief holiday. How it had changed! Now a vibrant modern society with a strong manufacturing base, Türkiye will clearly be a major world player in coming years.

We also had the opportunity to revisit Gallipoli and reflect on the futility of the 1915 campaign, the tragedy of my own family, and an Australian century of pointless wars.

Viet Nam, 2011

By 1975, Australia had been embroiled for over a decade in the Viet Nam War. *All the way with LBJ* …, Australian Prime Minister Harold Holt had proclaimed back in 1966 to United States President Lyndon Baines Johnson.

And so it was. Australia blindly followed its US master. Although the war became increasingly unpopular, our involvement dragged. Over 500 Australians died, with more than 2,000 wounded, and the war ended up costing Australia a staggering $218 million[52] [53] (approximately $3 billion in 2025 dollars). But even worse, Australians had contributed to the death of an estimated two million Vietnamese[54].

In 2011, we visited Viet Nam as tourists, eventually going to Ho Chi Minh City. In our travels we've been to some very confronting places – places that scream evil: Hiroshima, obliterated in 1945 by one of the two atomic bombs dropped by the Americans in the closing days of World War 2; the Jerusalem World Holocaust Remembrance Centre; and the Nazi death camps of Auschwitz and Dachau.

But the knowledge that we, as Australians (whether we served in the armed forces or not), were complicit in inflicting the horror depicted so vividly in the Ho Chi Minh City War Remnants Museum, still claws at our conscience. Millions of innocent men, women and children were slaughtered simply for the commercial gain of the political class of a remote super-power. I pray we'll never again allow such evil. And yet, in the 21st century, it's still happening.

Our first visit to Gallipoli was on 7 April 1975, almost sixty years after those fateful ANZAC dawn landings. Ironically, less than three weeks later, North Vietnamese troops dramatically entered Saigon (now called Ho Chi Minh City), defeating the South Vietnamese and, by association, the United States and Australia). Gallipoli had been repeated; Australia had been defeated ... again.

Gallipoli's Lone Pine Cemetery in 1975 was, for me, a turning point, the first time and the first place I'd really been confronted by the futility of war. The poignancy of the juxtaposition of our visit to Gallipoli and the fall of Saigon kickstarted our lifelong anti-war sentiment.

From that point on, the retreat from Gallipoli became symbolic of a necessary paradigm shift: a retreat from evil, when we pull back from the brink, turn our back on war and set a new course in the direction of peace. But so far, that goal has proved elusive.

Previous generations of Australians have heedlessly followed Britain into a series of remote conflicts: China's Boxer Uprising, the South African Boer War, the disastrous European

World War 1 and the European theatre of World War 2. Britain's post-war decline led to an unhealthy reliance on US "protection", based on the 1951 ANZUS Treaty of 1951. This has resulted, not in peace, but in our participation in conflicts scattered around the world, in places as diverse as Iraq, Afghanistan, Viet Nam and Korea.

My great-grandfather served in the Boer War, rising to the rank of major, and then to colonel during World War 1; my great-uncle, a sergeant, died a hero's death at Anzac Cove; my grandfather saw action in both World War 1 and World War 2 (including the 1944 Cowra breakout of Japanese POWs); my uncle (one of the first Australian officers to cross the Kokoda Track) was wounded and awarded the Military Cross [55] [56]; my cousin served in the SAS in Viet Nam; and my own father served as a commando in amphibious landings in Timor, New Guinea and the East Indies.

In short, my pedigree for military service was strong. But my father didn't talk much about his military service. Perhaps he chose not to remember the killing he must have witnessed and, quite likely, participated in.

Conscription was introduced in Australia in the 1960s to fill the quota of soldiers needed to satisfy the political promises made to help Americans prosecute their Vietnamese war. As a naïve nineteen-year-old, I'd willingly have gone, had my birthday come up in the conscription lottery.

But events don't always pan out the way you expect – fortuitously, in this case. I wasn't required to sign up. My lack of military service clearly limits my understanding of the moral and emotional pressures on those who must undertake the grim fighting that servicemen and servicewomen are compelled to execute.

But, on the positive side, this lack of focus on matters military enables me to contemplate the broader sweep of history.

As I write, my attention is particularly drawn to the disastrous events that unfolded in Afghanistan: the swift withdrawal of American (and Australian) support, the collapse of the government, the rapid Taliban victories, the frantic evacuations from Kabul airport and the appalling terrorist bombing by ISIS-K.

There was much media and public criticism of the withdrawal and the rescue missions, but this narrow focus on short-term tactical concerns puts at risk the proper consideration of the wider issues. In 2001, it was clear to anyone with even the most rudimentary knowledge of Central Asian history that a western invasion of Afghanistan would end in disaster. The "eagle" would be no more successful than the "bear" or the "lion" had been. In the latter half of the 2020s, it remains to be seen whether the "dragon" effectively fills the political vacuum.

Kyrgyzstan, 2016

2016 again, and I am on holiday in Karakol in Kyrgyzstan, nestled on the eastern edge of Issyk-Kul Lake, that huge reservoir of tranquillity. The history of Karakol is the history of Russian penetration of the region.

Founded on July 1 in 1869, it grew steadily with the arrival of Chinese Muslim Dungan refugees. Now, the twenty-first century tourists are the new invaders, besieging the old buildings, the wooden Russian Orthodox Cathedral (built to replace the previous stone building destroyed by earthquake), the timber Dungan Mosque with its intricate carvings, ingeniously built without the use of nails. But the Przhevalsky Museum, on the edge of Issyk-Kul Lake, offers the greatest intrigue.

Here in Karakol was our introduction to the players of the Great Game, those real people who lived the fantasies of Rudyard Kipling's fiction. The Great Game is the name given to the British and Russian intrigues and espionage as they vied for control of Central Asia in the 19th century, over 100 years before the similar American–British and Russian rivalry poisoned international cooperation in this same region again[57] [58].

In due course, I'd discover Younghusband, Stein, Stoddart, Conolly, Frunze, Bailey, Malleson, Dunsterville, Ibrahim, Enver – and Przhevalsky.

During the 18th and 19th centuries, Spain, Portugal and the Netherlands had suffered major losses of their overseas empires. France had been eclipsed by Britain, Russia and their allies in a series of wars, culminating in the rout of Napoleonic France in 1812 by the Russians, and in 1815 by the combined British, Prussian, Dutch and other allied forces.

By the late 1800s, Russia and Britain were the last two powers left standing, the leading players in the struggle for world domination – the superpowers of their age.

And now these players faced off in the Great Game. The Khyber Pass and the strategic corridors into Afghanistan, the rugged peaks and isolated valleys of the Himalayan chain, and the mysterious forbidding Tibetan Plateau provided the board on which this international chess game was played.

Przhevalsky versus Younghusband … the conquest of Tibet. That the former name of Karakol was Przhevalsk, invites explanation. Our 2016 museum tour started beside Issyk-Kul Lake, where a memorial is dedicated to the Russian explorer, Nicholay Przhevalsky, who died here of typhus in 1888. Already renowned for his journeys exploring Siberia, Mongolia, China,

Northern Tibet and Central Asia, Przhevalsky had sacrificed a life of comfort to his passion for exploration.

But his writings betray his adherence to the prevailing attitudes of European arrogance that accompanied such passion. He wrote: *Here you can penetrate anywhere, only not with the Gospels under your arm, but with money in your pocket, a carbine in one hand and a whip in the other. Europeans must use these to come and bear away in the name of civilisation all these dregs of the human race. A thousand of our soldiers would be enough to subdue all Asia from Lake Baikal to the Himalayas ...*

It is fitting that we, 21st-century citizens of the world, now repudiate such arrogance and inhumanity.

The Russian push into Tibet died with Przhevalsky on the shores of Issyk-Kul Lake, and it was a further fifteen years before their deadly enemies, the British, accomplished the first European penetration of Tibet to conquer Lhasa. From an early age, Francis Younghusband was destined to be one of the major players of the Great Game.

Born into a military family in India in 1863, Younghusband had, at twenty-four, participated with Henry James and Harry Fulford in a reconnaissance expedition in Manchuria and the Chinese Changbai Mountains. He then travelled west across China, along the old Silk Road through the arid Taklamakan Desert of the Tarim Basin to Kashgar, charted the Mustagh Pass, transited the Karakoram Range, Hindu Kush, the Pamir Plateau at the western end of the Himalayas, then continued south to Yarkand and Kashmir in northern India.

Perhaps one of the most celebrated incidents of Younghusband's career was his 1889 chance meeting, in the Yarkand Valley, with Bronislav Grombchevsky, a Polish officer in the Imperial Russian Army (and explorer and spy), who invited him to dinner in the Russian camp. Inhibitions suppressed by their shared vodka and brandy, the rival officers discussed the Great Game well into the night. After a show of Russian Cossack horsemanship was balanced by a demonstration of British Gurkha rifle drill, the opposing companies continued on their separate ways.

Younghusband, acting on the orders of the British Indian viceroy, Curzon, made other incursions into the Himalayas, culminating in the 1903 to 1904 invasion of Tibet. This well-organised and armed military invasion pitted rifles and machine guns against disorganised monks, armed only with flintlocks, swords and hoes.

The casualty count was five British and approximately 5,000 Tibetans killed. Younghusband forced the signing of the Treaty of Lhasa, only to have it subsequently repudiated by the British Government, which was, by that time, currying favour with the Chinese to promote coastal trade. International politics never was, and never will be, straightforward[59] [60] [61].

But I must return to our 2016 holiday. Travelling west from Karakol, the road skirts the northern shore of Issyk-Kul Lake, before exiting the valley through a mountain pass towards Shabdan in the Chong-Kemin National Park. A laid-back morning of horse-riding and sight-seeing preceded the resumption of the trek further west to the capital, Bishkek. Here the road significantly improves, compared to the pot-holed rural roads elsewhere in Kyrgyzstan.

Like other large cities of Central Asia, Bishkek is clean and tidy, complete with monuments and museums to commemorate the past twenty-five years since independence from the defunct Soviet Union. Although we weren't in the city for these celebrations, we were fortunate to witness the rehearsal: bands playing stirring martial music, precision marching and the salute taken from a couple of aged convertible automobiles.

Although an early-morning dash to the airport for our departure for Tashkent went smoothly, we received unsettling news. The Chinese embassy, close to our Bishkek hotel, had been bombed overnight by Uyghur separatists. Perhaps the tight security in neighbouring Xinjiang Province of western China had been warranted.

Asia–Pacific Region, 1985–2025

Clearing Tashkent airport in Central Asia, we met our new guide who proved over the next couple of days to be a most resourceful and caring travelling companion. First impressions of Tashkent were of broad, tree-lined streets, with hardly a trace of litter, for reasons that became apparent in the next couple of days.

For the time being, we settled down to a walking tour of the usual sights, first to the immaculate metro stations, trying hard to imitate the glitter of their Moscow counterparts, and then on to the Monument of Courage, commemorating the victims of the devastating 1966 earthquake.

This event wrought widespread devastation, destroying 80% of Tashkent, killing up to 200 people and leaving up to 300,000 homeless. Today, the only sign of the devastation is this monument, dedicated to the people who rebuilt the ruined city[62] [63].

The Tashkent earthquake and the subsequent Monument to Courage are reminders of both the fragility of human life and the resilience of the human spirit. Of course, natural disasters aren't confined to Central Asia, and devastating earthquakes, cyclones and tsunamis regularly wreak havoc throughout many parts of the world, including regions close to Australia.

For over four decades, my engineering career included the writing of Australian Standards, design manuals and building regulations. Many of these documents aim at ensuring the structural safety of buildings and other structures when subjected to extreme wind or seismic activity. While the importance of such standards, manuals and regulations shouldn't be underestimated, only when one visits the site of a natural disaster can the true scale of the human impact be appreciated.

On 26 December 2004, a massive magnitude 9.1 earthquake occurred off the Indonesian coast near Banda Aceh, triggering the Indian Ocean tsunami. The resulting waves rose up to thirty metres, the height of a six-storey building. Over 223,000 people perished (183,172 confirmed dead and 40,320 missing), over 600,000 homes were destroyed and approximately 1.8 million people were displaced. Through no fault of their own, these unfortunate people were just in the wrong place at the wrong time.

The generosity of the citizens of many countries resulted in huge rebuilding programs that mushroomed across the region, instituted by many NGOs.

By mid-2005, one such large NGO[64] had identified a need for technical auditing of their house construction, and management auditing of their program execution. I undertook two pro bono auditing assignments for this organisation – one to Thailand and Indonesia, and the other to Sri Lanka and India. The extent of the devastation I witnessed was overwhelming but so, too, was the intensity of the rebuilding programs.

But not all parts of this region were peaceful. Although the tsunami had temporarily submerged hostilities, they soon flared again in some hotspots[65].

The road approaching Trincomalee in eastern Sri Lanka was at that time lined with military watchtowers, spaced strategically about a kilometre apart, to provide desperately needed security against night-time raids by the Tamil Tiger (LTTE) separatist terrorist group. Although the government controlled the cities, the Tamil Tigers effectively controlled the countryside. Stickers on our vehicle proclaimed we weren't carrying guns, and a large flag demonstrated our status as representatives of a peaceful NGO.

Even so, our movements were partially curtailed. Our driver, a Muslim man, was prevented from entering one of the refugee camps for fear of sparking a riot among the displaced Hindu Tamil residents. It's difficult for us, from peaceful, tolerant Australia, to gauge the extent to which sectarian hostility clouds the judgement of so many people whose interests would be better served by compassion, cooperation and tolerance.

Fortunately, not all hostilities were resumed after the tsunami and reconstruction phase. Banda Aceh and the surrounding countryside had been notorious for violence perpetrated by the Free Aceh Movement (GAM) and government retribution, resulting in over 15,000 deaths over a thirty-year period. By the time of our 2005 visit, hostilities had ceased and an uneasy peace presaged a more permanent move from military activity towards political engagement[66].

In the early 1980s, I became friends with a leading Indian Christian theologian with a hands-on approach to practical pastoral care[67]. Through this initial contact, we have made many other lasting friendships with Indian nationals, many of whom we've visited in India and others we've hosted as they migrated to Australia.

Over a forty-year period, I've been privileged to visit India many times for work, tourism and humanitarian aid projects. India is the most exotic place imaginable, with a culture that can simultaneously appal and inspire. To know India is to know yourself.

I also became friendly with, and inspired by, a dynamic Australian philanthropist and future Senior Australian of the Year[68] [69] [70], who founded a leading Australian NGO and established micro-credit programs for the poor around the world. Such people were my role models.

In 1993, I attended an international NGO conference in Thailand. Here I met and became good friends with a fellow conference delegate and traveller, a retired British Ambassador to Indonesia[71]. The real highlight was our subsequent small-group trip through remote parts of the Philippines and Indonesia, including Sulawesi, Sumatra, Bali, Luzon and Mindanao.

This trip was a turning point in so many ways. We visited Manila's infamous Smoky Mountain (subsequently closed in shame by the Philippines government), where the poor had, at that time, lived, worked and died among the city's garbage.

But in the remote Mindanao city of Cagayan de Oro was where the inequity of poverty struck an indelible personal chord. As I stood in the sunlight on the edge of a putrid pool at the local garbage dump, a local man quietly carried out his daily ablutions close by. He was condemned to suffer the indignity of grinding poverty, while I luxuriated in the comfort and safety of undeserved relative wealth.

From that day onwards, I vowed to use my professional skills to benefit the poor – a commitment that led to leadership of an Australian international volunteer NGO[72] [73]. For over two decades, I served as the voluntary president and, for most of that time, was also the pro bono CEO.

The reward for almost three decades of pro bono work has been to witness appreciative villagers during the construction of water-reticulation systems in remote Solomon Islands, latrines in the Philippines, Papua New Guinea community health buildings and school buildings, funding of emergency housing in Fiji, and construction of cyclone anchorages for village housing in the Cook Islands.

But intangible benefits also accrue. To observe first-hand the diversity in social and demographic circumstances in each of these locations is truly educational. The declining population and infrastructure in Mangaia (traditionally known as A'ua'u Enua), the most southerly and remote of the Cook Islands, provides a striking contrast with the burgeoning population and strong social cohesion within the Papua New Guinea Highlands tribal groups[74] [75].

My first experience in the Solomon Islands, in 2007, was also in response to an earthquake and tsunami. Although this disaster was on a much smaller scale than the Indian Ocean tsunami, my involvement was more immediate, planning the execution of village rebuilding on the western end of Gizo Island. Of even greater significance, this trip served as the precursor to our much wider involvement, spread over many years, in building water and sanitation services in the remote islands of Ranongga and Vella Lavella.

My increasing involvement in development projects in the Asia–Pacific region led, incidentally, to a paid consultancy for the government of Kiribati. The international aid agency of the Republic of China (Taiwan) was constructing a large hospital on the remote island of Tabiteuea North. The aid project was a bid to curry favour with the Pacific Islands nation, as Taiwan became increasingly diplomatically isolated in the international community.

But the Taiwanese tried to cut corners, constructing the thirteen hospital buildings and forty-five small houses directly on the coral sand – *without building concrete footings*. What should the Kiribati government do? Accept the almost-completed project, or demand the buildings be demolished? My task was to advise the government.

After a week of inspections and rudimentary soil tests on site, and a further week in consultation in the capital, Tarawa, I recommended that the buildings remain, provided the Kiribati government closely monitor them and hold a significant retention bond to cover rectification of possible future problems.

While this advice provided a solution for the immediate structural issues, other problems were facing the Kiribati government. No funds were available for staff or equipment, the electrical supply was unstable and sewage disposal was polluting the groundwater, so the hospital stood unused for several years.

The Tabiteuea North hospital project serves as a warning of the many pitfalls surrounding international aid programs. When such aid is tied to international politics and diplomacy, there is always a risk that the outcome may not be in the best interests of the recipients.

Infrastructure construction should only be undertaken when there are commitment and capacity for the beneficiaries to properly use the infrastructure for its intended purpose. Beneficiaries (or their consultants) must be prepared to closely monitor the delivery of any aid package and must insist on the complete fulfilment of donor commitments. Infrastructure construction, whether in the form of aid or otherwise, and, no matter how remote, must be designed, constructed, supervised and inspected by competent, honest building professionals. These were the principles that guided our NGO[76] as we provided construction aid to the South Pacific during the next two decades.

Pro bono professional services work would take me to Thailand, Indonesia, India, Sri Lanka, Papua New Guinea, Vanuatu, Tonga, Timor Leste, Fiji and New Caledonia. Design and hands-on construction work engaged me in establishing and constructing prototype community buildings, village water reticulation, latrines, cyclone shelters and cyclone anchorages in Papua New Guinea, the Solomon Islands, the Philippines and the Cook Islands.

Of these, the most satisfying were in Papua New Guinea and the Solomon Islands. Here, the bonds of friendship, created as volunteer Australian professionals working closely with aspiring Indigenous village leaders to design and construct community infrastructure, lasted decades and transcended thousands of kilometres.

Papua New Guinea, 2015–2018

My most interesting pro bono project also occurred in response to an earthquake, this time in Hela Province in the Papua New Guinea Highlands. In 2018, a magnitude 7.6 earthquake devastated the area, killing over 200 people, but there were further complications.

Ongoing tremors were still occurring, and local tribal violence and banditry were contributing to continuing fatalities. Bands of local youths roamed about, armed with guns and machetes, and buildings were being torched. The United Nations aid contingent was evacuated pending the arrival of the army to secure the area over a week later.

I was there on a tight schedule to carry out pro bono building inspections of damaged schools, clinics, churches and houses on behalf of the Catholic diocese. After spending a couple of nights as a guest of the Catholic bishop[77] and the Capuchin Franciscan monks in Mendi, we decided to venture further west into the devastated region.

Three of us (an ex-pat Indian priest, my colleague[78] from the neighbouring PNG Western Highlands Province, and I) set out by road for Tari and Komo in Hela Province. The building inspections were successfully completed in four days, but not before we experienced a further tremor.

We also had to avoid violence and various perils, bypassing a burning building torched by disgruntled locals, meeting some gun-toting youths, being confronted on the road by a large group in full tribal costume and armed with guns, bows and arrows, off to do battle with a rival group, and hastily exiting one area when my frantic colleague called, "Get back in the car … someone is coming with a gun!"

Not all PNG experiences involved such excitement, though. In 2015, I was invited by my friend to speak (via an interpreter) at the "crying ceremony" for his deceased father. I was the only non-Indigenous person among the 600-plus Indigenous mourners, who individually and collectively were demonstrating great outpourings of grief. That my friend and his community had accorded me such an honour by inviting me to speak was humbling.

Much of this narrative describes the hardships faced by people who suffer because of war, violence and natural disasters.

But it's also a salute to the dedication of men and women who labour tirelessly through NGOs, churches and other organisations to help our neighbours in the developing countries of the Asia–Pacific region. Their efforts are pivotal in fostering goodwill among the diverse people of the world and will ultimately be key to ensuring the victory of peace over war.

Uzbekistan, 2016

Back to 2016, and resuming our walking tour of Tashkent, we moved from the Monument to Courage earthquake memorial to the precinct dedicated to the sacrifices of the soldiers during World War 2 (1941 – not 1939 – to 1945), mandatory in any former Soviet republic. And then it got interesting.

Due to a succession of Independence Day wreath-laying ceremonies, our access to the Independence Monument via the main entrance was restricted. Undeterred, we skirted the official activities by moving towards the side gate, only to be accosted not by the police, as expected, but by a couple of television crews.

"What do you think of Uzbekistan? What do you like about Tashkent? What would you like to say to the people?" … and so on.

Never the shrinking violets, and undeterred that we'd been in the country for a whole four hours, we rose to the occasion.

"Thank you for the warm welcome. What a beautiful city. Congratulations on twenty-five years of independence … blah, blah, blah …"

While we know roughly what we said, to this day we've no idea how the voice-over translated it. It must have been okay though, because there were no adverse repercussions. It was 31 August 2016, a significant date[79].

Like all modern countries, Uzbekistan enjoys the luxury of a fast train service, the new way to travel the Silk Road. The quick journey through the flat farmlands, from modern Tashkent to historic Samarkand, was both relaxing and interesting.

For nearly three millennia, Samarkand has endured invasion after invasion. Most likely founded between the 8th and 7th centuries BCE, the city was incorporated into the Persian Achaemenid Empire, from 550 to 330 BCE, as the Sogdian Satrapy.

Next came the Greek, Alexander, in 329 BCE, and his Hellenistic successors, the Seleucid Empire, the Greco-Bactrian Kingdom and Kushan Empire. The Sassanians conquered Samarkand around 260 CE, followed by the Hephthalites and the Turks, who were obliged to pay tribute to the Chinese Tang Dynasty.

During this period a number of religions flourished in Samarkand, including Buddhism, Zoroastrianism, Hinduism, Manichaeism, Judaism and Nestorian Christianity. Eventually the Arab Muslim armies of the Baghdad Umayyad Caliphate defeated the Turks to capture Samarkand around 710 CE. Ruled successively by the Arab Abbasids and then the Samanids, Samarkand eventually succumbed to the Turkic Karakhanids, who were followed by other Turkic peoples, the Seljuks and the Khwarazm-Shahs.

In 1220, the Mongol Genghis Khan (Temujin) conquered and pillaged Samarkand, which suffered a further Mongol sack by Khan Baraq.

In 1370, Timur (a.k.a. Tamerlane) expelled the Mongols and made Samarkand the capital of his empire. Following in the footsteps of Alexander and Genghis Khan, Timur set out to expand his empire from modern-day Türkiye in the west, to China in the east. While Timur went close to this goal, his achievements were ephemeral.

On Timur's death in 1405, the empire fractured, finally supplanted in 1505 by the Shaybanid Uzbek warriors, followed by Nadir Shah, the Ashtarkhanids and the Manghy emirs of Bukhara.

Samarkand passed to Russian control in 1886, was under Soviet suzerainty from 1925, and finally became part of independent Uzbekistan in 1991[80].

Of these invaders, Timur had the most lasting effect on Samarkand. Although the ravages of subsequent invasions, along with the natural elements, haven't been kind to his magnificent buildings, many have now been restored and serve as the symbols linking modern Uzbekistan with its Timurid past.

These include Timur's Mausoleum, the Registan madrasas of Ulugh Beg, Sher-Dor and Tilya Kori and the Mosque of Bibi Khanym, Timur's favourite wife.

Of religious significance, the Shah-i-Zinda avenue of mausoleums, constructed from the 9th to the 14th centuries, and then the 19th century, includes a mausoleum commemorating Kussam ibn Abbas, cousin of the prophet Muhammad[81].

On the death of Timur in 1405, his son, Shah Rukh, became ruler, based in Herat, with his sixteen-year-old son, Ulugh Beg, installed in 1409 as the governor in Samarkand. By 1411, Ulugh Beg was the sovereign ruler of the whole Mavarannahr khanate.

Ulugh Beg was no ordinary ruler; he was also a prominent scientist and an astronomer of note. Without the aid of a telescope, and working with a 36-metre-radius sextant built within his Samarkand observatory, he achieved remarkable results.

In 1437, Ulugh Beg compiled the accurate Zij-i-Sultani star catalogue of 994 stars and determined the length of the sidereal year as 365 days, 6 hours, 10 minutes and 8 seconds – an error of only 58 seconds. He later corrected this to 365 days, 5 hours, 49 minutes, and 15 seconds – an error of only 25 seconds – making it more accurate than Copernicus's estimate, which had an error of 30 seconds.

He also calculated the tilt of the Earth's axis to be 23.52 degrees, more accurate than later measurements by both Copernicus and Tycho Brahe[82]. However, from the perspective of modern Uzbekistan, it's 14th century Timur, not Ulugh Beg, who is the local hero.

With a fearsome reputation for cruelty, Timur was ruthlessly efficient in achieving his goals. For him, the ends always justified the means. The enormous and beautiful mausoleums, madrasas and mosques testify to his wealth and prestige.

It's said Timur was the role model for Uzbekistan's initial President, Islam Karimov. First as Communist Party boss during the Soviet era, and then as President during the first twenty-five years of independence, Karimov ruthlessly quashed all opposition to mould his country into a modern efficient state, with considerable success.

The IHF (International Hospital Federation), Human Rights Watch, Amnesty International, United States Department of State and Council of the European Union all defined Uzbekistan as "an authoritarian state with limited civil rights", and expressed profound concern about "wide-scale violation of virtually all basic human rights"[83]. In spite of (or perhaps because of) this fearsome reputation, Karimov appeared to be loved by a substantial proportion of the population.

The Uzbek national fetish for urban cleanliness is achieved by mobilising (or is it coercing?) large teams of cleaners (mainly women) to assiduously apply their labour-intensive sweeping skills to this task. Perhaps there's but a fine line between civic pride and mindless obedience.

Our second day in Samarkand, 2 September 2016, was disrupted. From mid-morning, we were amazed to see an incredible cleaning frenzy under way. Teams of women, some well-dressed and wearing high heels, others in more functional clothing, were literally hand-washing the pavements, sweeping and removing rubbish. And on a more robust scale, asphalt was being laid and concrete being poured, all under the watchful eye and supervision of the police and civil guards.

Clearly something had been afoot from early in the morning. As early as 27 August, there had been internet whispers that President Karimov was gravely ill (no, he had actually died; no, he was recovering; no, he was in perfect health). But still the government wouldn't clarify the situation. It was fascinating to follow the internet speculation as to whether he had – or hadn't – passed away.

President Karimov's 25th anniversary speech was read on television on 1 September by a presenter who stated that public support was helping him recover. According to a later government report, on September 2 President Karimov "… was in [a] stable neurological condition in a coma … He suffered another cardiac arrest at 20:15 UZT on 2 September and attempts to resuscitate him failed, and he was pronounced dead at 20:55 UZT"[84][85].

Yet we'd witnessed, a good ten hours earlier, the well-advanced program in Samarkand of concrete construction at the funeral site, the frenzied cleaning of the city, the laying of asphalt in access roads and the incredible build-up in security. While project managers deserve great respect, to have mobilised this level of construction and maintenance activity, even before the president's official death announcement, represents fantastic forward planning.

The news late on 2 September that the President had died and would be buried the next day in Samarkand, barely three kilometres from our hotel, wasn't necessarily welcome. The funeral would be a huge international event.

That night, Samarkand went into lockdown. Police and guards were bussed in from other cities and stationed at fifty-metre intervals along all the major roads. Unauthorised persons weren't allowed in, and any movement out was severely restricted.

Our main problem was there was no indication of how long the lockdown would remain in place. With travel commitments elsewhere, we decided it was time to break out. Again, blessing our foresight in travelling with only carry-on baggage, we trudged four kilometres to where we could hire taxis (at inflated rates) to drive us at high speed through the maze of Samarkand's back streets to where our ongoing transport was supposed to be waiting.

The vehicle lurched to a halt in a cloud of dust and shower of stones. Unexpected road repairs ensured no easy exit. Quickly reversing, the taxi was soon weaving its way back through the labyrinth of narrow alleys, carefully avoiding the army and police checkpoints. After two hours, when we had almost circumnavigated the city, we escaped the cordon and were free.

At no time were we in any significant danger, and the inconvenience was fully compensated by the experience, but this incident was disconcerting. That an entire people could be mobilised to such demonstrations of apparent "affection" was something reminiscent of Europe in the 1930s. Was the whole population still being manipulated from the grave?

And where was the media scrutiny of this sequence of events? Perhaps they were interviewing a pair of naïve tourists on trivia, instead of focusing on the deadly political manoeuvring that accompanied the ill health and death of an authoritarian president.

The excesses of the Central Asian authoritarian regimes are a stark reminder of the fragility of liberal democracy. While vote-rigging, intimidation and torture are the most obvious abuses inflicted by governments, ordinary people must also accept responsibility for compliant obedience as their freedom of independent thought is progressively stripped away.

People get the government they deserve, and must guard against the abuse of liberal democracy. Instead of wasting valuable airtime screening trivial interviews with a couple of ill-informed tourists, the Uzbekistan television media should have provided a much more valuable public service by investigating and reporting issues such as the power struggle leading up to and following the death of the president, and its implications for national security and wellbeing.

Media laziness and bias should be at the forefront of our concerns … we mustn't be brainwashed by a biased media. It was claimed the new president, Shavkat Miriziyoyev, won an overwhelming 88.6% of the subsequent vote. Not surprisingly, western monitors reported electoral fraud, with the Office for Democratic Institutions and Human Rights stating the election underscored the need for comprehensive reforms in Uzbekistan[86].

Let us hope the new president doesn't incite ethnic violence as a means of rallying the country. If he does so, the flashpoints will most likely be the Kyrgyzstan/Uzbekistan border and the Fergana Valley, both important as emerging choke-points in China's trade route expansion.

In many parts of the world, ethnic and religious differences are the trigger for violence and repression; individual fears and selfishness are reflected in national paranoia and national selfishness. Terrorism is now rife throughout the world, but it's born of (and feeds on) the intrigues and wars prosecuted by countries.

Our closest recent brush with terrorism was the tension of China's Xinjiang Province and the subsequent bombing of the Chinese embassy in Bishkek, both attributed to Uyghur separatists.

Just as the United States armed the Mujahideen (including Osama bin Ladin) to fight the Russians during the 1980s, so too China trained and armed Uyghur fighters for the same purpose[87][88]. China now has a major problem with armed Uyghurs.

The greatest threat to world security is state sponsorship of war and violence.

After the excitement of Samarkand, our holiday reverted to a reasonably conventional tour. The road climbed over the mountains to Timur's birthplace, Shakhrisabz, then south to within forty kilometres of the Afghanistan border, before turning west through the steppe to Bukhara.

Like Samarkand, the ancient city of Bukhara was a major trading centre of the Silk Road, and its wealth and power are reflected in the restored architecture. No tourist should miss the Ismail Samani Mausoleum, Khiva Gate, Friday Mosque, the towering Kalyan Minaret, Kukeldash and Abdul Aziz Khan madrasas, the Char Minar and the peaceful Lyab-i Hauz Pool.

But the highlight of Bukhara is the Ark Fortress, the former seat of power of the emir, and the backdrop for one of the grisly incidents of the Great Game. Colonel Charles Stoddart of the British East India Company arrived in Bukhara in December 1838, to thwart Russian expansion in the khanates of Khiva, Kokand and Bukhara. But Stoddart managed, with characteristic British arrogance, to offend the emir Nasrullah Khan, resulting in Stoddart's four-year imprisonment. After many months in the "bug-pit" dungeon of the Bukhara Ark Fortress, the emir gave Stoddart a choice: convert to Islam or sacrifice your head.

Stoddart chose the former, and from that time his conditions improved. He was moved to house arrest and recommenced his pro-British anti-Russian negotiations with the emir.

But in November 1841, events worsened. Captain Arthur Conolly, a devout evangelical Protestant who aimed to bring Christianity and British control to Central Asia, arrived on a lone rescue mission. He'd sought British Government assistance, but they were occupied otherwise, namely, forcing the Qing Chinese to import opium[89].

So too, the British East India Company was embroiled in the disastrous invasion of Afghanistan[90], which ultimately resulted in the rout of the entire British garrison (save one survivor) in Kabul on 5 January 1842. This event had dramatically demonstrated the British ineptness in controlling Central Asian politics and had dire consequences for Stoddart and Conolly.

Like Stoddart, Conolly had by this time managed to alienate Nasrullah Khan, and both Britons were to pay the ultimate price. On 17 June 1842, just five months after the British defeat in Kabul, first Stoddart, and then Conolly, were publicly beheaded in the square before the Bukhara Ark Fortress.

Despite public outrage, British interest was elsewhere and they didn't retaliate. Thus, the entire Central Asian region slipped from British influence to Russian control for the next century-and-a-half[91] [92].

Between Bukhara and Khiva, the traveller becomes painfully aware of the hardships that faced the trading caravans of yesteryear.

Thanks to a partially built new highway, the Kara Kum (Black Desert) and the Kyzyl Kum (Red Desert) are traversed in less than a day. Such a journey would previously have taken three months by camel, with oases providing periodic respite along the way. To the south, you can see Turkmenistan, across the mighty Amu Darya, the Oxus River, renowned from Alexander's Central Asian foray.

With a history stretching back millennia, the walled city of Khiva was once a key trading centre on the Silk Road. Substantially rebuilt in the past few centuries, Khiva presents the tourist with a smorgasbord of mausoleums, madrasas, mosques and minarets: Kunya-Ark Palace, the Madrasa of Muhammad Amin-Khan, the Juma Mosque with its ornately carved forest of timber columns, the iconic, unfinished Kalta Minar Minaret, the 19th century soaring Islam Khoja Minaret and so on[93].

The Mausoleum of Pakhlavani Mahmoud Rubais, the 13th-century Sufi teacher and professional wrestler, is a reminder this region spawned many poets, teachers, thinkers and scientists, which we tend to ignore in our focus on western modernity.

Our exit from Uzbekistan was via Tashkent again, where we farewelled our travelling companions. After a fortnight of full-on travelling, it was good to chill out for a couple of days, riding the Tashkent metro, exploring the shops and simply walking the leafy streets.

We thoroughly enjoyed our Central Asian trip. We'd witnessed the unfolding of some political drama and learned a lot about the people and their place in history.

As if to footnote this wonderful experience, while waiting in the crowd to be admitted to Tashkent International Airport, we witnessed an unfortunate man plucked from the crowd by the police and dragged away. We have no idea why, whether he was a terrorist or a tout, but we could hear him still screaming as he disappeared. Life is still fragile in many parts of the world.

China, 2017

All serious explorers of the Silk Road must visit Xi'an. From this ancient city of central China, we began the second year of our Silk Road odyssey, the two-year China/Central Asia/Russia/eastern Europe holidays.

For well over a millennium, Xi'an (Chang'an) was the on-and-off imperial capital of the Zhou, Qin, Han and Tang dynasties, only supplanted by Beijing in more recent times. From here the caravans would travel westwards with their precious cargoes of silk and other commodities[94].

Today, however, tourist interest centres a little further east on the mausoleum complex of the Terracotta Warriors. Unearthed in 1974, these 6,000 clay warriors and their 40,000 bronze weapons faithfully guarded the resting place of the first Qin emperor, Qin Shi Huang, for over two millennia, testifying to his imperial greatness – or so it seemed.

But what is greatness? Despite Qin Shi Huang's propensity to employ violence to crush his opponents, his dynasty lasted a mere fifteen years (221 to 206 BCE) before being supplanted by the Han Dynasty. Ruthlessness and vanity don't guarantee longevity[95] [96].

From Xi'an, we flew to Shanghai, that miracle of modernity, the true symbol of the Chinese people's hard work, coupled with government foresight and firmness. While the ruthless and brutal revolutionary, Mao Zedong, is still revered in the People's Republic of China, Deng Xiaoping was the true genius. Reputed as saying, "Keep a cool head and maintain a low profile. Never take the lead – but aim to do something big", Deng survived the Cultural Revolution purges of Mao and the Gang of Four to rise to be paramount leader between 1978 and 1989.

From this position, Deng orchestrated China's transition from an economic basket-case to a manufacturing powerhouse, setting it on the path to becoming the world's leading economy in the mid-21st century[97] . Rising as a testament to Deng's vision, Shanghai's Pudong district contributes over a quarter of Shanghai's GDP[98]. It literally gleams with glamour.

Russia, 2017

Continuing our exploration of the former Russian Empire, we flew to Moscow before continuing by train to St Petersburg, and then by coach to Tallinn, capital of Estonia; Riga, capital of Latvia; and Vilnius, capital of Lithuania. In those days, before the invasion of Ukraine, Russia was remarkably laid back, completely different from our expectations.

While we cannot realistically comment on the treatment of political dissidents in Russia (or, for that matter, elsewhere in the world, whether east or west), we can say our time wandering through the clean, modern streets of Moscow[99] and travelling its metro was no different from what we'd expect of our own country.

While we joined guided tours of the Kremlin, St Basil's Cathedral, the metro stations, churches, monasteries, museums and other tourist hotspots, we also had a refreshing amount of free time to do our own thing. As if to rebuff the repression of the Soviet era, churches appeared well attended, and monuments to class struggle and warfare were relatively rare.

From the modernity of Moscow, we embarked by fast train for the city of Peter the Great, called Leningrad in more austere times, but once again known as St Petersburg[100]. Here, the wealth of czarist Russia becomes fully apparent. St Petersburg hosts many iconic buildings, including the enormous orthodox Cathedral of St Isaac, and the colourful Church of the Saviour on Spilled Blood, built in the same onion-dome style as Moscow's St Basil's.

The final resting place of the murdered Czar Nicholas II and his family is in the austere Peter and Paul Fortress, across the River Neva from their former home in the flamboyant Winter Palace. This breathtaking palace now houses the inspirational Hermitage Museum, repository of many of the world's most treasured artworks. But it's just a foretaste of some of the other examples of czarist opulence.

The epic scale of the blue and white rococo external vista of the Catherine the Great Palace camouflages the beauty secreted within. Although gutted and vandalised in the dark days of Nazi occupation during World War 2, the interior has been substantially restored to its former richness and beauty.

But the magnificence of the St Petersburg architecture hides a more sinister story of cruelty, violence and inequity. A little upstream from the Winter Palace, our River Neva tour boat drew near to the historic naval cruiser, *Aurora*.

A century of international political struggle was heralded by a single shot from this warship in October 1917. The collapse of the Russian Kerensky government, the triumph of the Bolsheviks, the ascendency of Russian communism, the formation of the USSR, the 1949 communist victory in China, a plethora of other communist revolutions, the Cold War, Korean War, Vietnam War, and a host of other conflicts can trace their origin to that single shot.

In short, East versus West, while the gun was loaded by many over a long period, the crew of the *Aurora* pulled the trigger.

Australia, 2025

From the time we started our travels, I had a passion for the intersection of history, foreign affairs and politics. While one must account for modern context, the ancient relationships between countries tend to reflect the vanities, greed and ruthlessness of individuals, and they're a constant that transcends time and place. Lessons from the past can help us understand the present.

In 1984, well over forty years ago, I presented a discussion paper to the local federal electorate conference of one of the leading political parties. The synopsis of my paper, *Australia's Place in World History*,[101] reads as follows:

> "The Australian Government must carefully consider our place in world history when determining foreign policy. What is our long-term contribution to humanity? Can we best achieve it by close alignment with our traditional European and American friends, or should we draw closer to Asia and Africa? This paper recommends:

1. Australia must provide a cultural bridge between the traditions of Europe and America on one hand and Africa and Asia on the other.

2. We must specialise in a number of key high-technology industries in a range of disciplines demanded by our neighbours.

3. Most importantly, Australia must adopt enthusiastically the role of regional peacemaker. We must develop a genuine friendship with the people of many differing countries."[102]

Unfortunately, not until the upheaval of the 2020s, the Chinese trade tariffs and Donald Trump's catastrophic second United States presidency, did such considerations begin to permeate mainstream Australian political thinking.

The relationships between superpowers and their smaller client states are similar across the millennia. My paper drew on several ancient and modern historical events to demonstrate the consequences of the actions of various small countries, the most germane to Australia's relationship with the United States being the ancient relationship (2,200 years ago) between the small state of Rhodes and the Roman superpower. The paper stated:

"Up to 168 BC [sic], Rhodes had been a loyal ally of the 'superpower' Rome and had shared the spoils of previous Roman victories over its enemy, Antiochus. However, when Rhodes chose independently to mediate in another war between Rome and Perseus of Macedon, Rome was offended. Rhodes was deprived of its possessions and economically crippled by the paranoid Rome, thereafter fading from history."[103] [104] [105]

It seemed to me, in 1984, this would be exactly the fate of Australia if we continued in subservience to the United States. The longer we left the decision to act as an independent, mature country, the worse the consequences would be.

And then the Trump meltdown of 2025 occurred. The whole of the western world was forced to choose between subservience and independence. The 2025 federal election came and went. The Labor Party was returned with a huge majority, but what difference did it make to Australian foreign policy?

I've visited many countries, spread over all six of the populated continents. More important, I've visited and interacted with long-term friends in several of these countries over five decades.

Travel is an addiction that must be satisfied, like an itch that must be scratched. But how? A few photos, a diary entry and some shared memories? No, there must be more to it than that.

A lifetime of travel in exotic (and sometimes dangerous) lands must surely have a point to it. We meet so many people, some rich, some poor, some comfortable and some struggling. We witness history. Some of it is barbaric and violent, while some is uplifting and inspiring. We observe the cultures of distant peoples, and we start to understand ourselves. Most satisfying of all, we enjoy friendships across the world, as we share mutual respect with others. And if we are observant, we are able to peer into the past to see our own mistakes and the folly of our forebears, and thus we are able to look forward and see the possibilities of a brighter future.

Many of these travel experiences shape our attitudes to war, diplomacy and our place in the world and its history. I was old enough to be eligible for the Viet Nam draft, but lucky enough not to be called. The mind-numbing, confronting scenes of Ho Chi Minh City's American War Museum viewed forty-five years later in 2011 couldn't help but invoke a mixture of pity, sorrow and national shame.

In the 1960s, it had been all too easy to go "All the way with LBJ", too easy to forget we were killing and maiming ordinary people living in their own country.

The poignancy of our 1975 visit to the Gallipoli battlefield, just a couple of days before the similar western military debacle of final collapse in Viet Nam, was a life-changing experience, the start of my transition from hawk to dove, from nationalism to compassion, and from ignorance to wisdom. And now we're again faced with the aftermath of similar military debacles.

On a more positive note, it was encouraging to witness the extent of international goodwill extended in regions devastated by natural disasters such as tsunami, earthquake and cyclone. At the time, some of these affected regions had been recently subjected to violence by organisations such as the Free Aceh Movement (GAM separatist movement in Indonesia's Aceh Province) and the Tamil Tiger separatists in Sri Lanka.

So too, the international effort to rebuild the shattered villages following the Solomon Islands' 2007 earthquake and tsunami far eclipsed the ethnic violence that had previously plagued that island nation and occasioned the Australian-led RAMSI (Regional Assistance Mission to Solomon Islands) police intervention.

While there remained a detectable undercurrent of sectarian tension in Northern Ireland during our 2006 holiday, it was a far cry from the tanks and barricades we witnessed on our first visit in 1974, during the height of The Troubles. That such insular bigotry could plague a significant part of a major world power for so long almost defies understanding. Religious sectarian violence cannot be sustained in a modern, compassionate world.

At the time of writing, the most poignant recent examples of needless violence arising from blind bigotry and selfishness include the Israeli execution of the Palestinian genocide, the Israeli invasions (with American support) of Lebanon and Iran, the merciless Russian invasion of Uzbekistan, and the misery inflicted in Sudan, South Sudan and the Congo.

My personal experiences have fuelled a long-standing conviction of the evil of armed conflict. There can be few justifications for armed aggression.

Australians are too quick to step into world conflicts, too uninformed to understand the causes or the consequences, and too slow to learn from our previous mistakes. As tensions arise around the world in 2025 and beyond, it's chilling to speculate, "Where to next?"

Most Australians are irresponsibly ignorant of history, the genome of our culture. The world wasn't created in 1066 on Hastings Beach on a remote island on the fringe of the Atlantic. Nor did it start with a maritime conquest of the New World in 1492, the landing of a boatload of religious refugees in 1620 at Plymouth Rock, or the arrival of a convoy of criminals in the Antipodes in 1788.

Rather, we're the product of a series of long-intertwined cultures stretching back over five millennia of recorded history, and even further into the mists of pre-history.

Modern genetic fingerprinting is revealing remarkable surprises. Put simply, we aren't who we think we are. And the cultural links are even more illuminating.

Even worse than failing to recognise our own pedigree, we ignore and fear our eight billion neighbours. People are the same around the world. We all love our children, we all respect our parents, and we all strive for a peaceful world.

But we also fear anyone who speaks another language, dresses differently, or holds religious views not quite the same as our own.

Travel is one of the most important ways to combat bigotry and xenophobia. Unfortunately, we're often so mentally isolated that we equate world travel with a lazy week on a tropical beach or cruise ship, sucking down beers.

It's our responsibility to traverse the entire planet, meeting and encouraging others to do the same. Rather than seeking out our country's fellow citizens when travelling, we should try to befriend locals. Learn and practise a little vernacular; it's the effort that counts.

Liberally dispense hospitality, open your home and hearts to travellers, and graciously accept reciprocal displays of kindness and hospitality when they're offered. This is how lasting international friendships and understanding are born and nurtured.

Failure to critically analyse the current events swirling about us magnifies our ignorance. We wallow in the trivia and fake news fed to us by so-called media moguls, who'd sell their own citizenship for a couple more column inches in the global network of fear and misinformation.

Instead of the monochrome bias of the popular media, we should seek out a kaleidoscope of information from multiple media outlets, critiquing their sources and demanding balance. If you're fed enough garbage, you can grow to like it.

One of the more sinister outcomes of media bias is the dumbing-down of political discrimination. No longer do we seek out sustainable long-term policies that secure a stable and prosperous future for our progeny. Rather, we crave hard, uncompromising, so-called leadership as the substitute for visionary policies based on flexibility and compassion.

Mediocrity always trumps vision. Add to this, a combative two-party bicameral parliamentary system in which national governments risk dismissal every few years on the whim of a handful of swinging voters in a couple of marginal electorates. The case for a meaningful overhaul of our political system has never been stronger, but fear of the unknown paralyses initiative.

We're told we cannot develop our own manufacturing industries because our population is too small, and we cannot increase our population because there isn't enough wealth to go around. This is simply a ridiculous circular argument, fed by xenophobia and racism.

History is littered with societies extinguished by their failure to grow, failure to change and failure to learn. Stagnation is death. Our country has a wealth of natural resources, more than we can use and certainly more than we deserve.

Many who are not so fortunate would love to become Australian citizens with us, and it's in our mutual interest to share with them. Failure to do so will inevitably result in our conquest, not militarily, but economically.

More progressive societies, seeking our resources, will simply tempt us with a few "beads and trinkets" and then discard us. At best, our grandchildren could become an unenlightened, unskilled underclass of exploited local labourers, subservient to foreign-owned multinationals. We're a country of immigrants, each new wave stimulating our economy and revitalising our society. Now is the time to welcome new migrants.

We all make mistakes, and our countries reflect our collective errors. Just as greed corrupted the citizens of earlier empires, greed also corrupts us, the citizens of the smaller western democracies. We're induced to jettison our independence, to serve as the lackeys of the superpowers. Whether it be the all-powerful British Empire or its successor, the American empire, the parallel with historical experience is as appalling as it is inescapable.

Attitudes of the 21st century are not so different from the motivations of the 19th and 20th centuries. We've learned little from the preceding years of conflict. We Australians are still lured into foreign wars because we fear standing alone. Are we so immature that we still refuse to think for ourselves?

While we instinctively revere violent political and military events as those that shape our world, one must question whether they really merit the veneration they attract.

Stories of struggle, suffering and sorrow should cause us to pause and to contemplate our world. Profit-gouging by landed nobility or industrial capitalists, international intrigue by adventurers or diplomats, wars prosecuted by aristocrats or generals, empire-building by czar or president, 1825 or 2025, Russia, Germany, Britain or America ... What is the difference?

History tells of the cruel and indifferent exploitation by nations who believed themselves to be culturally or religiously superior. These have justified appalling atrocities, committed in the name of civilisation or religion, but really, just a smokescreen for self-interest.

But this realisation is just a beginning, not the end. A new vision for a cooperative, compassionate and caring world can emerge, one in which small and middle-sized countries are instrumental as peacemakers, but only if we, the ordinary citizens, recognise and exercise our responsibilities.

It's time for Australia to renounce state-promoted violence and to promote respect, cooperation and assistance throughout the region and the wider world. Australia must step up, not as a belligerent protagonist, but as a peacemaker. This is the only sustainable means of international interaction ... our last chance for survival.

ACKNOWLEDGEMENTS

I'd like to thank my wife Robyn, who for well over fifty years has been my loyal and loving friend and confidante, mother of my children and travelling companion. Without her flexibility and steadying influence, this work wouldn't have been possible.

During half a century of travel and international voluntary work, I've met and been inspired by many insightful and dedicated community leaders, volunteers and fellow travellers. Too many to list, and too inspiring to neglect, I extend to them collectively my heartfelt gratitude.

I'd also like to gratefully acknowledge all who have provided encouragement, advice and assistance in the preparation of this book, in particular the publisher, Aurora House, for recognising the timely significance of this work.

ABOUT THE AUTHOR

When does fiction become prophecy, and when does prophecy turn to reality? Can we change the future by learning from the past?

These are the questions that inspired Rod Johnston to write this book.

Rod Johnston is a concerned Australian, committed to making our country a safe and responsible contributor to international peace and prosperity during these increasingly turbulent times, for the benefit of our children and grandchildren.

He is a consulting engineer by profession, with well over fifty years' practical experience in the building and construction industry. For over twenty-five years, he has been president of a voluntary, not-for-profit NGO, constructing remote village infrastructure throughout the Asia–Pacific region.

Rod has a Master's degree in Engineering Science and in International and Community Development, and recently completed a semester as a university lecturer in Humanitarian Engineering. He lives on the New South Wales Central Coast with his wife, Robyn.

REFERENCES

1   https://www.abc.net.au/news/2025-04-19/united-states-china-tar-iff-trade-war-federal-election-future/105189008 Article by Laura Tingle.

2   https://en.unesco.org/silkroad/content/did-you-know-traditional-strategy-games-along-silk-roads-chess

3   Dalrymple, W., 2024, *The Golden Road – How Ancient India Transformed the World*, Bloomsbury Publishing pp 275-276.

4   https://www.abc.net.au/news/2020-12-17/australian-trade-ten-sion-sanctions-china-growing-commodities/12984218

5   https://www.abc.net.au/news/2024-03-28/china-government-offi-cially-abolishes-heavy-tariffs-on-wine/103644884

6   https://www.abc.net.au/news/2025-03-27/air-marshal-chief-com-fortable-chinese-warship-response/105100672

7   https://www.abc.net.au/news/2025-02-28/albo-doubles-down-on-response-to-chinese-warships/104994534

8   https://www.abc.net.au/news/2025-04-18/russia-has-a-long-history-of-friendship-with-indonesia/105191070

9   https://www.abc.net.au/news/2025-04-18/timor-leste-open-to-chinese-joint-military-exercises/105190596

10 https://en.wikipedia.org/wiki/History_of_Greece

11 https://en.wikipedia.org/wiki/Troy

12 https://en.wikipedia.org/wiki/Cassandra

13 https://shunspirit.com/article/psi-symbol-meaning

14　https://www.britannica.com/search?query=psi%20symbol&page=2

15　https://en.wikipedia.org/wiki/War_in_Donbas

16　https://en.wikipedia.org/wiki/Lies,_damned_lies,_and_statistics

17　Copeland, B.J., 18 March 2025, fact-checked by the editors of *Encyclopedia Britannica*, https://www.britannica.com/technology/artificial-intelligence/Is-artificial-general-intelligence-AGI-possible

18　https://en.wikipedia.org/wiki/Automotive_industry_in_Australia

19　https://en.wikipedia.org/wiki/2/4th_Commando_Squadron_(Australia)

20　Raby, Geoff, *Great Game On*, Melbourne University Press, 2024.

21　Johnston, R.K., 1984, *Australia's Place in World History*, presentation to the Berowra Federal Electorate Conference of the Liberal Party of Australia.

22　Ibid

23　https://en.wikipedia.org/wiki/Xiangqi

24　https://www.ccs.org.cn/ccswzen/internationalShipsList?columnid=201900002000000123

25　https://www.oxfordreference.com/display/10.1093/acref/9780191826719.001.0001/q-oro-ed4-00002794 Many have made this statement, one of the most poignant proclamations being by former British Prime Minister, Neville Chamberlain, on the eve of the Second World War: "In war, whichever side may call itself the victor, there are no winners, but all are losers." Speech at Kettering, 3 July 1938, in *Times* 4 July 1938.

26　https://en.wikipedia.org/wiki/Guangzhou

27　http://www.teamuse.com/article_010502.html Pratt, J.N.

28　https://en.wikipedia.org/wiki/Guangzhou

29　https://en.wikipedia.org/wiki/Dzungar_people

30　https://en.wikipedia.org/wiki/Xinjiang

31 Frankopan, P., *The Silk Roads – A New History of the World*, Blooms-bury, 2015.

32 Oresman, M., *Assessing China's Reaction to Kyrgyzstan's Tulip Revolution*, Analytical Articles, 2005 https://www.bing.com/search?q=tulip+revolution+uyghur&FORM=EDGENN

33 Barber, E.W., *The Mummies of Urumchi*, Macmillan, 1999.

34 McEvedy, C., *The New Penguin Atlas of Ancient History*, Penguin Travel Diaries, second edition 2002.

35 https://en.wikipedia.org/wiki/Tarim_Basin

36 Raby, Geoff, *Great Game On*, Melbourne University Press, 2024.

37 https://www.lusakatimes.com/2015/11/10/in-the-kitchen-with-kanta-nshima-kapenta-roasted-chicken-and-cabbage/

38 https://en.wikipedia.org/wiki/David_Livingstone

39 Ferguson, N. *Empire: How Britain made the modern world*, Penguin Books, 2003.

40 https://en.wikipedia.org/wiki/Joshua_Nkomo

41 https://en.wikipedia.org/wiki/Operation_Gatling

42 https://www.bing.com/videos/search?q=green+leader+raud+utube&docid=607991039932105230&mid=43F354237017D0BCD930 43F354237017D0BCD930&view=detail&FORM=VIRE

43 https://en.wikipedia.org/wiki/Kazakhstan

44 https://en.wikipedia.org/?url=https%3A%2F%2Fen.wikipedia.org%2Fwiki%2FCharyn_Canyon

45 https://en.wikipedia.org/wiki/Granada

46 http://www.marxist.com/portugal-40o-aniversario-de-la-revolucion-de-los-claveles-cuando-los-trabajadores-tocaron-el-poder-con-las-manos-en.htm

47 https://www.navyhistory.org.au/betano-bay-today/

48 Carlyon, L. *Gallipoli*, Pan Macmillan Australia Pty Limited, Sydney, 2001.

49 Herbert Howard Kentwell Fowles

50 Roberts, C., *The Landing at ANZAC 1915*, Book #12 of Australian Army Campaigns Series, published by Big Sky Publishing, distributed by Simon & Schuster, 5 March 2015

51 Stanley, P., *Lost Boys of Anzac*, University of New South Wales Press, Sydney, 2014.

52 https://en.wikipedia.org/wiki/Australia_in_the_Vietnam_War

53 https://www.awm.gov.au/visit/exhibitions/impressions/impressions#:~:text=The%20official%20estimate%20of%20the%20cost%20of%20the,of%20%24218.4%20million%20from%201962%20to%20March%201972

54 https://www.britannica.com/question/How-many-people-died-in-the-Vietnam-War#:~:text=In%201995%20Vietnam%20released%20its%20official%20estimate%20of,some%201%2C100%2C000%20North%20Vietnamese%20and%20Viet%20Cong%20fighters.

55 Lieutenant (later Major) Harold Jesser of the Papua Infantry Brigade (the Green Shadows) reconnoitred the Kokoda Track in January 1942, and then subsequently led the PIB A Company behind the Japanese lines as the main Australian army forces advanced up the Kokoda Track several months later from June 1942 onwards.

56 https://en.wikipedia.org/wiki/Papuan_Infantry_Battalion

57 https://www.britannica.com/topic/Great-Game

58 https://en.wikipedia.org/wiki/Rudyard_Kipling

59 https://en.wikipedia.org/wiki/Francis_Younghusband

60 https://en.wikipedia.org/wiki/British_expedition_to_Tibet

61 https://en.wikipedia.org/wiki/The_Great_Game

62 https://en.wikipedia.org/wiki/Tashkent

63 http://uzbek-travel.com/about-uzbekistan/monuments/earthquake-memorial/

64 Habitat for Humanity International, https://www.habitat.org/ap

65 https://en.wikipedia.org/wiki/List_of_non-state_terrorist_incidents_in_Sri_Lanka

66 https://en.wikipedia.org/wiki/Free_Aceh_Movement

67 Dr Vinay Samuel is a good friend and has been an inspiration to the author.

68 The author met and was befriended by David Bussau in the mid-1980s. They travelled and inspected microfinance projects together in Thailand, Philippines and Indonesia during 1995. David Bussau was awarded an Order of Australia and 2008 Senior Australian of the Year for his work in establishing and operating Opportunity International, a leading provider of micro-finance programs in developing countries around the world.

69 Tyndale, P., 2004, *Don't Look Back: The David Bussau Story*, Crows Nest, NSW, Allen & Unwin.

70 https://en.wikipedia.org/wiki/David_Bussau

71 Sir John Ford was the British ambassador to Indonesia from 1975 to 1978, and British High Commissioner to Canada from 1978 to 1981. https://en.wikipedia.org/wiki/John_Ford_(diplomat)

72 Partner Housing Australasia (Building) Incorporated, https://www.partnerhousing.org/

73 From 2001 to 2005, the author was Chairman of the NGO Habitat for Humanity Western Sydney, and for most of that time, was also a national board member of Habitat for Humanity Australia. In 2005, the small NGO became independent, changed its name to Partner Housing Australasia, and adopted the following vision statement: "Partner Housing Australasia is an entirely voluntary organisation, which aims to transform the lives of people living in Asia–Pacific villages by improving the cyclone, earthquake and tsunami resistance of their houses, clinics, schools and community buildings; and by providing clean water supplies and hygienic sanitation."

74 Diamond, J. *Collapse – How societies choose to fail or survive*, Allen Laine – Penguin Books, 2005.

75 https://en.wikipedia.org/wiki/Mangaia

76 Partner Housing Australia

77 Bishop Don Lippert is the Catholic Bishop of Mendi, and a Capuchin Franciscan monk. https://www.thefloridacatholic.org/faith/dose_of_faith/in-washington-u-s-bishop-shares-his-missions-work-in-papua-new-guinea/article_abcb33ce-0cf9-11ed-9672-d71b06df35ca.html

78 Kelly Kombra Peng, Manager of Vision for Homes (PNG) based in Mount Hagen, Western Province. https://visionforhomespng.com/

79 https://en.wikipedia.org/wiki/Tashkent

80 https://en.wikipedia.org/wiki/Samarkand

81 https://en.wikipedia.org/wiki/Shah-i-Zinda

82 https://en.wikipedia.org/wiki/Ulugh_Beg

83 https://en.wikipedia.org/wiki/Uzbekistan

84 https://en.wikipedia.org/wiki/Islam_Karimov

85 http://www.rferl.org/a/karimov-death-announcement-media-reporting-didn-t-die/27964184.html

86 https://www.theguardian.com/world/2016/dec/05/uzbekistan-elects-shavkat-mirziyoyev-president-islam-karimov

87 Frankopan, P., *The Silk Roads – A New History of the World*, Bloomsbury, 2015.

88 https://en.wikipedia.org/wiki/Afghan_mujahideen

89 First Opium War waged by the British against the Qing Chinese government, to force the Chinese to import British-controlled opium.

90 First Anglo-Afghan War

91 https://www.thoughtco.com/execution-of-stoddart-and-conolly-bukhara-195774

92 https://en.wikipedia.org/wiki/Arthur_Conolly

93 http://wikitravel.org/en/Khiva

94 https://en.wikipedia.org/wiki/Xi'an

95 https://en.wikipedia.org/wiki/Terracotta_Army

96 https://simple.wikipedia.org/wiki/Qin_Shi_Huang

97 https://en.wikipedia.org/wiki/Deng_Xiaoping

98 https://en.wikipedia.org/wiki/Pudong

99 https://en.wikipedia.org/wiki/Moscow

100 https://en.wikipedia.org/wiki/Winter_Palace

101 Johnston, R.K., 1984, *Australia's Place in World History*, presentation to the Berowra Federal Electorate Conference of the Liberal Party of Australia.

102 Ibid

103 ibid

104 https://warhistory.org/@msw/article/romes-humiliation-of-rhodes-and-pergamum

105 https://en.wikipedia.org/wiki/Battle_of_Pydna